D1564570

"A master storyteller…Danielle Skjelver delivers a powerfully unique and heart-wrenching tale that creatively weaves family compassion, deadly vengeance, and the brutal tribulations of daily survival in the Colonial period. She will send you back in time three hundred years to live the simple Puritan life and dwell with the native Americans… and after the entertaining, emotional, and sometimes shocking adventure, you may just want to stay. *The best* book I have read in twenty years!"

~ Lieutenant Colonel James Munroe
United States Marine Corps

"Before I read Danielle Skjelver's compelling novel, *Massacre: Daughter of War*, I thought I had a firm grasp on the realities of frontier life. I was wrong. Nothing in my experience and nothing in literature had informed me of the nature of an existence where death and the likelihood of death is so immediate. With the conclusion of this book, my conception of the exquisite and excruciating realities of early colonial America is forever changed.

This is a story that had to be told. It is about members of the author's family. It is about an important chapter in the history of New England. For that alone it was worth the telling. But the author's moving insights about human nature, the bounds of love and the pain of loss make this much more than a book of history. It is a book skillfully interlaced simultaneously with romance, adventure and horror.

Anyone with an interest in native Americans, colonial life, military affairs or the behavior of humans under stress will find this book hard to resist. If you think you know something of these topics, *Massacre: Daughter of War* will surely change your mind."

~ Edward Barnes Ellis
Author, *In This Small Place*

"I don't know when I have been so deeply moved, to the core of my being, page after page, sentence after sentence, phrase after phrase. Nor have I read, I don't recall, such a very satisfying book -- one that takes questions that matter so greatly to me, and carries them through so lovingly, so carefully, to amazingly healing and peaceful places of rest.

This wonderfully well-written new historical novel gave me a remarkably personal view/experience of what it was surely like to live through the events of the era around the 1704 Deerfield Massacre/Raid in western Massachusetts. The author has powerfully blended her own interest in family history into a well-researched awareness of the documented events of that period, casting it in a journal format. Gripping!"

~ Judy Holy
Author, *The Women Who Married The Orcutt Men*

"A writing style in the fashion of Jack London--Farley Mowatt... Danielle Skjelver has the unique ability to give 'life' to every name...every man & woman...every child. Each person is a story...each story is worthy of being told...worthy of being remembered."

~Randall R. Booher
LLB Resources

"*Massacre: Daughter of War* is not a book for the faint of heart. It is violent, graphic and chilling. But, Skjelver's book never loses its sense of historic heritage. And, it leads the reader through the dangerous intrigue and adventure of colonial life without pulling any punches. The often divergence of opinion of the French missionaries in Canada and the puritanical English is an important sidebar."

~ Lee Meade
Editor www.meadnewsletter.com

MASSACRE
Daughter of War

A Novel
by
Danielle Skjelver

Published by Goodwyfe Press
10 Harnett Road
Havelock, NC 28532
252-447-3780
www.goodwyfe.com

Cover illustration *Attack on the Pequot Fort, 1637*
Courtesy of New York Public Library Picture Collection,
The Branch Libraries, The New York Public Library, Astor, Lenox
and Tilden Foundations

Map by Digital Cartographics
www.digitalcarto.com

All scripture quotations are taken from the King James Version.
Copyright © 1982 by Thomas Nelson, Inc.
Used by permission. All rights reserved.

Childhood verses and prayers are from *The New England Primer*.
WallBuilder Press, Aledo, TX, 1991

Library of Congress Control Number: 2003116909

ISBN: 0-9748628-0-0

Printed in the United States by Morris Publishing
3212 East Hwy 30
Kearney, NE 68847
1-800-650-7888

Florence Pluma Waters Orcutt

1871 - 1962

My great-grandmother Florence Orcutt recorded all she
knew of her children's history. Without her notes, I
would never have discovered this story.
She gave flesh and blood to long forgotten names.

Preface

After my grandmother's death, I was given a copy of the family history notes that her mother Florence Orcutt had recorded. Among these notes were three sentences about one of my grandmothers three centuries ago, a woman named Hannah Hawks Scott, a woman who has haunted me ever since.

These people ~ specifically Hawks, Mead, Sergeant John Hawks, Joseph Baldwin, Martha Baldwin, Hannah Hawks, Jonathan Scott Sr., and Jonathan Scott Jr. ~ are my grandparents many generations back, and as such the reader will surely see these people through the eyes of a descendant writing about her own family. Yet I have tried to shatter the illusions it is so easy to hold in regard to one's own history. I wanted to know as deeply as I possibly could what our ancestors experienced, and I wanted to give that understanding, that empathy, to our future descendants as well.

Though based on actual events, this novel is first and foremost a work of fiction. Some places and events were merged or altered for the sake of flow and clarity while others are inventions of my imagination.

Ironically the most shocking events are those that actually happened. For instance, both the prologue and chapter three are based on specific first hand accounts. See the Author's Note in the back of the book for more.

The following elements of the story may be of interest to the reader:

FIRST NATIONS FAMILIES: Metacom, his family, Wequash, Uncas, and Awashonks were real people while Honors The Dead and his family are fictional. For the sake of clarity, Honors The Dead receives only one name in his lifetime. In reality, he would have had at least three names. The very name Honors The Dead is also fairly unrealistic, however it keeps the man's story in the reader's mind throughout the novel.

OF INTEREST TO GENEALOGISTS AND DESCENDANTS: The English characters were all real people. Modern descendants of the characters bearing the name Hawks spell their names both Hawks and Hawkes. In real life, Sergeant John Hawks and his brother Eliezer wrote their names Hawks, however the sergeant's daughter Hannah's name is recorded as Hawkes. It is all one family with the typical variations in spelling so common at the time. See Imogene Hawks Lane's outstanding work *John Hawks, A Founder of Hadley, Massachusetts* for more on this family.

The family trees include only those individuals specifically mentioned in this novel. Most of the English families in this novel had many more children than those listed in the trees.

I have changed the name of one character who was a real person, the daughter of Sergeant and Alice Hawks. In this work, she is called Sarah Hawks though her real name was Elizabeth Hawks.

A PLETHORA OF JOHNS AND MARYS: Common sense would have advised me to change the names of many more English characters, however this book was written primarily to preserve for our children a story about real people whose names are important.

The tradition of colonial days was to name children after members of the family alternating back and forth between paternal and maternal lines. Hence in the four generations this book spans, there are no fewer than seven males named John and two named Jonathan. Where possible I drop first names (John Hawks I of the Prologue is simply Hawks.), use titles (John Hawks II is Sergeant John Hawks.), or nicknames (John Scott, son of Joseph Scott, is Cousin John.) to help with clarity.

MUSKETS AND MEN AT THE PEQUOT FORT: The presence of the flintlock musket at the Pequot Fort is a possible point of controversy. While the flintlock per se would not have been at the fort, its forerunners were. As there were many different varieties of flint weapons and as the flintlock arrived in the colonies not long after the Pequot War, I chose to merge the forerunners into their mature form, the flintlock.

Regarding the characters Hawks and Mead, there is no proof that either man was at the Pequot Fort, but it is a distinct possibility given their locations, ages, status, and the general feeling among the public toward the action.

Though the involvement of Hawks and Mead is fictional, it sets the stage for the balance of the novel, for the attack on the Pequot Fort demonstrates how the English and Natives viewed one another.

It was at the Pequot Fort that the Natives and English first witnessed one another's battle tactics in their fullness. The English found the Native Peoples savage for their *means* of warfare ~ the Natives' imaginative and personal cruelty. The Natives found the English barbarous for the *extent* of their warfare ~ the English colonists' utter annihilation of a place as opposed to the killing of a score of people while taking the rest captive, and for the colonists' arrogant sense of superiority which precluded them from adopting Native children into their homes.

For an excellent resource on the differences in weaponry and warfare, see Patrick M. Malone's *The Skulking Way of War.*

WORD CHOICE: I have used politically incorrect words like "barbarian" with regard to the English because that is what the First Nations called the English, and "savage" or "Indian" for the First Nations because they are the words used by the colonists to describe the Native Peoples.

To some degree, I also tried to use the same inflammatory language that was used at the time. Without this, it is hard to see how people could do such horrible things to one another.

The word "nation" is used rather than "tribe" because that is how the First Nations viewed themselves ~ sovereign. In this early stage before the First Nations became subjects of the English Crown (some of them wittingly and some unwittingly), the English colonists saw the First Nations as sovereign as well. In these early days, "nation" was the word both sides chose when referring to specific groups of Native Peoples.

GRAPHIC VIOLENCE: Though it was not my aim, this book became a study of the word "massacre," for what the First Nations say is true. When white people slaughter hundreds of Indians, it is a battle. When Indians do the same, it is a massacre.

To our modern eyes, both the English and the First Nations appear barbaric. Both sides came to this conflict from warrior societies. Both sides trained for battle and expected to fight at some point in their lives. In the seventeenth and eighteenth centuries, the entire world was a barbaric place. Not to prepare to fight was to prepare to die.

To diminish the violence of the day would be a disservice to those who lived the pain and terror of these events. The horror of warfare, particularly eighteenth century warfare, is largely the point of the book.

These were frail and flawed, noble and beloved human beings just like us, but their world was vastly different from ours, and I suspect that very few of us, who today cannot imagine employing eighteenth century tactics, would have held then the same ideals we hold today. Ultimately the characters are simply human beings behaving quite normally in terms of their era.

For Renee

I went to the woods because I wished to live deliberately,

to front only the essential facts of life,

and see if I could not learn what it had to teach,

and not, when I came to die, discover that I had not lived...

I wanted to live deep and suck out all the marrow of life...

~ Henry David Thoreau

Hawks Family Tree

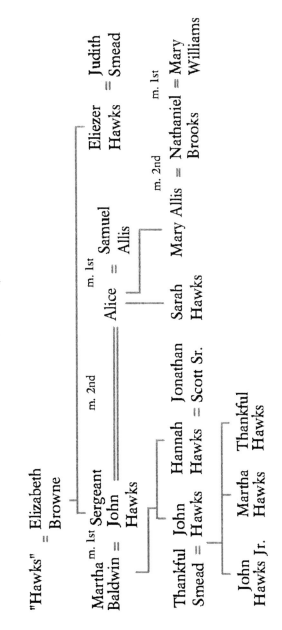

"Hawks" = Elizabeth Browne

Martha Baldwin ^{m. 1st} = Sergeant John Hawks ^{m. 2nd}

Alice ^{m. 1st} = Samuel Allis

Eliezer Hawks = Judith Smead

Mary Allis ^{m. 2nd} = Nathaniel Brooks ^{m. 1st} = Mary Williams

Thankful John Hawks

Hannah Hawks = Jonathan Scott Sr.

Sarah Hawks

Thankful Smead = John Hawks

Martha Hawks

John Hawks Jr.

Honors The Dead Family Tree

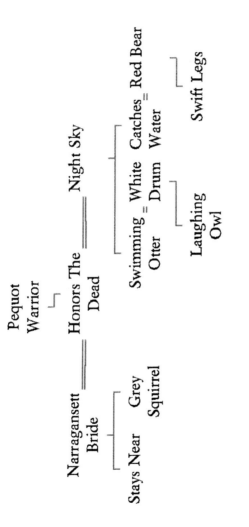

Pequot Warrior

Narragansett Bride = Honors The Dead = Night Sky

Stays Near   Grey Squirrel

Swimming Otter = White Drum   Catches Water = Red Bear

Laughing Owl

Swift Legs

Scott Family Tree

Edmund
Scott

Jonathan   Hannah
Scott Sr. = Hawks

Joseph
Scott

Jonathan   Rebecca
Scott Jr. = Frost
"Junior"

John
Scott

John
Scott
"Cousin
John"

John   Martha   Gershom   Eliezer   Daniel
Scott   Scott   Scott   Scott   Scott

Baldwin Family Tree

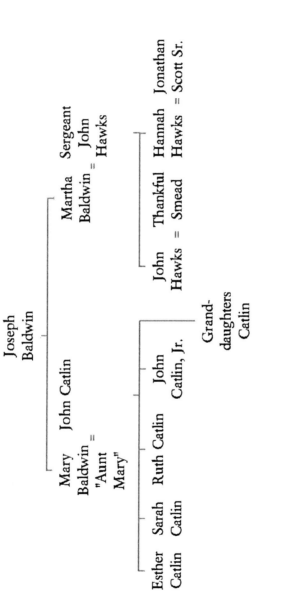

Joseph Baldwin

Mary Baldwin "Aunt Mary" = John Catlin   Martha Baldwin = Sergeant John Hawks

Esther Catlin   Sarah Catlin   Ruth Catlin   John Catlin, Jr.   John Hawks = Thankful Smead   Hannah Hawks = Jonathan Scott Sr.

Grand-daughters Catlin

Metacom "King Philip" Family Tree

Osamequin
"Massasoit"

Metacom = Wootonekanuske
"King Philip"

Son

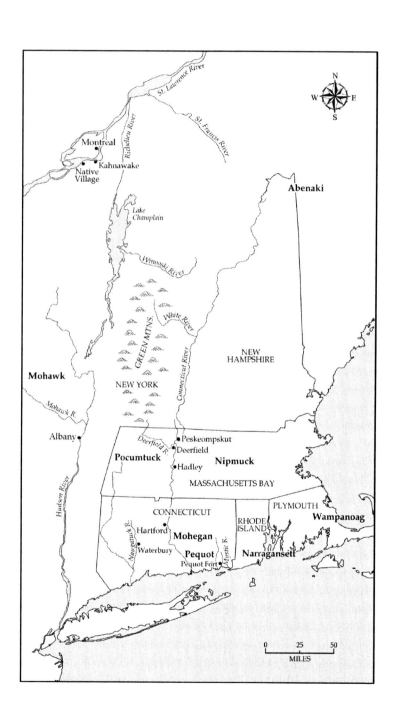

Prologue

Friday, May 26th, 1637
Mystic River, Present Day Connecticut

On a hill above the Mystic River lay a large stronghold of the Pequot Indian Nation sleeping in the illusion of safety behind the walls of their crude fort. Leaving gaps through which they could fire arrows, the Pequots had erected twelve-foot high vertical logs around their camp. Water protected part of the steep hill on which the fort stood. Patches of brush lined the base of the hill and the water's edge.

Hawks, a young Englishman, marched among his fellows through the thick northeastern forest just outside the fort. On this warm spring dawn he and his fellow colonists had marched for a few hours already and sweat now trickled down his back. The preceding night, the men had slept fitfully on the ground, having marched hard. Hawks had watched many of the men faint from the heat and hunger.

He lifted his hat exposing white-blond hair, and he wiped the sweat from his brow with the back of his arm.

Pushing his hat firmly down on his head, Hawks checked his musket. He examined the match, a thin gunpowder-treated rope attached to his musket by a serpentine clamp. To keep it burning, he blew the ashes from it, loosened the clamp and threaded the match a little further through the serpentine. With peculiar eyes the color of ice, he scanned the area around him, wondering how many hidden eyes were watching him.

Throughout yesterday's march, Narragansett and Mohegan warriors had moved in silence at the English flank. To Hawks, it seemed as though they were spirits. Hawks held the Indians in awe ... and fear. He had arrived from England seven years ago. He had never gotten used to the notion of savages living all around him. To some degree he mistrusted even those Indians allied with the English.

Hawks did not understand and did not particularly want to understand the intricacies of this war against the Pequots. He knew that somehow the English and Indians must live side by side, and the Indians did seem to understand force as a means of communication. After all, there were always Indian skirmishes here and there. Strength was something Indians respected.

It really did not matter to Hawks which Indian Nation was correct in this fight. What did matter to him was that the Narragansetts, ancient enemies of the Pequot Nation, were stronger and lived closer to English settlements than did the Pequots. Alliance with the Narragansett Nation meant relative safety for the colonists. That alone was good enough argument for Hawks. Besides, the Pequots were wont to make threats and were hardly innocent of shedding English blood. They had spent the preceding days preparing to set out on the warpath against them again.

The allied force of nearly five hundred Indians and seventy-odd English moved quietly from the forest into a cornfield, and the fort now came into full view. Tense, tired and eager, Hawks' nerves frayed as he walked among the rows of young cornstalks. Hawks had never killed a man, never engaged in battle of any kind. He was thrilled to have this chance to prove himself and protect his countrymen.

Knowing his captains to be honorable men who would avoid the killing of innocents, Hawks understood they were not attacking a group of men on an open field but in a village where women and children lived. He accepted that a few among the helpless would die. It was an unavoidable fact of war. He did not hate Indians, but holding a general mistrust of them, he knew the women would only raise their boys to resent the English. For Hawks then, the occasional death of a woman or child was not to be lamented.

The young Englishman was prepared to lose his own life in this fight. No matter the cost, he would not allow enemy savages to capture him alive. He knew Indians were notoriously creative in the torture of enemy prisoners ~ slowly peeling the skin off a man or burning him alive and piercing the blisters with sticks. Hawks shuddered at the imagination of savages. He would leave the fort a free man or dead. There would be no captivity for him.

Suddenly noting a difference in the eerie silence of the Narragansett and Mohegan allies who could walk for hours without so much as snapping a twig, Hawks glanced backward. Alarmed to see only a handful of warriors where moments ago there had been hundreds, he elbowed a fellow colonist by the name of Mead, then jabbed his thumb to the rear. Nonplussed, Mead looked behind them and cupped his hand around his mouth as he whispered, "Hawks, I heard they think we're going to run when we see how strong the Pequots are. They're just keeping out of the Pequots' sight until we prove ourselves. You know as well as I do that just because you can't see them doesn't mean they're not there."

As Hawks rolled his eyes in disgust, Mead continued, "See, their chiefs are still with us," and pointed at two braves walking through the corn ahead of them toward the English captains Mason and Underhill. "That's Wequash, sachem of the Narragansett Nation, and there's Uncas, sachem of the Mohegan People."

Captain Mason halted the allied force with an upheld hand. He and the chiefs, called sachems by their People, whispered briefly among the men in command. Watching the group closely, Hawks noted the difference between the English and Indian commanders. Mason, a short, stocky man sporting a carefully coiffed beard that came to a neat point just below his chin, wore an expensive buff suit of leather armor and held a shining steel helmet in the crook of his arm.

In stark contrast to Captain Mason, the lithe, smooth-skinned Indian sachems wore only loincloths. Hawks was always a little shocked by Indian nudity, and it seemed absurd to him that they could wear so little clothing especially in the presence of honorable English officers. Weapons hanging from straps here and there around their bodies, the Indians stood a full head taller than their white counterparts. They were perfectly self-sustained war machines, and Hawks could not help holding the Indians in some awe.

The sachems now returned to their band, still lurking in the surrounding forest where they would await the English attack. Captains Mason and Underhill knelt and the colonists all followed suit, each praying silently. Hawks prayed, "Deliver Thine enemies into our hand this day, O Lord."

Captain Mason rose and beckoned broadly with his arm, giving the order to proceed. Underhill's men split off from the group and moved quietly down a path around the hill to the opposite end of the fort. To ensure both ends of his match were lit, Hawks bent the end dangling from his musket up to the burning end that was clamped into the serpentine. With both ends burning, at least one end should stay alight throughout the battle. Mead, having no such preparations to make with his more modern flintlock musket, moved ahead of Hawks as they stole quietly up the steep hill.

Hawks heard a dog bark, followed quickly by an Indian voice inside the palisade sounding the alarm. "Owanux! Owanux!" The voice shouted the Pequot word for "Englishmen." Understanding that they were discovered, Mason immediately gave the command to fire. Instantly, Hawks heard the firing of those who had carried the flintlock into battle that day. Hawks crouched next to

Mead behind a bush on the hill, and while Mead was reloading his musket Hawks used his teeth to uncork his powder horn. Then, having poured powder down the barrel of his matchlock, he dropped a ball of shot down the muzzle and rammed the ball and powder tightly with a rod.

Now Hawks was forced to expose himself while Mead still crouched safely behind the bush. Aiming his weapon at the broad palisade wall, Hawks stood up and steadied his weapon on a rest which stood about shoulder height. The rest was an iron stand forked into a U at the top. Into this U, Hawks laid the end of his barrel. His weapon thus steadied, he poured a small amount of powder into the priming pan of his musket. He plugged the powder horn with the cork he held in his teeth and let it drop from his mouth so that it hung from his shoulder, ready for its next use. Checking his match again, he saw it still burned at both ends, and he blew the ashes off the end attached to the serpentine. Then, he squared himself behind the musket, pulling the butt firmly into his shoulder. He stood with his feet shoulder-width apart, his right foot a little to the front, his right knee bent, and his left foot a little behind him.

Hoping no Englishman behind him downhill would hit him in the back, Hawks aimed his weapon at the broad palisade wall. The gaps through which the Indians fired their arrows allowed musket balls to penetrate the palisade, and he could see Pequot braves gathering inside. Hawks' weapon was not as accurate as an arrow, but it was deadly when it found a mark.

As Hawks squeezed the long triggering lever against the butt of the musket, the serpentine snapped backward, dropping the lighted match into the gunpowder inside the priming pan. Through the tiny touch hole in the bottom of the pan, the gunpowder in the barrel ignited and shot the ball into the palisade. Hawks saw copper skin jolt, then reel backward. Surprised that he had hit anything at all, Hawks allowed a smile to flick across his face.

Despite a hail of arrows, Hawks could not seek cover and fire at the same time. Designed for the orchestrated battlefields of Europe and not the wilderness of the New World, the unwieldy matchlock required a standing rest. Hawks stood his ground as he reloaded and fired again and again. A torrent of shot slammed against the palisade wall, and the smell of sulphur filled the air.

Captain Mason ran forward with a few men to secure the entrance to the fort. The Pequots had barred the entrance with uprooted trees and branches. Arrows flew thick around the entrance as Hawks watched the men tugging and tearing at the barricade. An arrow pierced one of the colonists through the heart, and the man fell backward.

Hawks heard a constant whoosh of arrows whizzing past him, over him, all around him. He continued to re-load and fire as his English comrades hauled the makeshift barricade away. Arrowheads bounced off helmets and tough leather armor. Hawks saw several other men fall at the entrance of the fort. At last, the way was clear.

Hawks and Mead rushed up the hill, and stepping over their fallen comrades, the colonists poured into the fort.

Inside they found no Indians but plenty of arrows. Once the entrance had been breached, the warriors had run for cover, and now arrows flew at the English from behind domed, bark-covered wigwams.

With little success, the colonists ran through the village seeking braves to slay with the sword. Mason grew frustrated. He lunged into a bark-covered wigwam seeking anyone with the courage to fight and stumbled out seconds later scratched and battered. After several minutes of sustaining a barrage of arrows pelted at them with no recourse, many men lay injured and dead. Mason boomed, "Englishmen! These cowards do not present themselves to fight. They hide behind women and children." Mason paused and looked at his men. Then, he shouted, "Fire the place!"

A few feet to Mason's left stood a wigwam. Standing aside from the wigwam opening so as to avoid any attack from within, he reached inside and pulled out a burning stick from the fire pit. Then, he lit the wigwam's bark covering which caught easily. Turning around to face his men, he held the firebrand aloft and the Englishmen cheered as they sprang into action, darting from wigwam to wigwam, grabbing firebrands and torching the shelters.

Likewise, Hawks stooped to reach inside a wigwam and a wave of horror filled his belly as he glimpsed the small round face belonging to a terrified child of three or four years. He thought he had prepared himself for this. His pastor preached that New England was the Christian Zion and he had said there was a Scriptural precedent, in fact a necessity, of destroying the young as well as the old at times. 'It must be done,' thought Hawks as he averted his eyes from the child and grasped a firebrand. Quickly backing out of the opening, he shoved the flaming stick into the bark sheets covering the wigwam that contained the little child and God knows how many of his loved ones.

Grimly Hawks walked along a side lane, torching wigwam after wigwam. The dwellings were clumped so closely together that Hawks could fire two without even shifting his feet. Pequot warriors suddenly began to race through the streets and paths of the fort and Hawks thought with disgust, 'Mason was right. They finally fight like men.' Employing only swords now, the English found the place too tightly packed, and fighting too furious for their muskets to be of much use. As the English bumped against wigwam walls and stumbled over fleeing children, they cursed the closeness of the village. To Hawks, it looked like a war being fought in a closet.

Seeing that the English did not run from the fight, Narragansett and Mohegan warriors now rushed into the fort. Hawks heard their savage whoops pierce the air above the crackle of burning bark and the screams of women and children.

Finding himself in a small open space, Hawks spied first the topknot then the head of a brave examining him from behind the corner of a wigwam. Quickly stuffing his firebrand into the bark of a nearby wigwam, Hawks drew his sword and took a long breath. Heart pounding, he set his teeth, hissed and lurched onto the path of the Pequot warrior.

The brave had also come into the open seeking Hawks, and like most Indians he was more than a head taller than Hawks. Naked but for a loincloth, his hair spiked into a red and black topknot, he held his tomahawk menacingly out from his right side. Hawks held his sword with both hands now, willing all of his strength into the steel. The Indian raised his tomahawk with his right hand and brought it crashing down toward Hawks' skull. Hawks leapt to the side, escaping the blow, and slammed his sword into the warrior's left shoulder. The warrior's shoulder severed, he looked at Hawks for a moment, then raised his right arm again still holding the tomahawk and aiming anew for Hawks' skull.

Before Hawks could react, a Narragansett brave ducked under the Pequot's raised right arm. He wheeled around in front of the surprised Pequot placing himself between the warrior and Hawks. With both hands, the Narragansett man swung his stone tomahawk into the face of the huge Pequot. The Pequot fell backward, a puff of dust whiffing up around his body where he fell dead. The Narragansett brave stepped on the Pequot's chest and jerked his tomahawk free before pulling a knife from its sheath strapped to his calf. He grabbed the Pequot's topknot and sliced it neatly off, skin and all, and then beheaded the dead man.

Something caught the Narragansett brave's attention and he ran into the smoke. Though grateful for his life, Hawks was shocked at the Indian's savagery. As he stared at the gruesome sight, a naked little boy dashed out from behind the burning wigwam Hawks had lit before the engagement with the Pequot. The boy knelt beside the body of the Pequot warrior. Hawks watched in horror as the child pushed the severed, smashed head onto the body. Transfixed by the sight, Hawks could not move. Again and again, the persistent child tried to make the head stick. Suddenly, the child looked up at Hawks, and Hawks recognized him as the child from the first wigwam.

The child recognized Hawks too as he picked up his father's tomahawk, barely able to carry it, and rushed at the English menace. The boy had never seen hair that color, for though it was white, it was not the white hair of old men. This shining, white-gold hair covered the creature's chin and glistened on his arms. The boy thought the man must be part beast. As he rushed the Englishman, the boy was startled to find eyes the color of ice peering down at him.

The boy suddenly stopped in his tracks and Hawks grabbed the tomahawk tossing it to the ground. He held the boy's shoulders and looked him in the eye. Knowing the boy would not understand his words, Hawks spoke them for himself, "You leave us no choice."

The child blinked, shocked that the white-haired monster could speak, and as Hawks strode away, the boy watched him pick up a stick, light it on a burning wigwam and torch home after home. The boy reached down for the tomahawk again, but he felt an arm around his waist lifting him. He saw a blood-spattered Indian face, a face that did not belong to his People. The brave looking stoically ahead carried the boy toward the edge of the palisade. In the common Algonquin tongue, the warrior said to himself as though thinking aloud, "Honors The

Dead." Though the child understood the words, he did not yet know that he had just heard his new name.

Hawks heard a shout, and turning about he saw Mead waving his arms and pointing to the ground. Hawks looked down to see that someone had poured gunpowder along the edges of the wigwams from one end of the palisade to the other. Quickly, he jogged down to the fort wall where Englishmen gathered around Mason who, seeing his men were safe, touched off one end of the line of gunpowder with a firebrand. Captain Underhill, at the opposite end of the fort, lit the other end of the line.

In short order every wigwam was in flames. Screams and whoops filled the air as the sulphurous smell of gunpowder mingled with smoke. The fire raged, sending bark flying high into the billowing clouds of war above the scene, and Hawks thought to himself, 'We have kindled hell on earth.'

A few feet away, lining the palisade wall with their English allies, stood Narragansett and Mohegan warriors. Some had grown disgusted with the vastness of the destruction. Their red tomahawks hung in hands no longer willing to wield them. Though the English called them savages, at this moment the Indians saw the very essence of the word "savage" in these English barbarians.

None of the Indians had ever seen warfare on a scale such as this. It was not the manner in which the English killed; Indians were far more creative in their methods. It was not even the death of children. What appalled the Indians was the vast scale of death. The annihilation of an entire populace was a foreign concept. This English barbarism was new and their entire, unbounded carnage shocked and sickened many braves.

It was illogical; it made no sense to destroy an entire populace. In a way, each People needed the others. Even enemy nations needed to know that there were others out there from whom they could take corn or women or children when needed. War was a way young men proved themselves. It was a way to gain honor and to keep the blood strong with new women from different nations. When one nation saw starvation on the horizon, or perhaps when disease had devastated a group, they could raid another People to restore the balance of their own village. To honor a slain warrior, they could take prisoners whom they would slowly torture to death, or they might adopt a person into their homes to fill the void left by one who had died. Sometimes, they would just take slaves. In these raids, they would kill perhaps a dozen or a few score people, but never hundreds.

The braves watched Captain Mason give the command to shoot anyone fleeing the flames, and some of the younger warriors thrived on this unqualified carnage. Side by side, muskets and arrows mowed down Pequots fleeing the incineration. As the heat in the palisade soared, bowstrings snapped, leaving arrows useless.

Hawks loaded his weapon and steadied it on the rest. His match having gone out in the fight, he borrowed a light from the musketeer next to him. He secured the newly lit match in the serpentine, poured powder into the priming pan, aimed his weapon and positioned himself sturdily behind the musket's iron rest. He grasped the triggering lever and looked for a target. He saw a girl of about twelve running naked through the inferno carrying a baby girl in her arms. Hawks wondered if the child were her sister. He stood motionless, transfixed by the long black hair singeing off her head as flames licked her body. The baby squalled piteously as the girl ran straight toward her enemies lining the palisade wall. Hawks knew she was not thinking. He knew she was just running *away,* and he thought numbly, 'She does not understand. There is no 'away'.'

With muskets firing at fleeing Indians throughout the fort, Hawks could not tell which sound signaled her death. He saw a hole appear in her back, and he wondered if it had hit the baby as well. She stumbled with the force of the shot. She fell forward onto the baby. The baby stopped crying. The girl's hair was gone now and blisters formed on her skin. Hawks wanted to run.

Flames towered above the palisade and the little Pequot boy watched as village elders, cousins, and uncles raced crazily throughout the fort. Many ran headlong into the searing flames, preferring a fiery death to whatever torture their enemies might devise. In a matter of minutes, the fight was over, his village in flames, his family dead, his father undone. This was not the war of which the little boy had heard countless stories. This was something all together new. Standing among the fortunate handful of captives destined for adoption into Narragansett and Mohegan homes, the boy heard a teenaged girl whisper, "Who could do this? What kind of creature could destroy so many?" The boy knew the answer. These creatures were not men. They were monsters.

Frozen behind his musket, Hawks stood amid cheering Englishmen, Mohegans and Narragansetts. Like so many of his countrymen standing with him who had never seen battle, and like so many of the battle-tested Indian warriors, Hawks was shocked at the massive number of slain women and children. He wondered if it truly was only because the warriors had hidden. He wondered if perhaps his captain had anticipated this all along.

Blood everywhere, Hawks' hands were sticky with the stuff as he still clutched the musket he had been unable to fire in the final tempest of carnage. The smell of burning human flesh assaulted his nostrils. He tried not to breathe through his nose, but the air was so thick and heady that each time he opened his mouth to breathe, he could taste the stench.

He heard one of his countrymen vomiting a few feet away and Hawks suddenly wretched, then forced himself to stop. How dare he find revulsion in God's blessing?

The Pequots had made it plainly known they intended the colonists harm. His pastor had preached more than once the consequences Israel suffered each time they dealt lightly with their enemies. These Indians had shown open contempt for the Gospel and therefore deserved no quarter. He forced these thoughts through his mind. Precious few English had perished; this victory was truly a mighty one. God must have wanted it.

One of the English lieutenants announced, "In the space of one hour, men! One hour! We have killed six or seven hundred Pequots. Think of all the settlers who will keep their scalps because of what we have done here!" The men let out a mighty cheer, but Hawks could find no joy in such horror.

All around them the conflagration raged, consuming the palisade itself. Smoke blackened the sky. There was no escape from scorched corpses, headless bodies, and impaled children and women. Hawks looked upward trying to find the sky which was hidden from view by smoke and flame.

Hearing a peculiar sizzling sound coming from the ground, he looked down and saw a thin stream of blood flowing steadily over the dust toward his foot. He did not move. What was the point? He was covered with blood already. He followed the stream with his eyes and found that it stemmed from a broad wash of blood flowing through the center of the fort. And there was the source of the sizzling noise ~ fire licking at the wash, boiling and frying it.

Numb and empty, he stood rigidly primed behind his musket, still waiting to bring down the fleeing girl he had let someone else shoot. Mead laid a hand on Hawks' shoulder and said quietly, "It is over. God has delivered His enemies into our hand." The men looked at each other. Hawks straightened from his firing stance and relaxed his grip on the musket. Squinting, he looked upward again, searching for the sky still hidden behind clouds of red-orange smoke.

Chapter One

Saturday, October 30th, 1703
Waterbury, Connecticut Colony

Goodwife Hannah Scott, granddaughter of Hawks, enjoyed a rare moment of stillness. She sat on a stool just inside the great fireplace where an oven had been built into one corner. Today not being a baking day, this corner made a cozy place to nurse Gershom, her baby boy.

The Scotts lived in Connecticut Colony on the outskirts of a small village called Waterbury. Goodman Jonathan Scott had built their home on the very edge of the wilderness where they enjoyed a comfortable distance from their neighbors' watchful eyes. Having grown up with fathers who were active in civil affairs, both Hannah and Jonathan Scott disliked the petty squabbles of village life, nor did they like what they often viewed as self-importance veiled in public service. Thus, the Scotts kept to themselves as much as they politely could.

Their little tow-heads, four year-old John and two year-old Martha, napped on the trundle bed while their oldest child, seven year-old Jonathan, whom they called Junior, had gone to work in the fields with his father. Hannah treasured these moments of stillness, for they were very few.

Open shutters allowed bright autumn sunshine to stream through the square-paned windows and bathe the floor in light. Exhausted from waking every few hours to nurse Gershom, she leaned against the stone wall of the fireplace and sank gratefully into a productive kind of rest. Breast-feeding her babies was the only time Hannah could in good conscience sit doing nothing ~ not mending, not spinning thread, not grinding corn, not even reading the wonderful Word of the Lord. She smiled wearily, thanking God for this blessed rest from her many tasks.

Hannah allowed her thoughts to drift, and she wondered how her husband and son fared in the fields today. Married for nine years, her love for Jonathan Scott was comfortable, calm and deep ~ far from the desperate intensity she had felt in the beginning.

Hannah drifted back to the day she had first seen Jonathan Scott. She had met him in the fall on a day that had been so like this one ~ crisp, clear and brilliant. She had been sixteen, and none of the young men in her hometown of Deerfield, Massachusetts, had stolen her heart. Since her mother had died when Hannah was a baby, Hannah had spent most of her young life tending her father and brother. In all those years, her father had never remarried, and Hannah loved that he honored the memory of her mother in that way.

Having lived alone with her father and brother for so much of her life, she was used to the way men swaggered and boasted. She knew men behaved differently among themselves than they did among women, and she could spot a fib a mile away. Men had a difficult time impressing Hannah.

On the morning when she met Jonathan Scott, Hannah had stepped out onto the leaf strewn dirt path leading from her front step to the main road that ran through the Deerfield palisade. Ever guarding against the sin of idleness, Hannah carried her basket of mending looped on the crook of her arm. She shielded her clear, ice-colored blue eyes with her hand until they adjusted to the sunlight. The bright white-blond hair, which most of her family had inherited from her Grandfather Hawks, peeked out from under her coif. This simple linen cap covered most of her head, leaving a little of her hair visible around her face. In the back, the fabric gathered just at her hair-line, allowing faint wisps to grace her neck.

The bracing autumn air brought color to her countenance as leaves rained down from enormous maples and oaks. Red, orange, and yellow swirled before her, and color crunched pleasantly under her feet. 'Oh, heaven is a fall day,' thought Hannah.

David Hoyt, walking north on the main street, spotted her and started in her direction. Hannah could not help smiling at his obvious interest. Hannah liked David; but more than she liked him, she liked the effect she had on him. His infatuation with her swelled her pride and though she knew it was wicked to be prideful, she couldn't help it.

"Good morning, Hannah," David greeted her in his best attempt to ascend from the rank of childhood playmate to man. "Good morning, David. Shouldn't you be in the fields?" she replied. They talked casually as they went along.

When they came to the main highway, she turned toward the south end of the palisade and noticed that David reversed his course in order to accompany her. He was an attractive youth, and Hannah did not mind his walking at her side. They had not gone far before David's father spotted them. Having unexpectedly come up from the fields he scowled at David for loafing but said nothing to the young man, and David suddenly excused himself, "I've work to attend to, Hannah. I must be going." She nodded and watched him trot off after his father.

With regard to choosing a husband, Hannah's father, Sergeant John Hawks, had given her much advice. Hannah's role in the matter was limited to refusal of suitors, of course, for it would be unseemly to appear forward no matter how strong her attraction might be when she finally met a worthy man. Still, refusal was a great deal of power. Sergeant Hawks, an old soldier who had fought with his brother in King Philip's War, doted on his children. He and his wife had had a happy marriage and he wanted the same for their children.

God's Word commanded women to obey their husbands. Likewise, God charged each husband to love his wife as Christ loved the Church. It was Sergeant Hawks' observation that the latter charge was likely to be fulfilled only when the husband was deeply smitten from the start. So, to the chorus of advice, the old sergeant added something no one else would tell his daughter: "The man you choose will be your lord, Hannah. You will be subject to him just as you are subject to me." Sergeant Hawks admonished his daughter time after time, "Whomever you choose, above all, be certain that he loves you even more than you love him."

Preachers spoke on the importance of many things in making a sound choice for marriage. Among critical virtues such as industry and prudence, affection also ranked high. They often quoted the old maxim, "They that marry where they affect not, will affect where they marry not." Women were the weaker vessel in all matters, including sexual restraint. Men held a grave responsibility not to lure women into fornication or adultery. In their Puritan world, desire was a powerful force not to be treated lightly. In the wrong setting it could prove disastrous, but in its proper context, it brought blessing to a good marriage.

Hannah had spent enough time reading the Song of Solomon to know that God intended passion to be part of a Christian match, but she had yet to feel it tug at her own breast. Sometimes Hannah wondered if she were too particular in that regard. Her friends Thankful, Sarah and Esther thought Hannah ridiculous for not wanting David who came from so excellent a family. Everyone thought he was handsome; even Hannah thought so. She simply did not feel for him what her father described having felt for her mother.

Hannah continued down the highway through the palisade. She walked on the left side of the road as she made her way toward the Smead house which stood just outside the palisade. Hannah was on her way to meet her best friend Thankful Smead. Together they would walk down to Hannah's uncle's house. Uncle Eliezer Hawks had married Thankful's older sister, Judith. Thankful and Hannah helped in the busy household full of small children.

As she made her way through the palisade, she saw framed in the south gate three men riding into the village from the direction of Hadley, the nearest town. As the men came into view, Hannah took particular note of the man riding a chestnut horse on her side of the road. He was unusually large for an Englishman ~ tall and broad in shoulder like an Indian. He wore a dark brown doublet and buckskin breeches. As they came closer, Hannah saw him more clearly. His dark hair was tied back and he was clean shaven, revealing a strong, angular jaw.

Lest he be a married man, Hannah allowed not even the shadow of a smile to creep across her face. She continued on her way and watched him for as long as she dared, while intending to look away before anyone noticed her staring.

Hannah's intention was interrupted however, for as the men drew nearer, this target of her attention unexpectedly turned his eyes on her. Lightning shot through her chest as he locked his gaze with hers. Confidence flashed in his deep blue eyes and she froze in her tracks. He did not waver; he did not smile. He gazed frankly and powerfully at her. Breaking the stare just before he came abreast of her, he turned his attention back to his companions who had noted the exchange and smiled mockingly at Hannah. Disgusted and embarrassed, she rolled her eyes and resumed the trek to the Smead house.

∾

That evening Hannah arrived home from her uncle's house in time to prepare the evening meal for her father and brother. Whenever Hannah spent the day working at Uncle Eliezer's house instead of tending her father's fires and cooking, Aunt Judith gave her something to serve for dinner. Today Aunt Judith had given Hannah an apple pie and some pease porridge. Hannah was about to pour it into the great iron pot and start the fire to warm it when the old sergeant and her brother, John, burst eagerly in the door. Sergeant Hawks instructed Hannah to bundle some bread to take across the street to Uncle John and Aunt Mary's house. While her father rushed to pull his dirt-smeared shirt off and over his tow-colored beard, John dashed upstairs to the loft and did likewise.

Sergeant Hawks had heard that visitors from Connecticut had just arrived in town. Having come by boat to Hadley, they traded there for a few days, and then came to Deerfield on horseback. Visitors were rare and exciting events on the frontier. Hence, the old sergeant had invited himself and his family to dine with his brother-in-law, John Catlin, at whose home the men were lodging.

Her father explained none of this, so Hannah did not know the reason for the rush but she obediently gathered two loaves of bread and tucked her embroidery into her mending basket. After the meal the women would sit by the fire and Hannah would have the chance to learn from her aunt's skillful hands. She waited by the door while her father and brother rinsed their necks, faces and hands in a bowl of water and changed shirts, making many thuds and an occasional clatter. Hannah shook her head at the noise of her favorite men.

Her brother, John, held Hannah's arm as they walked across the ruts and tracks of the muddy meeting house common to their aunt and uncle's house. None could wonder if the trio were family as they walked together, for shocking ice blue eyes and thick white hair adorned all three of the Hawkses. Enjoying the cool autumn evening, Hannah looked forward to the cozy hearth awaiting her. Aunt Mary Catlin's hearth was her favorite in all the village. She loved her Aunt Mary, who was the sister of Hannah's deceased mother Martha Baldwin Hawks. Aunt Mary provided a strong connection to the mother Hannah had never known.

Sergeant Hawks knocked on the door, and the welcoming face of John Catlin appeared. A low fire cheered the dim home. Though it was still light outside, the day was coming to its end. The Catlins had been waiting for the Hawks family; everyone had already gathered around the table and Hannah quickly found her place at the table in the gaggle of Catlins. Standing between her cousins, Esther and Sarah, Hannah held their hands and kept her eyes lowered while she waited to adjust to the subdued light of the dim room. Fast friends and close in age, the girls squeezed each other's hands to repress giggles at absolutely nothing while John Catlin blessed the food and thanked their Lord. As was the case in most homes, seating was scarce at the Catlin table, so Hannah, her brother and cousins remained standing to eat while the adults sat down on benches and stools around the table.

The table was laid with a linen cloth, horn spoons, gleaming knives, and pewter plates. Bounteous pork, pottage, milk, and ale bedecked the long broad table. Though there had been nothing more than self-conscious teenaged femininity to trigger a fit, Hannah had to use every weapon in her arsenal to conquer the giggles for which she and her cousins would surely receive more than a verbal correction. She took several deep breaths, let go of her cousins' hands, and kept her eyes down as she ignored the girls, while focusing very hard on her pork.

Hannah suddenly heard unfamiliar male voices. They spoke of news from the Connecticut colony and talked of crops and Indians and trade. She suddenly realized who the men must be, for if there were more than one set of visitors in their tiny village, she would have heard it.

Keeping her head lowered so as not to attract their notice, she cautiously peered at the visitors. She was shocked to find her glance met by the same blazing blue eyes that had arrested her that morning. She froze for a moment, robbed of breath and unable to break his gaze.

Hannah quickly looked back down at her plate knowing that he still watched. Filled with both horror and elation she could not eat, and then her Aunt Mary added to

Hannah's self-consciousness, "Hannah, are you ill my dear? You don't look well, and you aren't eating."

Swallowing hard she surprised herself with a mere whisper for a voice, "I am fine, Aunt Mary. Thank you." She flushed with embarrassment and imagined the amusement she must be providing for the stranger's friends. Feeling dizzy, it suddenly seemed that her stays conspired to restrict her breathing. But she forced herself to breathe, for a weak, fainting woman was not an attractive thing on the frontier, and attractive was something she very much wanted to be this evening.

Mary said, "Hannah, please go sit on the settle. Tend to yourself, my dear." Nodding respectfully, Hannah picked up her mending basket and crossed the room to the fireplace. As she sat down on the settle, its high back shielded her from view. Grateful for a moment of privacy, she listened to the conversation at the table and discovered that the blue-eyed man was called Jonathan Scott. Closing her eyes she leaned into the settle.

After the meal Hannah moved from this coveted seat for her father and Uncle John. She picked up a stool and moved it into a dim corner to the left of the fireplace where she could still seek privacy in the weak light if in nothing else. The men brought tobacco pipes and sat around the fire, and her awkwardness flared anew as Jonathan Scott brought his stool from the table and sat down on her right.

On a normal evening every person, even five-year-old John Catlin Jr., would have been carding wool or tow, whittling, or spinning. But tonight was unusual for visitors were a treat, and hospitality allowed the Puritan men to have a relaxing evening with them. Hannah's brother and the older Catlin boys stood leaning against the wall and listened quietly to the men. The younger boys sat on the floor by the hearth, and the men chatted while the women quietly tidied up the evening meal. Hannah felt conspicuous as the only woman around the hearth, but she would not have given up her spot next to this beautiful man for anything in the world.

As she embroidered, Goodman Jonathan Scott would occasionally watch Hannah work, and her heart raced each time she caught him looking at her. Deep and dark, she thought his eyes were like water.

At length Esther quietly brought the remaining stool from the table and set it down for her mother on Hannah's left where she could sit near the fire. Aunt Mary sat down with her embroidery and young Ruth Catlin stood next to her as she began her dexterous stitching. Ruth watched Hannah from across her mother's lap, and whenever Hannah happened to look at the child, Ruth would beam. Hannah enjoyed Ruth. Though she had never been healthy, Ruth was known to be a bit of a spit-fire, and Hannah found herself relaxing a little in the presence of her dear little cousin.

Jonathan Scott watched the fire, his back spread broad as he rested his arms comfortably on his knees and intertwined his fingers. Though he never said a word to her, never crossed the line of impropriety, Hannah could feel his presence: quiet … relentless.

That night, Hannah lay awake on her straw mattress in the loft of her father's home. She had not even spoken to Goodman Jonathan Scott, and yet she knew without a doubt that this was the passion from Song of Solomon.

Somewhere in her childhood training, Hannah had heard of the great Martin Luther, the German Reformer who had paved the way for her own Puritan faith. Whether she had heard his story at her Grandmother Baldwin's knee or in one of hundreds of sermons she could not remember. She recalled that one of Luther's Popish foes had found his eyes confounding. The Catholic heretic had said Luther's eyes were as deep as a lake. She thought to herself as she imagined the stranger lying mere yards away that these were the eyes of Goodman Scott, deep and confounding. He intoxicated her.

∽

The next day, Aunt Mary knocked at the door and handed Hannah an egg. Puzzled by the proffered egg, Hannah thanked the matron who asked, "May I come in a moment, my dear?" "Of course, Aunt Mary," Hannah replied as she opened the door further and stepped out of the way for her aunt.

"Hannah, my dear, I know you do not need an egg, but I needed a reason to come see you. Before I begin, is there something you would like to share with me, my dear?"

Wondering what wrong she had done, Hannah responded with puzzled silence.

Aunt Mary continued, "Well then! I hope the directness of this observation does not disturb you. Let me assure you that I feel quite certain that I alone, among our family, noticed the situation last night."

Hannah searched her memory for any rudeness to her elders. Perhaps, she had taken too great an advantage of her aunt and cousins when they cleaned up the meal and she sat by the fire. That seemed unlikely, for her aunt was not one to push a girl to work when she believed the girl to be ill.

"My dear Hannah, the attraction between you and Goodman Scott is positively palpable." Hannah's jaw dropped. Shocked that her feelings had been so obvious, she sat down on the edge of her cooking stool. It was rude of her to sit before her aunt did. She looked up apologetically and invited Aunt Mary to sit on a stool beside her. Mary Catlin watched as Hannah's brow furrowed with embarrassment and distress.

Hannah's throat tightened and tears began to surface as she explained, "I said not a word to him, Aunt Mary! What did I do that was so untoward?" A tear slid down her cheek as she apologized, "I am deeply sorry if I embarrassed you or Uncle."

Surprised by this reaction, Mary Catlin slipped her arm around her niece's shoulders, "Hannah, you did nothing shameful. Not in the least!" She grasped Hannah's shoulders and turned the girl to face her, "Hannah, I have borne ten children and have seen more courtships and weddings than I can count. I know attraction when I see it, and I assure you that you did nothing wrong last night." She watched Hannah's face relax, and Hannah laughed a little as her aunt wiped away the tear.

Mary pulled her stool back a few inches so she could face Hannah more easily. "After you had gone last night, I engaged Goodman Scott in a little conversation. He is not married, though I expect he has had many opportunities. He is beautiful to behold, is he not?" Mary looked at Hannah with a girlish smile that Hannah had never seen on her aunt, and Hannah laughed out loud.

"He told me that he prefers the wilderness to town. He said that it is difficult to find a woman strong enough or even willing to live on the outskirts of town. Naturally, he understands the fear of Indians, but the Connecticut Indians do not seem to have the bloodthirsty nature of the savages who can't leave Deerfield alone. It seems silly for a woman to worry in Connecticut if you ask me. There is no danger there. I don't see why it should be so hard to find a good woman. After all he has established himself to support a family; he is strong; he comes from a good family, and … he is handsome."

Mary paused for a moment and studied Hannah's face. She loved watching someone fall in love, and she could see that it was about to happen for her niece. With a conspiratorial grin Mary added, "So, I told him that Sergeant John Hawks has such a daughter." Hannah's jaw dropped again.

"Aunt Mary!" she exclaimed.

"Are you not strong? Have you not taken care of your father and brother and countless cousins? Your love of the wilderness is as plain as day. You seek any opportunity to escape the palisade for the forest. Perhaps our Lord has caused Goodman Scott to wait for you, dear child. Perhaps Providence brought him here for the sole purpose of meeting you." said Mary with a wink.

Hannah had never seen this playful side of her aunt. It embarrassed her to no end, but she was grateful to her for talking to the stranger from Connecticut Colony.

≈

That afternoon Hannah sat on the front stoop hulling Indian corn and enjoying the bright autumn sun. All her life, her happiest memories seemed to have occurred in autumn. Hearing the heavy tread of a man approaching from the main road, she looked up and her hands suddenly suspended their activity as Goodman Jonathan Scott strode confidently toward her. The color drained from her face, and her mouth went dry.

"I understand your name is Hannah," Jonathan Scott said as he stood squinting through the sunlight at her. He wore no doublet and Hannah could see the hollow between his collar bones at the open neck of his linen shirt. His neck was strong and sinewy and his skin darkened from many hours working in the sun.

She started to stand up, but he stayed her with his hand, "Please sit. I came to have a word with you." Hannah swallowed hard. Her heart raced. Wide-eyed and feeling foolish, she looked up at him. Hannah guessed that

Jonathan Scott would be patient with her adolescent awkwardness but would not give a fool a second chance.

He continued, "Not being from the area, I don't expect that I will often have the chance to sit next to you. So, I believe I will take that chance now, if you don't mind." She nodded and scooted to the end of the stoop, setting the bucket of corn down as a barrier between them.

In this staunch little Puritan community, no man would dare sit and chat alone with another man's daughter unless he had an interest, however vague, in marriage. But they had just met and Hannah wondered how this could be.

Sitting down, he leaned forward and rested his arms on his large legs, just as he had done in front of the fire the night before. This seemed to Hannah to be his signature pose, and she thought it suited him well. She found herself unable to speak to Jonathan Scott in the same way she could to the more familiar boys of Deerfield and Hadley. It was not just that he was a stranger, for she had no trouble holding conversation with traders.

Unable to get so much as one word out to this man, Hannah waited for him to speak. When he did not, she resumed her task and desperately hoped she did not appear to be a fool. Jonathan Scott stared across the common. He seemed to be thinking about something. Hannah could feel his nearness and was grateful for the task of the corn to conceal the shaking of her hands.

They sat in silence for some time with only the pop and scrape of corn coming off dried cobs. Gradually Hannah grew more comfortable in his presence. She was grateful for his silence. Never having met him, it amazed her to realize she wanted Jonathan Scott to stay right there, forever, and simply be hers ~ her second body, strong and invincible. Sensing that she was being watched, she looked up from the corn and saw Jonathan Scott gazing steadily at her.

"You are a striking maid, you know." He waited for her to respond. "You do know that, don't you Hannah?" Jonathan Scott asked her with a smile. She shook her head. Vanity was a sin, and she had never heard such words.

Unabashed by Hannah's silence, he continued, "Your hair is most unusual. I have never seen anything quite like it. It shines around your face like a band of silver-gold, and your eyes ... why, I have never seen their equal. They are like ice. You could pierce a man's heart with such stunning eyes." He paused and examined her, shaking his head in awe. Tiny lines appeared around his eyes as he broke into a broad grin and calmly declared, "You are a beauty."

Hannah's brow furrowed slightly. Nothing could have prepared her for this. The first words this man spoke to her were the words rich men wrote to their wives. They were not the words farmers from the wilderness spoke to village maids. She was overcome by the simple, honest and sudden wooing of this man.

After a moment Jonathan Scott spoke again, "I will be leaving soon, and I do not foresee another trip this far north unless I have a reason to come. I have already seen much in you that pleases me, Hannah Hawks. Your elders tell me that you work hard, and I can clearly see that you are strong. Last night, I thought you were going to faint at the table, but you went out of your way to pick up your mending before you allowed yourself the chance to sit down!" He laughed and when Hannah still said nothing, he added with a smile, "And … you are modest, which has prevented you from speaking a word to me."

Hannah smiled and said, "Goodman Scott, you flatter me. I do not know what to say."

He laughed, "You are the first person to accuse *me* of flattery!"

The beaming pair chatted for several minutes. Then, just as Hannah was growing comfortable with him, he said, "I don't suppose you know where your father might be? I thought I might ask Sergeant Hawks' leave to court his daughter."

Hannah flushed again. 'What is wrong with him!' she thought. The smile had gone from her face. Not knowing how to respond, she looked back at the corn. She had met him only the day before. Though her attraction for him ran deep, she was more than a little offended that this man assumed she had serious interest in him so soon after their first meeting. 'Then again,' she thought 'he might never again find himself in Deerfield. Perhaps it is not so presumptuous.'

Rising to leave, Jonathan Scott said, "You are not pleased. I misunderstood …"

Hannah stood up, nearly knocking over the bucket of corn. "Goodman Scott," she cried. "I am not displeased! You simply overwhelm me." They were quiet for a moment before Hannah asked, "Can you not see how you might overwhelm a maid?" Their blue eyes met, and they laughed together in front of her father's home.

"Hannah, my boldness comes of necessity. Deerfield is a long trek from my farm. I have done with my business here, and there is no reason to return to Deerfield unless you give me one."

She blushed and stared at the ground for a moment. She looked back up at him towering over her. "You have a reason," she whispered.

Looking at her tenderly, Jonathan Scott said, "God guard you for me, Hannah." He turned and walked off to seek her father in the fields.

A gust of wind puffed down the Scott chimney blowing smoke in Hannah's eyes and jolting her out of her reverie. She stood up carefully so as not to wake Gershom and laid him in the cradle near the hearth to keep him warm. Then Goodwife Hannah Scott crossed the plank floor to her spindle and resumed the familiar hum of Puritan industry.

Chapter Two

Monday, February 28th, 1704
Deerfield, Massachusetts Colony

Snow wafted down on a grey day as three warmly dressed women worked in the chilly home of Sergeant and Alice Hawks. The three women had gathered at the small Hawks home while the Deerfield men worked and drilled outside with the soldiers who had come to protect the isolated outpost of just over two hundred fifty inhabitants.

Alice Hawks felt an errant strand of chestnut colored hair tickle her cheek, and she tucked it neatly back inside her coif. A little more than seven years ago, Alice had wed Sergeant Hawks. After the death of his first wife, he had waited to marry until both of his children had moved out of his home and started their own families. He was visiting Hannah and her growing family now in Waterbury.

In the drafty plank home, Alice stood at the large wheel and spun wool while her industrious daughter Mary Allis tended the temperamental bread-baking process. Mary was one of Alice's daughters from her first marriage.

Thankful Hawks, who had married her best friend Hannah's brother John Hawks, was knitting a new pair of mittens for her seven year-old son, John Jr. From many hours of work and play, he had worn his mittens beyond repair. Now young John was outside tending the animals with his father.

Thankful and John Hawks lived just a few yards away in a small house the old sergeant had built for them. Sergeant Hawks had built it within the safety of the stockade, and as did many families, John and Thankful had taken someone into their home because of the concern of Indian attack. A bachelor named Martin Smith now slept on the floor of their main room.

Many families chose to remain in their homes outside the stockade, preferring the risk of danger to the rank and close conditions of garrison life. Typically the Indians attacked the north end of town above the stockade. Because of this, those who lived south of the stockade did not believe that their danger was any greater than it was for those living inside the stockade.

Sergeant Hawks' large family was very close and frequently ate together, tended one another's children, and helped each other in fields. The extended Hawks family was spread throughout Deerfield, the head of each household choosing whether to risk living outside the stockade or to inconvenience his family and neighbors by bringing his large family into another man's home.

Feeling the draft from a window that was slightly ajar, Alice closed it. Even on these frozen winter days, there was the occasional morning when the stench of chamber pots was so overpowering that she had to open a window to offer some relief. Though she would have liked the protection of a soldier or two under her roof, their presence would have added considerably to the odor. There were also many larger homes to house the soldiers, and with her husband gone, it was out of the question to have men unaccompanied by their wives sleeping in her home.

Alice beckoned to Thankful, knowing that she would be pleased to see the visitors trudging down the path from the Williams house. Looking out the window, Thankful saw her husband's aunt, Mary Catlin, walking gingerly over the snow and frozen mud with her teenaged daughter, Ruth, and three granddaughters.

Under the tread of the soldiers, the snow melted just enough each day to create mud along the main road. Over night, the mud froze in the outline of boot prints, cart wheels and sleigh runners. It could prove a challenge to keep one's ankles from twisting, while horses had an even more difficult time. Thankful smiled, ever happy to see her wise and comfortable aunt. She went to the door and opened it, letting in a few flakes. From under her heavy wrap, Mary Catlin slipped an arm around Thankful's waist, gave her a squeeze and asked, "How are we all today?" Thankful replied, "We are well, Aunt Mary, and you?" She ushered her aunt and her entourage inside and closed the door.

"We, too, are well," said the old matron as she pulled a bench out from under the table. As she sat down with her mending, Thankful poured her a leather mug of cider she had been keeping warm near the fireplace. Mary Catlin opened her mending basket, which had a remarkable propensity for refilling itself, and Thankful asked her, "Do you come from Mister Williams' house?"

Mary set her fingers busily to work and said, "Yes, Thankful, we do."

Ruth worked from her sewing basket while she tended the girls who all sat down to card wool on the plank floor. The girls had found spots as close to the crowded fireplace as they dared without the threat of one of their mothers tripping over them with some delicious but dangerously hot treasure from the hearth.

The Catlin granddaughters sat quietly carding with their Hawks cousins. Thankful's daughter Martha, age four, was trying in vain to teach her younger sister how to card. Two year-old Thankful, called Baby Thankful, tried her best to learn but could only manage to send tufts of wool flying up her nose.

Six-year-old Sarah, daughter of Sergeant and Alice Hawks, tried to exert an attitude of benevolent authority over Martha and Thankful, but she was often rebuffed by toddling insolence.

All but one of the Hawks children had Hannah's white-blond hair. Little Sarah had inherited her father's eyes but had her mother Alice's dark hair. It was a beautiful combination ~ those singular, piercing eyes with Alice's rich brown hair. Sarah had met her half-sister Hannah only once or twice. Her mother said that Hannah's family had visited Deerfield when she was three, but Sarah did not remember. A year ago however, when she was five, she had gone with her father and mother to visit Hannah's family in Connecticut.

Her father was there visiting now. He had hesitated to leave them because the Indian attacks had come frequently that summer. But winter had arrived, and Indians never seemed to attack in the winter, for it was not the season for war. Winter removed the cover of foliage. Sarah's mother knew how much her husband wanted to see Hannah and Jonathan Scott's new baby, and she had encouraged him to go.

Sarah remembered her half-sister as a dear person and very loving. Hannah had taken Sarah berry-picking along with her children one afternoon. Hannah had eaten nearly as many berries as she picked, and Sarah remembered thinking with glee that Hannah was as bad as the children.

She had given Sarah her lessons while they were visiting. Sarah recalled that Hannah had focused intently on her while they worked. She had made Sarah feel uniquely precious. Sarah knew that she was loved by her family, of course, but Hannah … there was something about her that had made Sarah feel very valuable.

The women spoke of many things while they worked in the Hawks house that morning. They talked of the strange omen they had heard for two nights in a row. In the middle of the night, many throughout the village had heard trampling and stomping as though a great horde of Indians was running around the palisade.

In the morning, however, there had been no tracks, no sign that anyone had been there. Some of Thankful's siblings lived inside the safety of the stockade and some did not. Thankful feared for her sister, Judith, and for their mother who lived south of the palisade.

What did this omen mean, the women wondered. Was it God's looming judgment? Their pastor, the Reverend Mister Williams, certainly thought so. The Catlins had attended a special prayer meeting that morning, which Mister Williams had called.

Mary Catlin said that the text was Genesis 32:10-11 which read, *I am not worthy of the least of all the mercies, and of all the truth, which Thou hast showed unto thy servant. Deliver me, I pray Thee, from the hand of my brother, from the hand of Esau, for I fear him, lest he will come and smite me, and the mother with the children.*

Mister Williams had exhorted them to repent of any secret sins and to pray for the *true* repentance of each family in Deerfield, "All the prayer in the world will avail you nothing if you do not amend your life! How can our righteous and just God relent from punishment when we do not reform our lives?"

The women and girls worked in silence for the space of an hour. They inwardly battled fear and asked forgiveness for sins in silent supplication to God.

At first, the children were troubled by the women's obvious fear but as the hour progressed, the children's minds wandered. They were used to long periods without speaking. If their mothers were quiet, they were to be quiet as well.

Sarah looked around at the large cozy room as she carded. Her parents' bed, a simple table with a few stools and a bench comprised the large part of their furniture. A skilled carpenter, Sarah's father had made all of the furniture himself. In fact, he had even built their meeting house and all of the furniture therein.

Sarah's home was like most Puritan homes ~ crowded, loving, and filled with the clank and clatter of constant industry. Sarah's mother had created or bartered for everything in their home. Her father brought all the raw materials into their home, but it was her mother, Alice, who made them useful. Alice turned a stick into a broom; she spun useless puffs into yarn and thread. Everything, from the bread in the kitchen to the clothes they wore to the blankets under which they slept, her mother had transformed from something utterly useless. It seemed to Sarah that there was nothing her parents could not do.

Baby Thankful toddled over to her Great Aunt Mary, who laid her mending on the table and set the child on her knee as they proceeded to have a chat. Children were not allowed to speak much, but Mary Catlin enjoyed the chatter of toddlers.

She asked her grandniece about the weather, and Baby Thankful informed her that it was "methy."

"Why, yes, I suppose it is messy, Thankful. The snow gets very dirty with all the people and horses trampling it, doesn't it? Do you suppose we ought to clean the snow?"

Baby Thankful thought a moment, then nodded gravely, enjoying the opportunity to be taken seriously.

A few feet away, Sarah scowled at the idea but said nothing. Mary Catlin asked, "Sarah, do you disagree?"

"Yes, I do, Aunt Mary. A person cannot clean snow. Once it's dirty, it stays that way."

Aunt Mary asked, "Do you suppose that's like sin?"

Sarah brightened at the chance to show off her knowledge, "Yes! *In Adam's fall, we sinned all!*" she answered enthusiastically, as though it were a thing of joy.

Her aunt nodded and began quizzing her on her lessons, "Yes, Sarah, Adam's fall is for the letter A. What about the letter J?"

Sarah did not hesitate, declaring boldly, *"J: Job feels the rod, yet blesses God."*

"One more. Tell me C – from the Scriptures." Sarah thought a moment. Then, she said, *"C: Come unto Christ all ye that labor and are heavy laden and he will give you rest."*

Mary nodded again, "Now child, I should like to hear your favorite prayer."

Sarah recited it with confidence:

"Awake, arise, behold thou hast,
Thy life a leaf, thy breath a blast;
At night lay down prepar'd to have
Thy sleep, thy death, thy bed, thy grave.
Lord if thou lengthen out my days,
Then let my heart so fixed be,
That I may lengthen out thy praise,
And never turn aside from thee.
So in my end I shall rejoice,
In thy salvation joyful be;
My soul shall say with loud glad voice,
JEHOVAH who is like to thee?
Who takest the lambs into thy arms,
And gently leadest those with young,
Who savest children from all harms,
Lord, I will praise thee with my song.
And when my days on earth shall end,
And I go hence and be here no more,
Give me eternity to spend,
My God to praise forever more."

Mary looked approvingly at her niece and said, "You are an intelligent child Sarah, but you must guard your heart against pride. Remember the letter *S: Seest thou a man wise in his own conceit, there is more hope of a fool than of him."*

∽

St. Lawrence River Valley, French Canada

Far to the north in Canada lay an Indian village neighboring the large French-Catholic Indian town called Kahnawake. It was located on the St. Lawrence River. Situated about twenty miles west of Kahnawake, the little village comprised a mixture of people who had come mostly from the five confederated Iroquois Nations, the greater part of the population being Mohawk. Many of the people were former slaves of the Iroquois.

Inside the maternal family lodge, silver-haired Honors The Dead sat with his wife, Night Sky, on a wide, low bench draped in fur. Neatly tucked under the benches were stores of wood and family belongings.

The longhouse was divided by partition walls creating apartments for each family. Each apartment had three walls ~ an outside wall of the longhouse and walls on the right and left sides, leaving the apartments open to the central fires. Smoke escaped and light entered through gaps in the roof above the fires. The walls and crossbeams were hung with drying plants, skins, and all the necessities of their simple life.

Blankets draped loosely over their shoulders as the elderly couple leaned against the outer wall of the longhouse, Night Sky held their sleeping grandson wrapped snugly in soft furs. Night Sky was the matriarch of the lodge, which housed the families of her two daughters from Honors The Dead and the families of Night Sky's two daughters from her first marriage. It was cozy but not crowded, for their People could not produce the enormous numbers of children that European settlers did.

Honors The Dead savored these cold winter months even though they often meant hunger. In such a harsh winter climate, he was a little unusual in enjoying winter as much as he did, but he loved the enveloping warmth of the longhouse. He loved the safety, whether real or imagined, of being at home inside with his People. His People ... Honors The Dead thought about those words. He had known so many nations.

He had been born into the Pequot Nation, known to the neighboring Peoples as The Destroyers. He did not remember much of his life in the fort on the Mystic River. He had been only three or four years old at the time. He remembered his father, strong and tall. He remembered the great festivities the night before the attack. His father had planned to set out on the warpath the next day, and his mother had watched the braves proudly but not without worry. Instead, the warpath had come to them. He closed his eyes to repel the memory ~ the image of his butchered father, the flames, the peculiar hair and ice colored eyes of the man standing over his father ... the image would not fade.

He remembered the strong arm of his new father scooping him around the waist, and he remembered hearing his new name for the first time. He had been adopted into the Narragansett Nation, the People of the Small Point. In the foreign Narragansett camp that first night, he had been held close by a new mother who did not smell like his own, nor did she look like her. He had felt too numb to cry that night. That night had been his only opportunity to do so, for crying was weak.

Eventually, this new Narragansett father had told him that the ice-eyed Englishman had not killed his Pequot father. The news had not made the white-haired man cease to be Honors The Dead's enemy. The man had been at the fort that day. Therefore, the English barbarian had killed someone he loved, and over time this single man with the unforgettable eyes had assumed the mantle of all of Honors The Dead's enemies.

Nearly forty years later in King Philip's War, Honors The Dead had seen two Englishmen with the same bizarre coloring of eyes and hair. Honors The Dead had fought with his Narragansett brothers in the war of the great Wampanoag chief, Metacom, whom the English called King Philip. United for that brief time, the Indians had wrought much destruction on the settlers and had enjoyed a viable chance of beating the barbaric English.

He recalled that Metacom had taken a delegation to persuade the woman called Awashonks, squaw chief of the neighboring Sakonnet, to join their cause. Honors The Dead had visited the Sakonnet to hear Metacom's words. Metacom had spoken of his father, Massasoit, who had rescued the first Pilgrims from certain starvation. Massasoit had not lightly made the decision to help the English Pilgrims. He had seen their woeful state, and his heart had had pity on them, but why had they come and were they dangerous? He had seen their powerful muskets, and could not be sure that they would be friendly or trustworthy. However, if he helped them, the

Pilgrims with their muskets might help his People, greatly weakened by epidemics, against their enemies.

After speaking of his father, Metacom had said, "Ever since the English came to our shores, our People have done nothing but die. They die of disease; they die of rum; they die of starvation because the colonists' cattle destroy our crops.

"We are forced to move farther and farther toward the Man Eaters' hunting grounds. The English preachers convince our People to give up our customs. They treat us with little respect and call us savages. I say that *they* are the savages! We must drive them back across the sea!" The grief and rage of Metacom's words had given them weight in Honors The Dead's ears.

When the war broke out, the barbaric English had seemed genuinely insulted by Indian betrayal. 'Why does this surprise them?' Honors The Dead had thought. 'Perhaps they are stupid. How can they think the way they do? Their king, with his crown, has power because the English obey him even when his orders are unwise.'

Before the war, a chief near Plymouth had signed over the sovereignty of his People and had made them English subjects, but Honors The Dead knew that the chief could not possibly have understood the ramifications of what he had done. Native nations could never be subject to an English crown ... allies, yes, but subjects, no!

With the war raging, Honors The Dead had seen that the English understood the nations no better. The very fact that the English referred to Metacom as King Philip instead of just Philip showed that they believed that all the nations served him and obeyed his command.

Nothing could have been further from the truth. Metacom was Wampanoag, and Honors The Dead was Narragansett. Honors The Dead's People were not even subjects of their own chiefs, let alone the chief of another nation. Indians respected the guidance of their leaders because they were wise, not because of some ridiculous crown that could easily be knocked off a man's head.

Another thing that confounded him was that the English never accepted that the Indians had a *reason* for attacking them. To the English, his People were just bloodthirsty savages. Wherever Indians attacked, the English considered it the wrath of their O-God, and Indians were nothing more than mindless instruments of O-God.

Honors The Dead had wondered, 'Why can't they understand that it is not O-God punishing them? It is my People. *We* are punishing them.'

In an attack during King Philip's War, the English had burned the Narragansett Fort where Honors The Dead and his family lived. Honors The Dead had then taken his wife and two adolescent daughters to the safety of Peskeompskut, a fishing place just north of the then-abandoned English outpost of Deerfield. Many nations lay down the hatchet each year to fish side by side at Peskeompskut, and during the war Peskeompskut had served as a secluded camp where Metacom's allies made preparations for the warpath.

Honors The Dead recalled that when the English barbarians attacked Peskeompskut, he had suddenly caught sight of two white-haired Englishmen across the camp from him, one bearded and one clean shaven. Then, he had seen his wife and daughters.

At that moment there had been a hopeless distance riddled with fighting men and fleeing women and children between himself and the two ice-eyed, white-haired men. Honors The Dead had watched in horror as the clean shaven barbarian decapitated his wife with a sword. The bearded one ran his younger daughter through with his blade. His older daughter had fled, and as Honors The Dead ran toward her, another Englishman shot her in the lower back.

Honors The Dead had been able to kill and scalp the shooter, but his daughter had died soon after being wounded. As for wreaking revenge on the white-haired men, there was little opportunity, for they had been but a flash in the melee and were quickly gone from his sight. The grief had overwhelmed him, and he had never fully recovered from the loss.

After that battle, the allied Indians had found themselves hunted like animals. There was no safety wherever they fled. If the English did not find them, the Man Eaters did.

Known to the Narragansett and other nations as the Man Eaters, this People was allied with the English who called them the Mohawk. They called themselves the People of the Longhouse. They were of the great Iroquois Confederacy, and while they had formally stayed out of

King Philip's War, they harassed Metacom's men from time to time.

The Mohawk had finally caught up with Honors The Dead's band of twenty-odd warriors, torturing most of them to death, roasting and eating some of them. They had allowed Honors The Dead to run the gauntlet, which was torture in and of itself, but it also enabled him to become a slave if he survived.

And he had indeed survived the whipping, pelting line of Mohawks. He had run with stoic courage, and they had made him a slave. After three summers, the Mohawk had found him worthy and had adopted him as one of their own.

Later he had gone on a trading expedition to see the Mohawk Nation's brothers at Kahnawake. There, he had seen that the French priests dwelt among the Indians; thus the Indians were allied with the French in most things. This had pleased Honors The Dead, for the English were enemies of the French, just as they were his enemies.

The French priests' complete abstinence from women astounded Honors The Dead. While Indians restrained themselves sexually in that they did not rape captive women and did not display their affection, sex was still something a man needed. As a proudly stoic man, he respected the French priests' self-control, and he found a good thing in their God called Christus.

Though the priests did not approve of many of his People's ancient ceremonies, they did not prohibit them. These priests did not ask Honors The Dead to stop being

Indian as the English preachers did. The English required an Indian who converted to Christianity to give up his Indian-ness, cut his hair, move into a European style house, stop wearing Indian dress, stop hunting … stop being Indian; but, even then, he could never become the equal of an Englishman. They were too proud. These French priests simply lived among the People and taught them.

From the Frenchmen, he could receive this great God called Christus. The idea of one God with three persons, the Breath of all life … it gave him chills to think of such power resting in the hand of just One. He had come to love this Christus in a quiet, confident way. He enjoyed the rituals of the Church as well, and the rhythmic Latin tongue lent gravity to the Mass.

But, even as he accepted the new faith, Honors The Dead could not reconcile everything the priests taught, for what was the need for purgatory if Christus' sacrifice was sufficient for all? He wondered about those who had died before hearing of Jesus. However, Honors The Dead did not allow such conundrums to muddle his thinking. He was simply glad to know this Christus and was glad that the priests had come.

These were his People now, the Kahnawake Mohawk. Here he had met Night Sky, who had taken him to her village west of Kahnawake. She had borne him two daughters who were both mothers now themselves.

Their younger daughter, Catches Water, sat cross-legged on a deerskin near one of the cooking fires in the center of the longhouse. She wore moosehide leggings and a deerskin mantle with the soft fur against her skin. In her lap, she held a large flat-bottomed dish in which she ground dried corn into a fine powder called nocake.

Her husband, Red Bear, had gone on the warpath with the French, Huron and Abenaki. The French and English kings were battling for control of Acadia and New France as part of the larger European conflict known to some as Queen Anne's War and to others as the War of Spanish Succession.

Though there were roughly as many French as Indians in the war party of more than two hundred fifty, it was expected that the Indians would do most of the fighting and dying, as was often the case in these things. Catches Water imagined the nocake sustaining her man and giving him strength to return to her. She knew that there would be many days when he would survive on the corn powder alone.

Her babe awoke, and Night Sky entertained him for a few minutes. But soon he cried and Night Sky carried him over to her daughter, who set down the corn and took the babe. Catches Water drew her thick raven hair behind her shoulder and brought her son close to nurse. Closing her eyes and rocking a little, she felt the tingling surge of her milk letting down. With her abundance, she hoped this boy would grow strong. An elder chosen to name their child had called him Swift Legs because he kicked more than most wee ones. Her husband thought the child would be fast and strong, for the boy seemed impatient to learn to use his legs.

Breathing deeply, she savored the scents of her home ~ wood smoke, venison, corn, and animal hides. The wind howled outside, but they were warm and cozy. The longhouse preserved most of the heat from the fires. The heat stayed in the building rather than going up a chimney as in European homes.

It made for a smoky home, but it was certainly warm. Catches Water opened her eyes and looked down on her son gazing up at her as though she were the most fascinating creature alive. To him, she was indeed. When he saw her soft, lustrous eyes looking back at him, he smiled a great toothless grin. She laughed and stroked his cheek.

Catches Water missed her husband. She imagined him now walking silently across ice and snow. Tall and strong under his mantle, his muscles were precisely carved beneath his copper skin. His head was plucked clean except for a patch at the back. This patch of hair was pulled taut, greased and interspersed with feathers to stand proudly like the tuft on a blue jay.

He was a stunning man. Catches Water adored her husband. She wondered what he would bring her from the spoil ~ an iron pot, perhaps, or a fine coat with silver buttons… She knew he had wanted to go, but she would have traded all the English loot in the world just to be sure he would return. She smiled with bittersweet hope as she thought of their son against Red Bear's smooth, bare chest. She wanted him home.

The day moved along easily. Though diminished with so many of their braves gone, the sounds of life filled the longhouse. Children played and squealed with delight as they threw snowballs outside. Here and there a dog barked.

Inside the longhouse, now and then one of her cousins would stir the pots that hung along the cooking fires; her nieces and nephews snacked on succotash and dried meat; her sister and half-sisters stitched leather and chatted; but mostly people just sat ~ sat and talked, sat and listened, and sometimes just sat.

There was no hurry. Work was a part of life, but it was not the purpose of life.

Swift Legs had stopped nursing now, and he cooed at his mother. He made an O with his mouth as he peered wide-eyed around the longhouse kicking all the while. Whenever his eyes lit on his mother, he beamed.

Catches Water enjoyed her son for quite some time before returning him to her mother, who received him with the joy only a child can bring. Swift Legs looked about, kicking his legs and craning his neck. When he caught the eye of his grandfather, the babe's body jumped with excitement, arms and legs flailing.

Night Sky smiled at Honors The Dead, who nodded and laughed. How he loved this child. He looked at his daughter, who had resumed the task of grinding corn. She looked up, and their eyes met. The love and contentment in his face was unmistakable.

Catches Water knew the pain of his life. He had shared the story with her and Red Bear one brilliant autumn day.

Afterwards, Red Bear had told her that her father's words had burned into his heart. Red Bear told his wife that one day he would avenge her father; and more than that, he would restore her father's peace.

As the day faded, families took to their own apartments. Catches Water reluctantly left the fireside and retired. She lifted the heaping furs and tucked Swift Legs into the softness against the outer wall of the longhouse so that he would not roll out of bed. She was grateful for her family sleeping throughout the longhouse. What would she do if she were all alone with her baby in a big European house? It was inconceivable to be so alone. She loved her People.

Their home was warm and snug even against the extreme walls. She lay down next to her child and drew him close to her as she covered her body with heavy furs. She nursed him as they drifted off to sleep, sinking into softness and comfort.

In the frozen night, Red Bear moved quietly among the warriors and French soldiers. The war party of over two hundred fifty carried tomahawks, clubs, muskets, and hopes of spoil and a triumphant return with many captives. They would make their final preparations for the attack on a mountain overlooking the sleeping English town of Deerfield known to the French as "Guerrefille" meaning Daughter of War. Their snowshoes slapped and crunched softly as they passed through the snow-clad forest, almost specter-like, fading from one hill to the next. Even the French had grown quiet as they drew nearer their destination.

Red Bear's heart pounded ~ his own silent drum of war. Through the darkness, through the trees, ascending the last mountain they made their way. Closer, closer...

Chapter Three

Tuesday, February 29th, 1704
Deerfield, Massachusetts Colony

In the dark hours before dawn, six year-old Sarah found herself unable to sleep. With her father gone and winter still in full force, Alice, Mary, and Sarah all slept in the big bed on the first floor. In the frigid room, she was grateful for the warmth of her mother and sister. Sarah snuggled against her mother's side. In her sleep, Alice stroked Sarah's dark hair as Sarah rolled her head back against her mother's hand.

The day's talk of omens and Indians had frightened Sarah. The pastor was sure that the town was about to be destroyed. Staring into the darkness, she wished her Papa, the old sergeant, were there to protect them. She knew that she was safe when Papa was nearby. At sixty-one, he was old compared to her friends' fathers, but he was still strong and was something of a local hero from King Philip's War. The way he blustered about gave her confidence.

Though she was not entirely sure what great sins her family and neighbors had committed, Sarah hoped that God would forgive their village and spare them the great calamity which their pastor was so certain loomed ahead.

After some time, her favorite prayer drifted into her mind. Its mercy comforted her as it thrummed in her head. She allowed the rhythm of the words to rock her like a babe as she tried to sleep:

JEHOVAH who is like to Thee?
Who takest the lambs into Thy arms,
And gently leadest those with young,
Who savest children from all harms,
Lord, I will praise Thee with my song.
And when my days on earth shall end,
And I go hence and be here no more,
Give me eternity to spend,
My God to praise forever more.

Sarah thought she heard the same soft thump of footsteps on the snow that she and the other villagers had heard the two preceding nights. She slipped out of bed through the top of the covers, careful not to let in any cold air that might wake her mother or sister. She crept to a stool below the window, climbed up and peered through the slats in the shutters. Her breath caught as she saw to her horror that real creatures were making the sound of footsteps tonight. Pouring over the palisade wall and even through the gate were scores of savages and soldiers. The snow had piled so high on the northwest end of the palisade that they simply walked right over the wall and dropped down into the sleeping village.

Sarah ran to the bed and frantically shook her mother awake. "Indians! Mama! There are Indians outside!" Alice blinked. She realized that Sarah's nightshift was cold and that she had been out of bed. This was no nightmare. Alice threw off the covers and set her bare feet on the cold plank floor. She ran to the window and watched, stunned, as an enemy against whom she had no defense, loped toward their house. 'Where is the watchman? Why is no one defending the town?' she thought.

From the direction of John Hawks' house, they heard the cellar door slam shut. Alice' head snapped toward the direction of her step-son's house. She shut her eyes in relief, and whispered to Sarah, "I think your cousins made it to the cellar."

The thud of a hatchet in their door jolted Mary out of bed. Immediately it was followed by whoops and screams and more thuds and cracks. Sarah heard her mother whisper, 'My God, there is no defense,' as she rushed the girls away from the door into the corner next to the fireplace. Alice grabbed a poker and squared herself in front of her daughters. Standing in the freezing room in her nightshirt, she held the poker with both hands, waiting for the savages.

Wood splintered and chipped; within mere moments, the door had split. A copper hand reached through the chasm in the door and pulled free the heavy plank that barred it. Sarah heard the door hit the floor with a whack. She clutched the back of her mother's nightshirt and buried her face in it as she heard the soft thumps of heavy moccasinned men striding toward them and then a hideous crack. Suddenly, her mother lurched forward. Sarah, still holding her dress, fell onto her mother's legs.

She felt a hand grab her hair and pull her to her feet. A pair of black eyes peered out of a face painted half black divided down the nose line and splattered with blood. The brave looked intently at her eyes and examined her face. The man's head was plucked smooth except for a tuft in the back. Sarah put her little hands up and clutched his fist where he held her hair. He jerked her to his right side and held her there with one hand. Pointing at her sister Mary with his hatchet in the other hand, he spoke to the other three men in a language Sarah could not understand. Standing next to the Indian, Sarah tried to look down to see what was wrong with her mother, but he held her hair so tightly that she could not see. Sarah saw that in the dead of winter, they wore no shirts, only war paint and leggings. The Indian who held her hair said to Mary, "Dress."

Mary took Sarah's hand and the Indian let go of her hair. Sarah was finally able to see her mother who lay face down on the floor, the iron poker useless at her side. Blood poured from her neck which was strangely twisted and rent where it met the shoulder. As she followed Mary, Sarah slipped in her mother's blood and fell. She yanked her hand out of Mary's, her mouth tightly set, eyes ablaze with terror and wonder. As she got to her knees and lay across her mother's back, she clutched the broken body.

The Indian with the half painted face then squatted next to the body and placed his knife against her scalp. With both arms, Mary quickly grabbed Sarah around the waist and yanked her up. Mary lost her footing in the blood and stumbled onto one knee as she turned Sarah's head away just before the sickening slice and rip hissed in their ears.

As Mary helped Sarah to dress, the Indians used firebrands for light and began rifling for loot upstairs and down. Sarah kept turning to look at her mother with the gash and horrible bend in her neck. She wanted to go to her, but there was nothing but obedience for the moment. She must dress and wait. Then as Sarah began to whimper, Mary knelt down to comfort her sister. She put her hand gently over Sarah's mouth, and said, "You must not cry. Mama is in heaven; she is happy even now."

Her words did nothing to quell the whimpers that were fast becoming sobs. Mary lifted Sarah's chin and forced her to look in her eyes. "Sarah," she said roughly, "Do not irritate them. If you would live, you must hush." Sarah sucked her breath in hard through her nose. She looked in Mary's eyes and found strength there. The tears did not stop, and she quaked, but she was quiet.

The Indian who had slain their mother took Sarah by the hand and shoved Mary out the door into the faint morning light. Mary tripped but regained her footing in the snow. As she emerged into the screaming melee, Sarah's little face went grey with disbelief. Her pastor's prophesies had never created nightmares so horrific as the hell all around her. Her entire world was on fire. She kept reaching backward for her mother's hand. Where was her mother? Sarah could not think. She shook her head to shatter the vision of her impotent mother on the floor, never to follow her. 'God, where is my mother! Please,

please, God, I *need* my Mama!' she silently besought her Creator.

The girls and the Indian stood outside Sergeant Hawks' house, and Sarah looked toward her pastor's house next door. She saw an Indian emerge carrying one of the Williams' six week-old babies by her feet. The baby cried the pitiful, visceral wail of a newborn. Sarah heard Mary whisper, "Jesus…" as the brave walked to a spot a few feet away from the corner of the Williams' house. He swung the babe into the air. In surprise, the infant stopped crying. Then the brave swung the child in a swift, downward arc against the corner of the house. The babe's skull cracked against the wall, and her brain slid down the corner as the Indian dropped her on the ground.

Mary began to reel but caught herself. She bent over and put her hands on her knees to keep from fainting. Sarah saw her sister gasp for air. Tears flowed freely from Mary's face, but not a sound escaped her.

Mary turned her contorted face toward Sarah's and then grasped her hand. Everywhere Sarah turned, blood-stained snow mingled with butchered and smashed bodies, human and animal. Hogs squealed piteously and sheep bleated as they burned alive in the villagers' barns. This was hell. Sarah was sure of it. Her voice trembling, she whispered "O God, forgive us. Please don't be angry anymore."

French soldiers and Indian warriors ran out of houses bearing all manner of pewter and iron trophies. Sarah looked back to see her house afire with her mother inside. Behind it, John and Thankful's house burned as well.

The door was still barred. 'That's peculiar,' thought Sarah. Then she realized with horror that her cousins and their parents were still in the cellar under the house. She opened her mouth; she wanted to scream, but she could make no sound. Her tears ceased to flow. This was hell, and she was not dead. How was that possible?

She grew weary of the relentless scenes, sounds, thoughts and prayers slamming together in her mind. Her head to one side, Sarah stared vacantly into the conflagration. All the people who loved her were running or dying or fighting or burning. Nearly all the buildings that had stood as bastions of her security now hissed and crackled with no more will to stand than logs in her mother's fireplace. Sarah's hand grew limp in her sister's as reality drifted away. Sarah saw no more; she felt no more.

&

The morning was now half spent. The war party with its captives had departed ~ the captives now gone beyond hope of rescue. Some of the men at nearby Hadley had seen the red glow of Deerfield's incineration and had come to her aid. These men at first had some success against the retreating war party. Threatened with the killing of captives, these Hadley men now waited outside the palisade walls to ensure that the enemy was gone. The survivors still kept their hiding places as well.

Completely alone and numb, Mary Catlin sat in the snow surrounded by blood and burning ruins. She was alive because she had offered water to the commanding French officer. For this demonstration of Christ's love, she had received criticism from all those beset and attacked by his forces. From the man himself, she had received her life.

Every single person she could see was dead. Her children and husband, her grandchildren, everyone of her family was dead or taken captive.

She wrapped her arms around her knees, rocking slowly back and forth, and whispered, "God... God... God..." Mary Catlin wondered 'How could we have been so sinful, so proud, so preoccupied with the treasure of this world? How could I have been so sinful? With all of the warnings and omens You gave us, and still we did not repent, Lord. We have no one to blame but ourselves.'

Mary knew that there was no punishment in heaven, for there she had Christ, her advocate, to cleanse away her sins. If God would not relent from worldly punishment of sin, she knew she could find reprieve if she occupied this place no more. In Christ alone, in Heaven alone, would she find rest from the horrors of this world... and she would be reunited with her dead children. A sob escaped her. Then reaching her hands heavenward she cried from the depths of her agony, "My God!"

Thursday, March 2nd, 1704
Waterbury, Connecticut Colony

The dawn ushered in a bright and hopeful sky as the old sergeant kissed his grandchildren farewell. Sergeant Hawks slapped Jonathan Scott's back and brushed Hannah's cheek tenderly with his hand before mounting his horse. "I don't know when I'll make it back here. I shall try again next year. I love to see you all. He looked at little Martha and winked, "You're a prize, you are, my dear," then he blustered, "And the lot of ye mind yer mother!" Beaming, he trotted off, taking care of his horse on the snow.

The road to Hartford, whence he would wait for a boat on the Connecticut River home to Deerfield, was really just a wide path in most places, and Sergeant Hawks took care. Where the trees were not so thick, the sun warmed the snow, making the path slushy on the frozen ground. Sometimes, sleigh runners had sliced rivulets in exposed mud. They froze making the way difficult for his horse to keep its balance. There were patches which the sun had not reached in weeks; these were slick and treacherous.

Sergeant John Hawks was a happy man, blessed beyond measure. He missed his daughter Hannah already and longed to see her children more often. He had found a good friend in her husband as well. 'Would that they lived in Deerfield,' thought the old man. Sergeant Hawks knew that his daughter had chosen a good man and that she would be cared for come what may. Still, he missed her a great deal.

As he traveled on sometimes quickly, most of the time not so quickly, he ruminated on his family. He thought of how peaceful Alice looked as she read the Bible each evening. Though reading was difficult at night, it was her favorite time to read the Word. Winding down for the day, she was most receptive to the Lord's teaching and with night approaching, most needful of His comfort. She would make the most of the firelight, leaning in toward the light and warmth. He wondered what his family was doing now. Perhaps they were spending the day with Thankful. What were John and John Jr. doing? Life was not so busy for the men since the town was staying inside the palisade. For months, they had been pestered by Indian attacks. Their crops had been poor because they had never known when the Indians would attack. This year had been very difficult that way.

His granddaughters Martha and Baby Thankful came to mind. 'Now, what do you suppose they are up to?' the old sergeant wondered to himself. Perhaps they had found a cat to pester with relentless cuddling, he chuckled. His step-daughter Mary might be tending the fire or plying her needle.

And Sarah, ah, Sarah... shining, bright little Sarah, always ready to spout off her lessons. There was something about a child born into a man's old age. Patience and time were gifts he gave more freely; he doted on this greatest blessing of his life. It was like the heaven of having grandchildren only getting to have her with him all the time. Perhaps now Sarah sat on the hearth leaning against the stone wall of the fireplace; perhaps she sorted wads of tow for her mother to spin.

Imagining her head tucked down and her eyebrows raised, he whispered, "My God, how I love that child. Thank You, Lord," and he resisted the temptation to spur his steed on over the unpredictable path.

ৡ

Thursday, March 9th, 1704
White River, Present Day Vermont

The sun was low in the sky, and Red Bear's snowshoes were sinking from the weight as he walked stoically carrying both his pack of loot and little Sarah Hawks on his back. She seemed strong enough to Red Bear and certainly fared no worse than any of the other children, but her survival on the arduous journey all the way to Night Sky's longhouse was not guaranteed.

The party of more than one hundred captives with their Native captors had split into small bands while the French continued their journey alone. That morning, Red Bear's band had left the Connecticut River. The river ice had easily borne Sarah and the other captive children as they rode on sleds pulled by dogs. Though the wind had been bitter without the protection of trees, the snow on the river was minimal, and Red Bear had not had to carry Sarah. Now they headed northwest along the shore of the White River, where the snow had gotten progressively deeper. The White River was wild and had not frozen over. The snow on its banks was so deep that little Sarah found herself sinking in it up to her chest. Thus, Red Bear now carried both his pack and the child.

Perched on top of his pack, Sarah was wrapped tightly against Red Bear's back with a blanket around the widest part of his shoulders and knotted at his chest. Red Bear had chosen Sarah for his captive when he had seen her eyes. Immediately, he had recalled his father-in-law's stories of the family he called Ice Eyes.

When they had been traveling along the Connecticut River with Sarah riding on a sled and Red Bear easily bearing the weight of his pack, he had envisioned the smile on Honors The Dead's face when Red Bear would stride into camp with a new granddaughter for him, one no doubt descended from the same pale-eyed barbarian who had caused Honors The Dead so much pain. Ah, that would be restoration indeed. He thought of his wife's happiness as well, and he recalled his promise to restore peace to her father's heart. When he had seen the beautiful child in that English house, Red Bear had thought the day had come.

However, Red Bear now found himself faced with a choice. His pack was filled with heavy valuables made of iron and pewter. He simply could not carry both his pack of booty and the child. He could take the child and risk that she might not survive the journey. If he did this, he would have to leave his pack on the trail, and all of the loot would be lost.

Red Bear's only alternative was grievous but virtually risk free. He could choose the pack and leave the child. But he could not simply leave her to struggle in snow up to her chest where she would die of exposure if she were not first torn apart by animals. Thus, if he did not take her with him, Red Bear would have to kill her.

He struggled now with the choice, for despite his better judgment, he had grown fond of the little girl. Throughout the day, Red Bear weighed the two options as he fell farther and farther behind the small band. While a captive was even more valuable than any booty, he wondered how he could justify the gamble of choosing to keep the child when she might not even survive the journey. If she died along the way, how could Red Bear return home empty handed? How could he rob his family of the booty expected from the warpath? But if she lived… what joy she would bring to Honors The Dead. She would be restoration incarnate.

❧

The next morning, the small camp rose from beds of pine boughs over snow. Among the Indians, Deerfield's pastor and two weary, starving children obeyed the command of survival as they got to their feet to face another hopeless day. Knowing that there would be no breakfast, Sarah stood next to her pastor as she waited to be strapped onto her master's back for the day's march. Yesterday, Sarah had lost sight of her sister and cousins when her master had joined one of the smaller bands. Sarah had never felt such isolation, and now her pastor and a neighbor child were her only comfort.

Wrapped in a blanket stolen from her parents' bed and given to her by Red Bear, her master, Sarah stood still.

She kept quiet, ever quiet, attempting to go unnoticed. Being noticed was something that vibrant little Sarah had started to avoid; on this trek, she had seen the consequences of capturing the attention of these people. She wanted to cry, but fear held her in check. She was not sure that what she had seen had really happened, that her mother was really gone, but here she was waking up with snow for a pillow each morning. It must have happened. She clutched the blanket against her face. She could still smell her mother on it even after ten days of wind and snow.

Sarah watched as her master strode toward her, his face stoic and unreadable as always. He bent over and set his shoulder against her waist, lifting her easily, and walked into the woods. Sarah had seen captives disappear with Indians before on this trek; she knew what was about to happen. Her heart raced, and her eyes grew wild with terror as she craned her neck to see anything. All she could see were her master's snowshoe tracks, pine cones on snow, and great grey boulders. Sarah began to pray. She mouthed the words silently at first:

"Awake, arise, behold thou hast,
Thy life a leaf, thy breath a blast;
At night lay down prepar'd to have
Thy sleep, thy death, thy bed, thy grave."

Her silent prayer became a whisper as her face bobbed against the wool blanket on her master's back.

"Lord if thou lengthen out my days,
Then let my heart so fixed be,
That I may lengthen out Thy praise,

And never turn aside from Thee."

Red Bear's snow shoes slapped against the crust of snow as he carried her farther away from her fellow captives. Sarah whispered the prayer mechanically now, the familiar words soothing her as she thought of her fellow captive, Mary Brooks, who had been slain earlier in the week for her frailty after a miscarriage. Mary Brooks had known she was going to be killed; she had had no fear; and she had surrendered completely, even cheerfully, to God's will. A glimmer of peace flicked in Sarah's heart. 'If I die and go to heaven, I can see my Mama,' she thought. Her heart thrilled at the thought. Tears of hope and fear sprang to her eyes, and she allowed them to flow freely, knowing that whether or not she annoyed her master made no difference now.

"So in my end I shall rejoice,
In Thy salvation joyful be;
My soul shall say with loud glad voice,
JEHOVAH who is like to Thee?"

Red Bear put his hand out behind himself for balance as he carried Sarah down a short, steep drop. She thought to herself with sudden, fervent joy so strangely mixed with terror, 'Jesus *will* save me from hell. He *will* send me to heaven if only I believe, and I believe! Mama, Mama... I can have you again!'

"Who takest the lambs into Thy arms,
And gently leadest those with young,
Who savest children from all harms,
Lord, I will praise Thee with my song."

Red Bear walked around a large grey rock. He bent over and laid Sarah on the snow. Her face wet with unashamed tears, she looked up at him, fearing the pain, but her heart thrilled at the hope of embracing her mother again. She continued to whisper,

"And when my days on earth shall end,
And I go hence and be here no more,
Give me eternity to spend,"

With no change in countenance nor even so much as a pause, he raised his hatchet over his head.

"My God to praise forever more."

Red Bear slammed the steel blade into her face, crushing her skull. He took hold of her hair, now splattered with blood and brain, setting his knife to what remained intact of her skull, and jerked upward. Wiping the blade on Sarah's tattered dress, he sheathed the knife, and tucked her scalp into the pouch containing her mother's chestnut hair. Then Red Bear strode back the way he had come.

Now able to continue the march home, Red Bear knew that one day he would indeed bring restoration to Honors The Dead, and his face betrayed no sign of weakness, no evidence of the struggle within.

૭

Friday, March 10th, 1704
Deerfield, Massachusetts Colony

Eliezer Hawks stood with his older brother before the charred ruins of John and Thankful Hawks' home. Beneath his grizzled beard, Sergeant Hawks worked his jaw and stared numbly at the cellar where his grandchildren with John and Thankful had suffocated beneath the now collapsed floor boards. Charred with rivulets and cracks, the great timbers of the ceiling had fallen in on the floor. They lay askew across the length of the burned out first floor room. Eliezer laid his hand on his brother's shoulder. Feeling the touch, the old sergeant crumpled to his knees and wept.

Next door, his own home also lay in ruins. His dear wife was dead, his daughter and step-daughter taken captive, "God, how could I have been absent? Why have You left me alive?"

Ironically, the stockade had been the most dangerous place to be that fateful night, for that was where the Indians had attacked, simply walking up the snow banks to the top of the palisade and dropping down within its walls. Fifty-six souls had departed the earth, and one hundred nine men, women, and children had been taken captive. Many would not survive the journey to Canada. Eliezer's home, situated farthest south of the stockade, had been spared, and all of his immediate family were alive.

Eliezer knelt next to his brother and said, "There is still hope for little Sarah. For she is among the captives and has her cousins and big sister to care for her on the march. We will ransom her, my brother." Sergeant Hawks nodded, then shook his head at the thought of his small child struggling toward Canada through the snow.

"How could I have been gone?" he said through tears. "Eliezer, I have searched my memory. I do not recall any omens when I left. Yes, we were on alert, but it was winter. Indians never attack in winter!" He shook his head and whispered, "How could I have been gone?"

Eliezer did not know if his words mattered, but he did all he could to provide comfort, "My brother, God always has a reason. Hannah will need you. Imagine the grief and wonder that will beset her when she learns that her family is destroyed. But she still has her father, has she not?"

Eliezer continued, "*We* need you. Stay with us awhile, brother. Help us defend this place, for the enemy will surely return. The King will not allow us to abandon the settlement, for that would mean conceding a victory to the French. You are old enough that the colonial government will allow you to leave. You *could* go and comfort Hannah, live in the safety of Waterbury. Yet think of all of us here who are forced to defend this town. Many of the men here fought with you and me in King Philip's War. We still have some of the garrison soldiers, and Connecticut Colony has promised to send more than one hundred men."

Eliezer spoke softly now and with gravity, "The enemy will return, brother. God spared you to defend His people. This is the reason you live."

Out of the corner of his eye, Sergeant Hawks saw his first wife Martha's sister stumbling toward him across the common. Her cheeks sunken and skin grey, Mary Catlin laid her arm across his back and knelt at his side. Sergeant Hawks reached his hand up over his shoulder, and Mary took it as she looked darkly into the ruins of her brother-in-law's house. Alternately keeping silent vigil with the dead and praying for their precious captives, the three stayed there for some time, knees freezing in the cold as they wept staring hopelessly into the ruins of the sergeant's and his son's homes.

After some time, his face swollen from tears, Sergeant Hawks stood and helped Mary to her feet. Eliezer stood with them and took Mary's hand. The old sergeant looked over to his own blackened floor where his wife had died. It was visible through the great chasms in the walls and gaps in the ceiling. Sergeant Hawks said to his younger brother, "How fares Judith with the loss of her sisters and mother?"

Eliezer shook his head and answered, "It is a hard thing to survive, my brother." The ruins of Deerfield, great blackened towers that had so recently served as sturdy homes and barns, stood witness to the three as they clung to each other in their grief.

❧

Wednesday, July 12th, 1704
Deerfield, Massachusetts Colony

The old sergeant had written to his daughter gently informing her about her Aunt Mary who had died of grief just a few weeks after the attack. He named her many friends and neighbors taken or killed. The letter seemed to him a list of all whom Hannah knew and loved. Her brother with his children and wife Thankful, even some from Thankful's childhood family, Hannah's step-mother Alice, Alice' son from Hadley who had been killed in the attempt to rescue Deerfield, so many cousins, so many friends…

He continued his letter telling her of hope for Sarah and Mary who had been taken captive. All of the children among her Uncle Eliezer and Aunt Judith Hawks' family had been spared. In closing, he told her of his intention to stay and help protect their remaining family and friends. He blessed her and thanked God that she had married Jonathan Scott who lived in the safety of distant Waterbury.

This morning, Sergeant Hawks was on his way with the other men to the meeting house common to receive their first pay since the February attack. Though not allowed to abandon Deerfield, and forced to carry out the duty of soldiers, the men had not received the pay of soldiers. Small though it would be compared to most of their usual incomes from farming and craftsmanship, they welcomed it.

The work of guarding the garrison left little time for the peacetime occupations which would have supported their surviving families. They had little remaining livestock, for the Indians had killed all they could in the attack. Their stores from last year's harvest were paltry because the threat of Indians had kept them out of the fields a year ago as it did now. The colonial government still required half the taxes of the impoverished outpost despite the fact that half of its breadwinners had been killed or taken captive leaving behind needy survivors. To support their families, the men of Deerfield had gone deep into debt in the nearby settlements. Now added to their overwhelming strain was the very real threat of arrest for debt.

As he walked, Sergeant Hawks felt a heavy hand on his shoulder; he turned to see his brother. He started to smile to share the relief of the whole town at receiving some pay, but a grim look met his brightness. He did not allow himself to think what was already creeping into his mind. Sarah's return was his only hope; she had to come home. Eliezer's hand still on his shoulder, Sergeant Hawks' looked hard at him, not willing to receive the unspoken news. Eliezer shook his head, and the old man's eyes pleaded with his brother, who could offer only sorrow. The old man asked, "How?" Eliezer softly said, "With a hatchet." Sergeant Hawks nodded and walked away. Eliezer considered following his brother, but he expected that the old sergeant did not want this pain witnessed by anyone but his Maker.

Having clung so tightly to the hope of her ransom, the news of Sarah's death robbed Sergeant Hawks of his will to live. The dream of holding his little Sarah again had been his escape when he walked through the burned out reminders of his grief. He hated himself for allowing her to be killed in the snow, and he hated the Indian who did it. He ran out through the gates of the newly fortified palisade, and sought refuge in the woods to the north. As he ran, images of wolves tearing at her dead body, birds picking at her tender form, taunted him.

Leaving the palisade on his own was a foolish thing to do, but he welcomed, even invited, death to deliver him from this pain. The French in Canada, pleased with their success, had sent war parties to harass the settlers and friendly Indians all along the Connecticut River valley. They had done their job well, killing one here, taking another captive there. Filled with rage, the old man did not care. He wanted to fight the whole lot of them. He wanted them to come into the open and fight like men which they had never done, always ambushing men and boys at work or traveling families. Had they no honor?

When he could run no further, he bent double, gasping for air. Waiting for his breathing to return to normal, he scanned the dense greenery all around him, hoping to find Indians. He found none. Suddenly he felt a tight column of rage well up from the pit of his belly, and a low growl escaped his lips. Straightening his back, he threw his hands behind his head and clutched his hair. He opened his throat and roared against the savage wilderness that had devoured his child. How he wished the enemy would come on, let him stab and cut and kill. He dropped to his knees and wept, holding his head in his fists as great wracking sobs shook his frame.

At length, he walked slowly back to the palisade, defeated and ready to die. He collected his pay and walked numbly to his brother's barn to saddle his horse and ride to Hadley to pay his debts. The other men had already gone ahead, but there was no reason for the old sergeant to wait until tomorrow to ride in the safety of other men. He did not care if he lived or died, but he was not going to allow a day to pass before he cleared his name of debt.

As one of the men required to stay in defense of Deerfield while the others rode to Hadley to discharge debts, Eliezer was cleaning his stalls. Eliezer knew that he could not stop his brother from riding alone, so he handed him a saddle for the big bay mare. Then Eliezer leaned on a post and watched his brother mechanically tighten, test, and tighten again the girth strap under the mare's belly. At length, Eliezer broke the silence, "There is some good news. Your step-daughter Mary is alive, and so are…"

The weary old man interrupted, "Thank you for the news. Mary is dear to me indeed. But tell me no more, Eliezer. For God forgive me, at this moment, I have no wish to hear whose children are not dead."

Weary in heart, Sergeant Hawks mounted his horse and set out alone on the path toward Hadley. He had gone perhaps twenty minutes, his pain subsiding into a welcome numbness, when his bay mare skittered backwards and yanked the old man back to reality. He gently reigned her to a stop and examined the trail for anything that might have caused her to slip. Seeing nothing and thinking she may have sensed danger, he peered into the thick brush surrounding them on both sides of the path.

Seeing nothing, he squeezed his calves gently to prompt her forward. The mare walked only a few yards before shying again to her right. She pranced anxiously, and once again he calmed her, bringing her to a tenuous standstill.

Sergeant Hawks shut his eyes in weariness at the omnipresence of the enemy. He knew they were there. Of course, it could be a wild animal, but he doubted it. His life meant nothing to him now, but he was tired and did not want his death to come at the inventive hands of savages. The old sergeant wanted to turn around and go back to Deerfield where he might lie down, never to get up again. He empathized perfectly with his sister-in-law Mary's wasting away from nothing more than sorrow.

But then Eliezer's words came back to him, "We need you." He thought of his nieces and nephews who yet lived; he thought of all those left in Deerfield. He thought of the men who had gone on to pay their debts and would return this way, and he gently urged his horse forward. Defeated though he was, he thought he could manage at least not to waste his death. If he was going to die, he might as well do it defending those whom he loved.

Having ridden this path hundreds of times, the old sergeant knew that just ahead it would take a steep decline through a ravine with a stream running through it. He knew it was the ideal place for an ambush. If he did not scatter the Indians, even at the expense of a tortured, diabolical death, there would be yet more grief in Deerfield tonight. He decided that he must go on.

He knew that he had to make the Indians believe he was the head of a troop and not alone. He also knew that he would not be able to make it through the ambush to gather men from Hadley. If the ambush was truly set, the Indians would mow him down before he ever reached the other side of the ravine.

When he was within a hundred yards of the ravine, Sergeant Hawks wrapped one hand tightly into his horse's mane, weaving her coarse hair around his fingers and clutching it tightly. He spurred the mare to a gallop as though he led a large company of men, clamping his body against hers and leaning into her neck as she gained speed. The power and weight of her great form thundered against the worn trail.

By the time he reached the ravine, his mare was at a dead run. She coursed down the steep hill, her hooves kicking clumps of mud high into the air behind her. Nearly to the bottom of the hill, shots exploded, and his mare reared up. As the mare dropped down, the old man felt a sharp burn as a bullet grazed his hand.

Having no idea how many Indians lay in wait, he wheeled his horse around to face the onslaught. As he spurred her directly into the bushes, crashing through dense brush, he boomed in his command voice, "On, men! After them!" He pushed the mare forward, then he reared her up and brought her forehooves crashing into the brush on the left. Then pulling her back, he plunged her toward the right. Suddenly he saw a score or more of

Indians, and much to his relief, they were scrambling to retreat. He boomed out commands and made as much noise as he could with the mare's thunderous hooves creating a sound like many horses.

When he believed that all of the enemy were gone from the roadside, he plunged into the brush and followed the two trailing Indians into the woods until the foliage became too thick for him to proceed.

Then turning his mare around, he made for the road and thence to Hadley, galloping all the way. He could not believe that with all of the bullets that had flown in the first and only volley, he had merely been grazed. God had used him to save lives that day ~ even on that very sad day. An old man, grizzled but still strong and lean, he had saved the lives of countless kinsmen, and he remembered Eliezer's words, "The enemy will return, brother. God spared you to defend His people. This is the reason you live."

Chapter Four

Friday, October 22nd, 1708
St. Lawrence River Valley, French Canada

Clouds eddied above; the brilliant leaves of red, gold and orange rained down with each new gust of wind. Free for a moment, warm and vibrant colors swirled through the air before lilting gently to the brush below. Periodically, the wind would toss the leaves back into the air where they danced a moment more.

The younger villagers still wore little or nothing at this time of year, but in their old age Night Sky and Honors The Dead felt the chill. The pair sat with their daughter on a fallen log, their backs to the river.

'Soon the geese will come,' Honors The Dead thought to himself. 'The geese will be so abundant that they will darken the sky.' Honors The Dead loved the great cacophony of geese, for their noise meant food for his People in the coming cold months.

Looking around the camp on this lazy day, Honors The Dead spotted Red Bear playing lacrosse with the other warriors. Women chatted with each other and played with the village children. There was no reason to seek tasks when one could relax and enjoy God's gifts of family and friends on this beautiful day. Indeed, what greater gift could Honors The Dead offer God than to savor what God had given him?

Honors The Dead looked over to Night Sky's longhouse where God had blessed him for so many years. He thought of the great honor Red Bear had brought to their clan. On a pole outside the longhouse hung many scalps. Among them were a long chestnut colored strand of hair and the fine dark tress of a child.

Honors The Dead recalled the day his son-in-law had returned from the Deerfield raid, bearing much spoil. Red Bear had told him that one of the scalps had come from a beautiful pale-eyed child who could only have come from the family called Ice Eyes. Red Bear had taken the girl to restore Honors The Dead's heart and to avenge him for all his loss at the hands of the Ice Eyes. But the child had not been able to walk in the snow, and Red Bear had made a hard choice.

Honors The Dead could tell that it had grieved Red Bear not to bring home a new grandchild to replace the spirit of the daughters Honors The Dead had lost in King Philip's War. It grieved Honors The Dead as well, to hear how close he had come to having the child in his home.

His neck stiff with age, Honors The Dead leaned forward and turned his torso to peer at his daughter, Catches Water. She sat quietly on the log with her parents enjoying the spectacular show of leaves raining down on their village. The weather being yet warm for the season, Catches Water was bare-chested wearing only a deerskin skirt that wrapped around her hips. Tiny lines of amusement appeared at the corners of her eyes, and Honors The Dead followed his daughter's gaze to see what had caught her attention.

At a safe distance several yards from where the men played their game, a group of boys imitated the warriors. Swift Legs, now having seen four summers, pushed and tumbled and ran among his cousins and friends. The boys, some naked, some wearing a loincloth, knocked each other down as they ran.

Eight year-old Laughing Owl, another grandson who lived in Night Sky's longhouse, suddenly stopped in the middle of the running boys. He slammed his hands indignantly on his hips and shouted, "You're not doing it right!" Laughing Owl was promptly knocked down by an older boy running with purpose as the game went on unheeding Laughing Owl.

The braves' match now over, Red Bear broke off from the men and ran toward Swift Legs, carefully darting in and around the boys. He scooped Swift Legs up in his arms, sweeping him off his feet and high into the air. The child laughed as his father ran a few paces from the boys' game. Red Bear dropped to the ground on his back, holding Swift Legs against his chest. Then he rolled over laying the child in the soft grass. Swift Legs giggled as they wrestled.

Seeing that the boys were not going to cooperate with him, Laughing Owl picked himself up and ran over to his Uncle Red Bear and Cousin Swift Legs. Laughing Owl jumped onto his uncle's back and held the warrior's neck. Red Bear grabbed Laughing Owl's legs and swung the boy's body under his arm and around his torso. When Laughing Owl would not let go of his neck, Red Bear and Swift Legs tickled the boy relentlessly. Laughing until he was gasping for air, Laughing Owl finally let go of his uncle's neck. The three collapsed on the grass, smiling as they caught their breath.

✍

That night, in the dim light of fading coals in the longhouse fire pits, Red Bear lay against Catches Water's body. Swift Legs slept on an adjacent bench in his parents' apartment. Red Bear lifted Catches Water's arm, straightening it above his face. As he held her hand in his, the warm light reflected a faint sheen of oil, which Catches Water often rubbed into her skin. Red Bear looked at the bones of her hand ~ so graceful, so beautiful.

He turned her hand to look at the palm, which was strong and rough. Catches Water worked hard in the fields; she followed her warrior on the hunt, and her hands attested to her worth. Slowly rotating her hand back and forth at the wrist, Red Bear passed his gaze over her arm and watched the play of muscles beneath her skin.

The warrior brought his wife's hand to his lips and kissed it. Catches Water turned her head, her black hair loose and flowing as she looked into her husband's eyes. Seeing that Red Bear's eyes were free of desire, Catches Water marveled at the unusual nature of her man. A stoic brave, he was powerful and reticent; yet he brought such intimacy to their union.

Tonight, her warrior simply loved her and wanted to touch his bride. Red Bear stroked Catches Water's cheek, then closed his eyes and drifted off to sleep. Lying on soft furs next to her husband, their son on the next bench, and her family sleeping throughout the longhouse, Catches Water felt warm and safe. She was surrounded by love.

Waterbury, Connecticut Colony

While Goodwife Hannah Scott cleared the table, her husband Jonathan Scott gathered the children around the door frame and marked off their heights with his knife. Not knowing how to write, Jonathan Scott handed his knife to his father-in-law to carve initials next to each child's mark. Sergeant Hawks carved each letter with care, and as he carved "Jn" for nine year-old John who had grown the most, the old man remarked that the lad was nearly as tall as his older brother Junior.

John beamed as his father, grandfather, and Uncle Joseph tousled his thick shock of white hair. It felt good to do something well, anything at all. To John, it often seemed that no matter how hard he worked, he could never do anything as well as Junior.

The excitement over, the Scott family gathered around the fire where Hannah mended and Martha pounded fragrant nutmeg. Jonathan Scott taught his older boys to whittle while Baby Daniel slept in his cradle, and three year-old Eliezer sat on the floor in the center of the group, shelling peas and valiantly battling his fast drooping eyelids.

Jonathan Scott's older brother Joseph planned to spend the night with them after having helped Jonathan Scott all day. Joseph had brought his teenaged son John, whom they called Cousin John. Now they sat on the settle next to Hannah's father, Sergeant Hawks, who was tamping his pipe.

Sergeant Hawks had stayed on at Deerfield until the government had released the younger men from garrison duty. Sergeant Hawks had been living with the Scotts for three years and had settled nicely into life as grandfather to his daughter's six children.

The old sergeant loved his grandchildren all, but nine year-old John and seven year-old Martha held a special place in his heart. Martha, of course, reminded him of his dear daughter Sarah, for she looked remarkably like her, and she was now only a year older than Sarah had been when he last saw her.

The cause of the old man's affinity for John, however, was not so obvious to him. Sergeant Hawks thought it might be partly because the lad was named after him, or perhaps it was that John was one of only two tow-heads left among the sergeant's grandchildren. All of his son's children had shared his strangely colored hair, but among Hannah's children, only John and Martha bore the old man's likeness in that regard.

Yet, it was more than that. In these years since the destruction of his family, Sergeant Hawks often found himself mired in inescapable melancholy. For whatever reason, the mere presence of his grandson John was enough to lift the old man out of the misery of memory.

This same boy, to whom God had given the balm to soothe the sergeant's broken heart, had a strong tendency to find himself in trouble. It hurt the old man to watch John follow such a mischievous path, for the punishments were brutal.

John's older brother Junior was the first born child. Junior excelled in everything to which he set his hand, and their grandfather had watched John grow rebellious in the shadow of his older brother.

Sergeant Hawks felt that the cause of this rebellious streak was that John was a left-handed child. It was a known fact that left-handedness left the door wide open for witchcraft and devil worship. These tendencies could manifest themselves in different forms of rebellion throughout a left-handed person's life. For the sake of the individual and the whole community, the correction of left-handed children must begin the moment the condition was noticed.

This training was difficult for John, and he found it difficult to accomplish the standard tasks that all children were required to perform with their right hand. Next to Junior, John looked like a fool, and Sergeant Hawks knew that this exacerbated the tendency toward rebellion inherent in every left-handed person.

School was difficult for John because the act of writing did not come easily for him, and their schoolmaster had tied John's left hand behind his back to help him resist the urge to write with it. The boy did enjoy reading, however, and frequently offered to read the daily Scriptures for the family.

Sergeant Hawks honored his grandson's desire to contribute in the few areas where he excelled. He wanted to help the boy adapt to life as God expected him to live it, so the old sergeant spent as much time alone with John as he could.

One afternoon several months ago, Sergeant Hawks had taken down his old flintlock musket from above the fireplace and had taken John out alone to teach the boy how to shoot. Sergeant Hawks had tried to teach John to shoulder the musket in his right shoulder, but as he watched his grandson's frustration, Sergeant Hawks had gone against his better judgment and allowed the boy to shoulder the weapon on the left.

That reckless concession on the part of Sergeant Hawks had bonded the boy to him. Now the old man counted it a great blessing to watch his grandson's skill develop, and the two of them went off alone to hunt whenever they could find both the time and a proper excuse.

Hunting was a great secret between the old man and his grandson, for hunting was seen as an idle pursuit in the eyes of many Puritans including the boy's father. Many colonists persisted in the belief that game was something to be traded from poor folks and savages.

Though he disagreed, Sergeant Hawks knew that nothing would come of arguing ~ only time could pull such people out of their stubbornness ~ so he and his grandson John kept their secret.

Around the fire that evening, a comfortable silence rested over the family with only the slice and chip of Jonathan Scott and his boys' whittling. The fire popped and hissed, and Hannah checked to see that Eliezer sat at a safe distance from the flames. The night was chilly, and drafts flowed in through the walls and up the chimney, causing most of the heat to run out into the starry night.

Hannah watched her husband patiently teach their sons, his great form silhouetted by the flames. Often when they sat like this in the evening, she would gaze at his quiet, powerful form.

Though Waterbury remained untouched, Indian attacks had continued throughout the frontier in these years of Queen Anne's War. Hannah thought of the nights when Jonathan Scott and her father heard suspicious sounds. They would close the shutters and bolt the door, then sit with muskets primed, facing the door and waiting for an attack.

Jonathan Scott's physical power, his protection of her and their children never ceased to amaze Hannah. True, it was his duty and the natural tendency of a man to protect his own. Still it awed her. Jonathan Scott glanced up and returned her gaze. The left corner of her mouth lifted into the faintest smile as contentment passed unspoken between them.

Joseph broke the peaceful silence and said, "Sergeant Hawks, tell us about King Philip's War. We understand you were at Turner's Falls."

The old man raised his shaggy eyebrows and puffed thoughtfully on his pipe for a few moments. At length, he removed his pipe from his mouth and said, "Yes, that was the summer after my Hannah was born."

Sergeant Hawks winked as he pointed at Hannah with the bit of his pipe. "Hannah was born in the Hadley garrison while King Philip's War yet raged. 'Tis fitting that she should be born in a garrison town, for she comes from a family of courageous men, who shrink not from the tomahawk of our savage enemies. My father, Hannah's Grandfather Hawks, fought at the Pequot Fort. The blood of many a valiant man flows through Hannah's veins."

Sergeant Hawks turned to his daughter and said, "Hannah, I'm sure ye recall your Aunt Elizabeth who died when ye were about seven."

When Hannah nodded, the old man proceeded, "Her husband was killed in King Philip's War, and their son, your cousin was taken captive in ninety-six. He worked the fields for a bunch of idolatrous nuns in Canada, but God delivered him. They sent him to France and then on to England. The lad arrived back in his home only two years later. Quite a story, that one," he said peering at his audience through a puff of smoke.

"To answer your question, Joseph: yes, I was at Turner's Falls with my brother Eliezer. Before the war, we called Turner's Falls by its Indian name, Peskeompskut. So many of my family fought on that day ~ my sister Mary's first husband, Experience Hinsdale, was a guide for Captain Turner. Experience lost his life that day, leavin' Mary a widow.

"My sister Sarah's husband, Philip Mattoon was there with us as was my sister Joanna's husband, William Arms.

"My second wife Alice was the widow of Samuel Allis, who fought with us and died on that day. Our friends, our neighbors, many of the local men fought together at Turner's Falls." His brows furrowed as he drifted back to that day.

"Many captive English were held at Peskeompskut. A few hundred Indians had gathered there from many nations. The Narragansetts, whose fort our men and allied Indians had burned in December, had fled there. Many of Philip's men were there making ammunition and repairing weapons. Nearly everyone there, even the women and old men, had a task that supplied Philip for the warpath.

"The homes of many settlers had been burned to the ground as King Philip's War raged. God used the filthy heathen to punish us greatly. The Lord chose an efficient scourge, for the heathens had no shame. Sometimes when they had killed our English settlers, those savages would dig up bodies buried by grieved loved ones, and mutilate them anew."

The old man paused a moment before shaking his head and saying, "At length, however, God relented and gave us the upper hand. One of these successes was the attack on Peskeompskut. We were living in Hadley at the time, for Deerfield had been burned and abandoned. One stormy night in mid-May, about one hundred-fifty of us rode north for twenty miles through Deerfield, burned and abandoned as it was for much of the war. We rode most of the night, passing the mournful sites where many of our men had died in ambush. Near the falls, we left our horses with a few men to guard them, and we climbed a hill above the enemy camp.

"That morning, the Indians were all sleeping soundly. Being the gluttons that savages are, they had stuffed themselves the night before on roast beef and milk. About a week earlier, the Indians at Peskeompskut had stolen seventy head of horses and cattle from English settlers. Fortunately for us, their gluttony had made their sleep very deep.

"We quietly swarmed into the camp, placed our musket barrels just inside the wigwam doors, and then we all fired. Many were killed in that first volley. As the Indians began to run, several drowned in the river as they jumped into canoes and overturned them. At first, the Indians yelled, "Mohawk!" because they were so confused and assumed we were their ancient Iroquois enemy.

"As the braves gathered to launch a counter-assault, they left their women, children, and grandparents to our swords and muskets." The old sergeant was silent for a moment, the destruction of the day coming back to him. His forehead wrinkled with pity, but he had no regret.

"It had to be done. Had we left them, they would have raised up their little boys to war against us all over again. This rebellion had to be quashed, and we were the ones to do it. That day, we made an end of many savages, certainly a few hundred. We burned the enemies' wigwams, we threw into the river the forges they used to fix their weapons, and the lead with which they made ammunition.

"Eventually, the warriors came on, and it was a rout. In the retreat, which I am ashamed to say can barely be called that, for it was anything but orderly, our brave Captain Turner was slain. It was a great blow to lose him." The old man knocked the ashes of his pipe into the fireplace.

As he refilled it, Sergeant Hawks continued his story, "We fled all the way through and past Deerfield at a dead run, some on horseback, some on foot. The Indians had managed to kill several of our horses including my own, but God saw fit to preserve your Uncle Eliezer's mount, which he and I shared. Not everyone behaved honorably however, for there were many a dastardly English horse thief that day.

"The warriors followed us all the way to Deerfield, screaming and hacking at those they could catch. Once past Deerfield, we were able to slow our pace. By the time we reached Hadley, we had lost forty men."

The bit of his pipe disappeared into the old man's beard. He puffed a few times and watched the shadows dancing on the beamed ceiling before continuing, "So it came at a great price, but we destroyed a major enemy stronghold and greatly limited King Philip's capacity to fight. In terms of the entire war, it was a stunning blow to the Indians, although a few weeks later the savages attacked our garrison at Hadley. I've quite a story to tell about that, but it is late, and we shall save it for another night."

Joseph asked, "It is indeed late, but do you know what happened to King Philip's family after he was killed? I recall a great fuss about his wife and son, but I was just a lad at the time."

Many times Hannah had heard the stories of her heroic kin, but she had never thought about the fate of King Philip's family. She urged her father to tell it.

Sergeant Hawks nodded and said, "There was indeed a great fuss about Philip's wife and son. When they were captured, no one knew what to do with them. Some wanted to hang them, but they recalled that God's law allows no son to be put to death for the sin of his father. However, there were those who argued that this child ~ only nine years old at the time, the same age as ye, John ~ participated somehow in the war. Now, I find this rather hard to believe. On the other hand, leaving the child of so great a threat as Philip alive would have been a monumental risk. The Indians would have sought to make him a chief and the whole bloody war would have been acted out again a decade later.

"So what to do with them… The debate raged for eight months while the boy and his mother sat in prison with their brethren malefactors. Ultimately, the ideal solution was determined ~ deportation to Barbados, there to be sold as slaves. Since the start of the war, the colony had made quite a lot of money from the sale of Philip's Indians. This helped offset the great cost of Philip's rebellion.

"The mystery, however, lies here. About the time that Philip's wife and son set sail on a slave ship, Barbados decided that it had had enough of our savages and made a law refusing to accept them. They found our Indians violent and completely untrustworthy as slaves. Rather than submitting, our Indians had a tendency to kill their masters. Frankly, I hope I would do the same, myself. At any rate, by the time Philip's wife and son reached Barbados, this law had long since gone into effect.

"The slave ship's captain could not leave them there, so what did he do with them? Well, he has never said what he did, and no one has asked. It is a bit of a touchy matter ~ a lot of money he lost, ye know."

The old sergeant stopped there, assuming that everyone understood what he left unsaid. Young John scowled at his grandfather a moment as he waited for the story to proceed. When he realized that the story was over, John said, "Grandfather, what do you think happened to them?"

Sergeant Hawks looked at his grandson and wished the lad had not asked the question. The old man took his pipe out of his mouth and leaned forward, resting one elbow on his knee. "I don't think it was pretty, John."

The boy continued to look at him expectantly, indicating that this answer did not suffice. The old man sighed and said, "Only two things could have happened. The captain may have done a generous thing and used up weeks of precious food supplies to take the slave cargo to Africa where they could be set on dry land in relative safety with a fair chance of survival.

"That would not have been particularly wise, however, John. You see, all of his men were expecting to be paid. How was he going to pay them when he could not sell his cargo?

"Now, if on top of that, the captain were to stretch their journey weeks beyond their food stores, thus causing starvation conditions for his men, he would have been asking for mutiny."

Sergeant Hawks watched his grandson to see if the lad had discerned the only other alternative. When it was clear that the child did not understand, the old man reluctantly added, "More likely, my boy, the captain threw them overboard."

❧

As John lay in bed with Junior and Eliezer that night, he dozed off into a fitful sleep and dreamed that he lay on his back in the dark cargo hold of a slave ship. Tired and hungry, he was chained to a wooden shelf. There was another shelf above him, and as he craned his neck he could see in the faint light that there were rows and rows of these shelves all holding Indians.

In his dream John wondered how he had gotten there, for he was not an Indian. He turned his head and saw his mother, who was chained to him, ankle to ankle. She was naked except for a skirt, and John could see that she was terribly thin as she touched his hand.

He dreamed that suddenly a hatch at the far end of the hold opened and sailors poured down the stairs. They unlatched the bonds that held the top shelf of prisoners to the wood and led them up on deck, all of them bound together at the ankle in one long human chain.

John clutched his mother's hand. A thunderous rattle, as though a chain were banging against the ship, terrified the boy as it vibrated the floorboards of the deck above. Then came the skidding of bare feet on the deck followed by screams and splashes.

It all stopped as suddenly as it had begun. The hatch darkened with sailors again. They loosed the bonds on Hannah's ankles and wrists, then John's. From John's shelf, the sailors grabbed the feet of Indians and pulled them down to the floor.

John and Hannah were next, and Hannah hit the floor with a thud. Still chained to her, John followed suit and landed on his back, knocking the wind out of him. The sailors gruffly lifted them to their feet and led the long chain of slave cargo toward the light.

In his dream, John caught his mother's hand and she walked in front of him. As they struggled up the stairs, the weight of their chains impeding them, John grappled to keep hold of his mother's hand. For a moment when they reached the deck, she fell and her hand slipped out of his. She quickly restored the connection as she stumbled to her feet.

Suddenly in the sunlight for the first time in weeks, searing pain shot through John's eyes. He clenched them shut, but the light was still too much even through his eyelids.

When all of the slaves on their chain were on deck, the thumping of boots and shuffling of naked feet on wood ceased, creating an eerie lull before John heard the first scream and splash. Then the thunderous rattle which John had heard in the cargo hold began anew.

He clutched his mother's hand with all his strength. John saw those ahead of him slip onto their backs one by one as the chain dragged them to an opening in the ship wall where they plunged into the sea.

As the chain tightened against her ankle, Hannah's hand flew out of John's as she fell backward onto to the floor. John forced himself to lurch forward, painfully twisting the chain against his ankle. He grabbed Hannah's hand and pulled himself toward her. They slid swiftly across the deck toward the open wall. As he clutched Hannah's hand, John's knuckles banged against the floor boards of the deck, the skin rubbing off them. They sped through the opening in the ship wall, fell through the air, and plunged into the water below.

Coursing down through the salty water that stung their eyes, the panic of death hit mother and son. Frantically John dug his nails into his mother's hand to maintain the grasp. Involuntarily, they opened their mouths to breathe and received water for air. Their eyes bulging in the fight to breathe, they maintained the physical connection until at last the struggle ended, and their hands slipped apart.

In his dream, John watched the darkness surround his mother and himself as they descended to the deep. John saw that the chain's pull slowed as it neared the pile of bodies on the ocean floor. Among the Indians with their long black hair, John saw his white hair waving in the water as the bodies sank. Down they fell, reaching the bottom gently, and John watched as his body rested on his mother's.

Suddenly sitting up in bed and gasping for air, John awoke to the sound of his own scream. His brothers sat bolt upright next to him, and Hannah rushed up to the loft. She leaned down and held John's face in both hands.

Wild-eyed, John looked into his mother's blue eyes. He touched her cheek, and then her hair to ensure that she was real.

Hannah sat down on the edge of the bed and pulled John close. She told his brothers to go back to sleep, and she stayed there, rocking her boy in her arms, until he drifted back to sleep.

Chapter Five

Thursday, November 4th, 1708
Waterbury, Connecticut Colony

Huge maple and oak trees towered overhead as a band of sixteen Abenaki quietly walked through the woods. Brothers of the Kahnawake and allies of the French, these Abenaki warriors had come down from Canada to harass English settlers.

One of the Indians spotted an English boy across the Naugatuck River. The brave held up his hand, and the others stopped behind him. The group watched from the cover of thick brush along the river's shore as a boy about nine or ten years of age dropped to one knee and aimed his musket at a concealed target. The Indians noted peculiar white hair peeking out from under his broad-brimmed hat, and then they heard the familiar explosion of gunpowder. The boy flinched backward only slightly, demonstrating both that he was strong and that he had placed the musket perfectly in the hollow of his shoulder. They watched the boy cautiously rise to his feet and creep toward the object of his shot.

As he disappeared into the underbrush, the Indians waited to see if his shot had been true. Though the boy would make a fine captive, the warriors would not be able to capture him, for the river was too fast and deep.

A moment later, the boy emerged bearing a fat raccoon. Surprised, the Abenaki braves looked at one another and smiled their approval. Few settlers hunted; they looked down on it as something reserved only for the poor among their people.

The boy walked to the river's edge, where he stood his musket on end and balanced it with one hand. Holding the coon in the other hand, he rested a foot on a rock and straightened his back. Standing next to his musket, which was a bit taller than he, the Abenaki thought that he looked rather pleased with himself. The boy stared across the river at the place where the Abenaki crouched in the brush. He did not appear to see them; he seemed simply to be enjoying the moment. While he looked thusly in their direction, the sun caught the boy's eyes and the warriors were startled to find that he had eyes the color of ice. They had never seen eyes like that on any man of any nation.

The Abenaki braves watched the boy sit down on a rock just above the river's edge, proudly laying the coon across his lap. When the boy shifted his attention and gazed at the water, the Abenaki warriors silently slipped away.

Slate grey clouds formed a canopy, making the world appear smaller. All the colors were more brilliant to John on overcast days ~ green looked greener, and autumn's vibrant colors pierced the grey horizon with jubilation.

John sat by the river for some time. He enjoyed doing nothing. Nothing was not something John got to do very often. In fact, nothing was not something John should be doing at that moment. He was supposed to be in school.

School was not easy for John, for he had felt a fool from the very first day. As a left-handed child, John always required special correction, which caused the other children to tease him cruelly.

Though most of John's academic lessons were nothing short of torture as far as he was concerned, he found great pleasure in reading. John's home offered only one form of literature ~ The Bible ~ and while it was hardly a nine year-old boy's idea of an enjoyable read, its voluminous pages provided him with a rare opportunity to shine in his brother's shadow.

John often read aloud from the Scriptures for his family, and while the ponderous Book often did not hold John's attention, he had discovered that the mere act of sitting with the Bible on his lap brought a smile to his parents' faces.

It was not all show however, for Scripture had a powerful effect on John. He did not understand everything he read, of course, but occasionally he would come across a passage that seemed to leap bodily off the page, plunge into his chest, and clutch at his heart.

Sitting on the rock now, birds chirping sweetly over the roar of the river, John recalled a Scripture, "Be still and know that I am God."

At his age, John found it impossible to know when stillness became idleness. Today for instance, John knew that his father would whip him for indulging in the sin of idleness. Yet John wondered what God thought. For John had gone into God's creation seeking comfort from what He had made, seeking assurance amid the rushing river and rustling leaves.

John's grandfather was now ailing, and John feared that he was going to lose the only man who seemed to understand him. The boy knew that he was a disappointment to his father. Yet he could bear this as long as Grandfather was there to share the secret that he was superb at something.

John never fell short in his grandfather's eyes. His staunch old grandfather nurtured the boy's natural affinity for the wilderness and hunting. The old sergeant recounted heroic stories demonstrating the value of English scouts in King Philip's War. When his grandfather shared these stories, John believed that what appeared to be his only skill was indeed a worthy one.

John dreaded the idea of going back home in the afternoon, for it was not just the sin of idleness that merited a whipping but also worrying his mother and sneaking out of the house before anyone awoke that morning. Of course, school tomorrow would bring yet another round of punishment.

A twinge of guilt gnawed at John. He knew his mother must be worrying about him. Queen Anne's War had raged nearly all of John's young life, but the boy did not worry about his safety, for Waterbury never seemed to be a target.

The people of Waterbury did not share nine year-old John's confidence. In fact, the government had forbidden even friendly Indians to hunt in the vast area northwest of Waterbury. Whenever John and his grandfather went hunting, they had to ride south along the Naugatuck River in order to fire a weapon without raising a general alarm in town.

Even in his naïveté John understood that the unpredictable nature of Indian attacks made it nothing short of reckless for a young boy to venture alone into the woods with nothing but a horse and a musket. Worried as he knew his mother must be, John was not yet ready to return. Right now, John needed to be exactly where he was.

The boy left the rock and walked to the tree where he had tethered his horse. John strapped the musket to the saddle and led the gelding along the river's edge. Not wanting to part with his prize for a moment, he held the coon in his free hand rather than stowing it in the saddle bag. Daydreaming and exploring, the boy and his horse wandered along the river's edge for much of the day.

At length, John reluctantly mounted the gelding and began the ride home. This day of freedom and solitude had done much to calm John's racing worry over his grandfather. It was worth the price he was about to pay.

❧

Friday, November 5th, 1708
Waterbury, Connecticut Colony

In the wilderness near Waterbury, Jonathan Scott's elder brother Joseph was finishing the work of clearing his new patch of land. He had had to obtain special permission to live so deep in the forest where a man had not the watchful eyes of neighbors to keep him from sin.

The townsmen had approved his request so long as Joseph gave account of how he spent his time whenever he was asked. The townsmen also required that Joseph attend weekly spiritual services regardless of how long the journey took him.

With the help of family, the trees had been felled and cleared away earlier in the week. Today Joseph worked alone, his teenaged son John, whom everyone called Cousin John, having gone to help Joseph's brother.

As Joseph picked up a large rock, setting it in the wagon hitched to a dark mare, he thought he heard a breeze rustle the leaves. With just a few more rocks, he would drive the horse to the edge of the field where he would unload them.

Joseph worked near the base of a huge boulder called the Rock House. The sun shone on the stone face, a great dull ballast in the midst of yellow and vermilion leaves.

The day was crisp and clear, and warming to the work, Joseph had shed his doublet. He hoisted a flat red stone and carried it toward the wagon. Suddenly Joseph froze, for he was surrounded by half a dozen painted, half-naked Indians.

He heard a terrible, lone whoop; then came a heavy blow to Joseph's chest. All of the warriors began to whoop, filling the air with hideous sounds. Gasping for air, Joseph kicked wildly at the hands that grabbed his limbs.

Dragging him through the scrub of his new field, the Indians pinned Joseph to the ground at the base of the boulder. Leaves crunched under his back as the Indians held his arms and legs down.

While their companions restrained the settler, two of the Indians used stone tomahawks to drive four makeshift stakes into the ground around Joseph. The braves held down each limb until it had been secured to the stakes with long straps of buckskin wrapped several times around the wrists and ankles.

When they felt that Joseph was secure, the Indians stood up to survey their work. They whooped incessantly, raising their tomahawks and muskets as they jumped around him. Wide-eyed with terror, Joseph awaited his fate. He dared to hope they might take him captive, and he kept quiet so as not to infuriate them if that were the case. If they took him captive, he had a good chance of survival and ransom.

One of the warriors standing at Joseph's feet drew a long slim blade from a sheath attached to his calf. The unsmiling Indian waved it gracefully, tauntingly in front of Joseph, who reassured himself by recalling tales of captives in which Indians sometimes threatened without killing.

The Indian slowly moved around to Joseph's left side. He lowered himself onto his haunches and looked into Joseph's eyes for a moment. Frantically Joseph watched the man's eyes for a clue to his intentions, for some sign of mercy. The man seemed to be considering something, or perhaps he was just prolonging Joseph's horror or perhaps trying to find something in Joseph's eyes.

Then the brave, his eyes still on Joseph's, moved on his haunches behind Joseph's head. Joseph craned his neck to maintain eye contact, hoping that the Indian might see something to cause him to relent. His face like stone, the Indian put one hand on Joseph's forehead, bracing his head to the ground, and with the other hand set his blade against Joseph's scalp. Joseph felt a jerk and a terrible sting as his own forelock appeared before his eyes, held aloft by the whooping savage.

Joseph understood now that he was not destined for captivity, for a scalped man was a dead man. These Indians meant to destroy him. As all hope of mercy vanished, he knew it mattered nothing if he annoyed the Indians, and with all his strength, he began to yell, "Help!"

The small company of Abenaki warriors whooped even louder, for the more noise they created, the greater a war party they would appear to be to the nearby settlers.

Knowing that they stood deep enough in the wilderness to cause fear of an ambush and that the Waterbury settlers had little force in the area, the Abenaki felt confident that no one would attempt to rescue this captive.

Sent down from Canada by the French with a mission of psychological warfare, these Abenaki men knew that the moment they could get their captive screaming, he would terrify the local settlers, and thus the braves would have achieved their objective.

All along the frontier, English settlers had abandoned their homes and farms, all that they had worked for. Now the braves hoped that this man would coax a few more settlers to leave, but as long as he was yelling instead of screaming, he did not serve their purpose. So they set about to remedy the situation.

Joseph watched in horror as another warrior on his right side squatted down and made a deep slit on Joseph's forearm. The brave cut just enough to slip two fingers underneath and grasp the wet, bloody skin. Digging his fingernails into the skin in order to grasp it firmly, the Indian began to pull backward, slowly ripping the skin away from Joseph's body.

His neck muscles straining to lift his body off the ground, Joseph saw his skin tearing away from his arm. As he pulled frantically at the bindings, panic set in. The image of his body without its wrapping exploded in his mind, and he screamed shamelessly. Joseph's neck still straining as he tried to pull at the irresistible tethers, the Indian continued to peel and pull until he had a strip about a foot long. Then he neatly sliced off the end and dangled it over Joseph, whose contorted face was rendered more hideous by the red patch of bone on his forehead where there should have been skin and hair.

The warriors whooped as the brave continued to play with the strip of skin, and another resumed the work on Joseph's arm. Joseph screaming in horror and pain, the warriors took their time. Hour by hour, strip by strip, they peeled away Joseph's skin. They danced and waved the strips; all the while, the face of the great rock amplified the sound of Joseph's torture throughout the area.

❧

Out of breath, Jonathan Scott flung the door open, ran into the house, and grabbed his musket. Seeing Hannah standing at the hearth, Jonathan Scott told her, "Cousin John and I heard screaming. It sounds like there's a war party." The door was still open, and suddenly a horrible shriek pierced their ears.

Hannah's hand flew to her heart as she asked, "Who do you suppose it is?"

Just then, Cousin John rushed through the open doorway, and Jonathan Scott answered his wife, "I know not, but I fear it may be my brother. He was working alone today at his new field, the one near the Rock House."

From his place on the settle, the old sergeant asked in a low voice, "What do you mean to do, Jonathan?"

Puzzled by the question, Jonathan Scott answered defensively, "Why, I mean to save whoever is up there screaming for his life!"

Sergeant Hawks calmly asked, "Are ye goin' to do this alone then? Or perhaps ye might take Cousin John with ye so that ye can both die along with the poor fellow losin' his life as we speak."

Cousin John could not believe his ears, "That could be my father, Sergeant Hawks, and I'll gladly give my life to save him. I should be ashamed if I didn't!"

The air suddenly filled with renewed screams, the old man nodded at the lad, honoring his courage, "Lad, you do as you must, but I would have a word with my son-in-law first."

Sergeant Hawks turned his attention to Jonathan Scott and looked hard at him, "You're a big man Jonathan, but it matters not how great a man be when it's an ambush the savages have laid. The savages are trying to lure us in. Who wouldn't go to the aid of such pitiful cries? I'll tell ye who would not go to that poor wretch's aid: Sergeant Hawks."

The old man leaned forward and his voice crescendoed into its old military thunder, "Listen to the tenor of those screams, man! The wretch is doomed already! Neither you nor Cousin John nor any army can save the life of a man that far into torture."

Narrowing his eyes, Sergeant Hawks' tone grew ominous as he asked, "And what happens if that war party descends on Waterbury or on this very farm? Who will defend your family? Are ye thinkin' I can do it without ye?"

The screams came almost constantly now, and knowing that the boy was likely hearing his own father's death, Sergeant Hawks looked at Cousin John, "Even if it is your father, lad, there's naught ye can do to save his life, but ye can do him proud by protecting Aunt Hannah and your defenseless little cousins. Would your father not be proud of that, Cousin John?"

While the young man considered his course of action, the wiry old soldier got to his feet, crossing the room to stand before his son-in-law. Laying a hand on Jonathan Scott's shoulder, Sergeant Hawks spoke with compassion, "The choice is before you, Jonathan. For the sake of a doomed man, be he your brother or no, will ye martyr yourself and make a widow out of my Hannah? Or will ye pray with me? Will ye do heavenly battle for the man's soul? And will ye help me prepare the defense of this house?"

Jonathan Scott stood for several seconds, the musket still gripped in both hands. At last, Cousin John said, "In conscience, Uncle, we cannot abandon Aunt Hannah." As he listened to the unending pleas of the tortured man, Jonathan Scott turned to his nephew and nodded his assent.

∽

In the shrieking sunlight, Jonathan Scott's brother met his end. Thinking he was dead, the Abenaki warriors had left their handiwork to horrify the settlers who would find him. All the skin torn from his face and body, Joseph lay unbound and barely breathing, begging God to take him.

The sun high overhead burned into his exposed eyes, which had no eyelids as defense. "Dread God please," he tried to form the words though his lips had been ripped away. Joseph had not the strength to cry out anymore, not even to his God. The man simply lay still and waited for the pain and horror to end. At last, the wretched mass of flesh, sinew and bone slipped into blessed release.

Chapter Six

Wednesday, March 1st, 1710
Waterbury, Connecticut Colony

Hannah Scott sat on a bench facing the fireplace while Martha in a clean shift, sat on a stool in front of her. With Jonathan Scott working in the barn and two of the boys at school, John and Martha had stayed home from school to help Hannah. After lunch, Martha had received the rare pleasure of a bath, and now Hannah combed her daughter's hair.

Hannah wondered how Cousin John fared. Thankfully, the Indians had not attacked Waterbury on that awful day more than a year ago, but the Scotts had quickly learned that their own Joseph had indeed been the victim.

In the wake of his father's death, a furious Cousin John had marched north under Colonel Whiting against the French and Indians in Canada. Hannah thought about him often and prayed for his safe return.

Sergeant Hawks' health had almost entirely returned, and he sat on the settle reading a letter. A few feet away, John was weaving a new pair of suspenders for himself while five year-old Eliezer pounded spices. Having removed his shoes, Little Daniel surrendered in the battle against idleness and began to play with his toes.

Hannah allowed herself to linger about the business of tidying Martha's hair. It was such a tender time, and she knew Martha enjoyed it as much as she did. The fine locks, gently curling as they dried, slipped loosely through Hannah's fingers like bands of silk.

As her father read quietly to himself, he paused now and then to give Hannah the particulars, "My sister Sarah's new husband, Daniel Belding, along with your Uncle Eliezer have seen action and were among those who valiantly defended Deerfield from yet another attack, this one by nearly two hundred French and Indians." He looked up from scanning the page and said, "Do you remember Daniel Belding, Hannah?"

Hannah nodded and said, "His first two wives were killed by Indians, weren't they?" Her father replied, "Yes, and many of his children were wounded, taken captive or killed outright in '96. Such a shame. I think my sister Sarah will be a boon to him.

"Anyway, apparently the damned French papists and their savages had planned to sack and destroy Deerfield yet again, but our men were alerted and drove the bloodthirsty bastards back into the woods where they belong." The old man shook his head and said, "'Tis no surprise that the French call our Deerfield 'Guerrefille.'"

Seeing Hannah's puzzlement, he asked, "You have heard that before, haven't you Hannah?" She shook her head, and Sergeant Hawks explained, "In their flowery tongue, 'Guerrefille' means Daughter of War." As she comprehended the French mockery, a look of anger and deep offense swept over Hannah's face.

Not wishing to delve into the old wound, Sergeant Hawks pretended not to notice his daughter's fury. He paused a moment, his finger on his lip as he tried to find news to fill the silence before Hannah spoke, "Ah... I see here that sadly your cousin John Arms was wounded in that action and was for some months a prisoner of the Indians. But he is now safely in Albany, though the government has agreed to hold him there pending our release of a particular French officer back to Canada. We shall have to remember him in our prayers, for though he is among his own now, he still has not his freedom, and his captivity has left him deep in debt."

Scanning the letter as he spoke, the old sergeant continued, "Ruth and three more of your cousins, all Aunt Mary Catlin's granddaughters, have chosen to stay among their captors." He shook his head and said, "Glad I am that Mary Catlin is not alive to know such pernicious rejection."

The old sergeant read silently for a few moments, then announced with enthusiasm, "Your step-sister Mary Allis, the Lord be praised for her ransom, has chosen Nathaniel Brooks for a husband! Well, that is wonderful," the old man said smiling and nodding his head. He continued, "You remember Nathaniel Brooks,

Hannah. His first wife's name was also Mary …" he trailed off, and a far off look came over his face.

Sergeant Hawks could deal with most of the promptings that caused his mind to drift back to the attack on Deerfield, for if he would stay in touch with those who still lived in Deerfield, he must deal with such promptings. Knowing however that Mary Brooks presented the one link against which her father had no mental wall of defense, Hannah tried to distract him cheerily saying, "Yes, Father, I remember Nathaniel. He will make a fine match for our Mary!"

The old man nodded and stared blankly at the paper. Understanding that her father must be pulled out before he sunk into a season of melancholy that could last days, Hannah quickly finished Martha's hair. Then she crossed the room and sat on the settle next to her father. She picked up the letter and began to read to him. As she read of Mary's dress and wedding feast, and how happy she was, the old sergeant began to brighten.

The balance of the letter brought good news, and he returned to his confident, hopeful self. When she reached the end, Hannah folded the letter, laying it neatly on his lap. Patting her father's knee, she rose to begin preparation for the evening meal.

A few minutes later, John laid down his tape loom and walked over to his mother who stood at her worktable.

When she had acknowledged him, John asked her quietly, "Mother, do you need my help with anything… something outside perhaps?"

Whispering so that no one else could hear, Hannah asked, "Do you wish to speak to me alone?"

John nodded, and as she sliced beef into bite sized pieces for pasties, Hannah thought about what they might do that would take them away from other ears. Convenient cold lunches, pasties were usually reserved for field work only, but they were so delicious when hot that Hannah occasionally made a double batch so that she could treat her family.

Hannah considered how to avoid idle hands while chatting with John, for at this time of year most of her work took place in the house, which provided no privacy. She stepped back and forth between the table and the fireplace to drop the beef into a large iron kettle. Returning to the table, Hannah began preparing the crust, and as she scooped flour into a great bowl, she suddenly felt a commotion about her feet. She stepped back and looked down to find Martha slapping her skirts. "Martha!" Hannah exclaimed.

Knowing the terrible danger of burns, John dropped to the floor and helped his sister extinguish the flames which had consumed several inches of their mother's hem. When the children were certain that the fire was out, a breathless Martha replied, "Yes, Mama. It is out now."

Having helped her daughter up, Hannah put her arm around her daughter's shoulders. "What would I do without you, my dear? And thank you too, John," she said as her son got to his feet.

Hannah turned around to see if her father had noticed the uproar, but he had dozed off. She smiled at her daughter, "Tell me Martha, do your friends put out as many fires on their poor mothers' hemlines as you do?" Mother and daughter laughed while John shook his head at the dangerous business of cooking.

Martha returned to the task of mending with which she had occupied herself before the crisis, and Hannah quietly said to John, "'Tis too early for it, but I suppose we could go break up the soil in the garden while the stew for the pasties simmers."

About half an hour later, Hannah instructed Martha to tend her younger brothers and the stew. While John went to fetch the hoes, Hannah went out the front door to the garden. Finding the wind too brisk in spite of her woolen waistcoat, Hannah went back inside for her wrap. When she returned, John was waiting for her. Taking a hoe from her son and setting to work, Hannah gave her son permission to speak.

"Mother," John began tentatively, "Who was Mary?" Hannah looked blankly at John. There were so many Marys; she wondered which one he meant. John clarified, "The Mary from the letter Grandfather was reading ~ not your step-sister Mary, but the other one."

"Ah, that Mary…" said Hannah. Taking a deep breath, she dove into the facts that would never be mere facts. "She was Mary Brooks, and she was killed on the way to Canada just three days before my sister Sarah. Mary Brooks' name always forces your Grandfather to think on

Sarah's death. It was simply too much for Grandfather today. She was his light, you know."

Recalling the legendary piety of young Goodwife Brooks, Hannah leaned on the hoe, "Mary Brooks had just miscarried her baby. She was too weak to keep up on the march, and she knew that the savages intended to kill her." Hannah turned her gaze back to John, who saw, in light of the present topic, a most incongruous peace appear on her face. Hannah resumed her work with the hoe, "But Mary was not afraid because she knew that Jesus loved her." Her eyes misty, Hannah smiled at the thought, "That's all there is to it, John. The Indians killed her; she knew it was coming; and she had no fear. Such faith…"

Unsure how to proceed, John was quiet for a moment, for the attack on Deerfield was a subject that did not often come up. Whenever it did come up, the topic died down immediately. It was simply too painful for Grandfather. John wanted to ask so many questions, and in this private moment his mother seemed willing to answer them. Finally, he asked, "Mama, after God caused the Indians to destroy Deerfield, what made Mary Brooks think that Jesus still loved her?"

Hannah tenderly looked at her son and said, "John, does your father punish you when you do wrong?"

"Yes, Mother," answered John.

"Your father punishes you, yet your father loves you, and just as Jonathan Scott is your earthly father, Jehovah is your heavenly Father. He is a God of justice and must punish evil, but that never diminishes His love for us." Hannah watched her son to see if he understood. After a moment, she added, "These things are hard, John. That is why Mary Brooks was remarkable. Few have peace at such a moment."

The pair were quiet as they worked together enjoying a rare moment alone. John asked, "What did our family do? What did they do to anger God?"

Hannah kept hoeing as she answered, "I do not know, John. Only God knows the heart. Perhaps they did not love Him as they appeared to. For some, perhaps it was only a show. It could have been so many things."

As she worked, Hannah's head swam with lost family, dear friends, neighbors, even her old admirer David Hoyt. The list seemed to have no end. So often it seemed unreal, impossible. Yet, they were all gone ~ her brother and his dear children; his wife Thankful, once her best friend and then sister-in-law, now long since gone ~ Thankful's mother and two of Thankful's sisters as well ~ Aunt Mary, Hannah's only link to her mother ~ Father's wife, Alice, and of course, Sarah... Memories of them all swirled around in Hannah's mind, faces fading in and out, scenes of tenderness and cheery industry mingling together.

After a silence of several minutes, John spoke again, "Mother, since Grandfather's brother, Uncle Eliezer's whole family was spared, does that mean that they were better people than Grandfather or Aunt Mary who lost so many children?" Afraid of offending his mother, John was desperate to know why God had done this to his family. He cautiously ventured, "Did Uncle Eliezer love God as much as God wants, but Grandfather did not?"

Hannah had never thought about it quite like that. She raised her eyebrows and shook her head, "It is not so simple as that, John. Neither you nor I can know who truly loves God; only God can know."

Relieved at his mother's lackluster reaction, John listened eagerly. "You see, God caused the savages to take Deerfield's own minister captive, and many in his family were killed or taken captive. To the unending torment of our minister, one of his children even now chooses to remain among the savages. Did our Uncle Eliezer please God more than the minister, John? I think not. These are hard questions, John. It is good that you think so much on the Lord. Often, John, the answers simply will not come to our mortal minds. In such moments our only comfort is to be still and know that He is God. He *will* be exalted among the heathen, and on this we must rest."

Just then, Martha ran outside carrying a barefooted Daniel under one arm, the wind billowing her petticoat. "What is it, Martha?" asked Hannah.

"The stew, Mama," she replied. Handing the hoe to John, Hannah walked back in the house. The pot was suspended over the fire by a hook, which hung from a great iron lug pole spanning the width of the fireplace. Martha had tended the fire a little too well, and the stew was now boiling. Daniel's mischief, which took on new and different forms every time his mother was absent, had distracted Martha from the task of stirring the pot. Around the inside edges of the pot, the stew had begun to burn giving off a sickly sweet odor. Timidly Martha said, "I am sorry, Mama."

Hannah shook her head and said, "The stew will be fine, Martha; only the edges have burned. It is no small task to manage a little one, a fire, a stew, and your other tasks all at the same time. You will get the knack of it in time. If anyone should be scolded, it is you, little one," Hannah said as she scowled at Daniel. "You must allow your sister to work." Embarrassed, Daniel lowered his eyes.

Dispersing the logs under the pot, Hannah diminished the fire, and she stirred the stew to allow heat to escape. Tending other duties, Hannah allowed the savory beef mixture to cool considerably before ladling it onto circles of crust. She folded one side of the crust over the over and pinched the edges together to seal each half moon.

Hannah placed the half moons on a long-handled platter, and taking care of her skirts, carried the platter inside the fireplace. After sliding the pasties into the oven and flipping them off the platter, she shut the oven door and returned to her work table.

She tidied up the table and sat down at the small spinning wheel she and Martha used for spinning flax into linen thread. Dipping her fingers in a small bowl of water, Hannah began twisting the fiber and pumping the pedal with her foot. From time to time, she glanced up from her work to check on her father and children.

As Martha sat with her head bent over her mending, tight little curls at the back of her neck peeked out from under the linen coif. Hannah smiled at her daughter. All of the

Scott children had blue eyes; all of the boys shared their father's strong jaw; her children were robust and they were unusually tall.

In their dim house, Hannah watched John working diligently on his new pair of suspenders. Though he could be a bit rebellious, Hannah was proud of her son. She had never seen a child devour Scripture as he did. On rainy days, he would find a rare moment of free time to set a stool in the corner of the fireplace and read God's Word. It was a quiet thing with him, almost an escape.

Looking at John's fair hair, piercing eyes and square jaw, Hannah thought to herself, 'So like your grandfather and so like your father.' She could see both of her favorite men in John's nature as well as in his countenance. In this boy, her father's daring mixed with her husband's quiet strength.

John's left-handedness, which accounted for his occasional recklessness and rebellion, was a serious concern for the family. Left-handed people were known to have a propensity toward witch-craft and devil worship, and therefore left-handedness was something that must be corrected. This correction was difficult for John. When he had been little, Hannah had forever been whacking his hand with a spoon for reaching with his left hand instead of his right.

It was hard for him to learn to use his right hand, and Hannah could tell that the correction and his lagging behind in school embarrassed him, but for the security of his soul and the spiritual safety of the village it must be done.

Hannah knew that John received teasing from his older brother and from the other children at school. It hurt her to watch John struggle in his older brother's shadow. No one expected John to be able to perform a task as well as Junior, who was two years his senior, but John expected it of himself.

Hannah rose to check the pasties, now golden brown and inviting. Using the platter to get them out of the oven, Hannah arranged the pasties on a wooden platter. Hannah called to Martha, who quickly obeyed and spread the table with linen while Hannah held the platter. As Hannah laid the platter of pasties on the linen, Jonathan Scott and the boys walked in the door, Junior and Gershom having arrived home from school just as Jonathan Scott came in from the barn.

Together Martha and Hannah set the table and poured milk and ale. Without delay, the family gathered round the table for a quiet meal together. Jonathan Scott sat at the head of the table, Grandfather at the foot, and Hannah sat next to her husband while the children all stood.

After dinner, Hannah and Martha cleared the table while the men and boys took a few moments to talk about the day. Jonathan Scott bounced Daniel on his knee until the boy giggled, and Junior told his father and grandfather about school.

When Hannah and Martha had finished, Jonathan Scott fetched the Bible from its box, set it on the table, and sat down before it. All had grown quiet as they waited to hear the Word of God. The ability to read Scripture was crucial in the spiritual development of everyone including girls, thus Hannah and Martha both knew how to read. Writing, however, was not so critical a skill for the average colonist. Unlike his sons and father-in-law, Jonathan Scott had never had the opportunity to learn to write, but he could read.

Beginning at the sixth chapter of Romans, Jonathan Scott read through the eighth chapter. Aware that he might be quizzed to demonstrate that he had been listening, John sat on the floor by the hearth and did his best to concentrate. He caught each word, but as was so often the case, he found their meaning confounding.

It was not solely the fear of being quizzed that caused John to pay attention however. Frequently some word or phrase would shout to him, and for days it would mill around with his thoughts just as did the passage, *"Be still and know that I am God."*

As the reading came to an end, John heard something remarkable, *"Yet I am persuaded that neither death nor life, nor angels, nor principalities, nor powers, nor things present nor things to come, nor height nor depth, nor any other creature, shall be able to separate us from the love of God which is in Christ Jesus our Lord."* John had heard it before; in fact, it was among the Scriptures he had been required to memorize. Yet, tonight it seemed strangely new and unfamiliar.

After the reading, everyone set to work, and the Scott family home was filled once again with the sounds of industry ~ the pump and whir of the flax wheel where young Martha spun; the rustle of fabric as Hannah mended britches and shirts; the thud of wood against the plank floor as Jonathan Scott and the boys constructed a bucket.

Just before bedtime, Jonathan Scott said with a smile, "Come, children! It has been months since we last measured you. Line up at the door." Jonathan Scott marked each child's growth on the doorpost, and Grandfather smoking his pipe walked over to carve initials next to each mark. Laughing, the old sergeant said, "Why Junior and John, you are nearly as tall as I!" The sergeant was of about average height at five and a half feet tall, and he added "It must be your father's height ye've got. Ye'll both be as tall as savages, ye will."

Upon hearing the news that he had grown an inch, five year-old Eliezer beamed. Hannah grabbed the boy around the waist and sat down with him like a babe in her lap. "You're not so big!" she said to the giggling boy. Jonathan Scott announced prayer time, and kissing his mother good night, Eliezer slid off Hannah's lap as the family knelt.

After prayers, Martha, Eliezer, and Daniel undressed to their long shirts. The children folded their overgarments neatly as they climbed into the trundle bed pulled out from under their parent's bed. John followed his brothers as they climbed up to the loft.

John undressed and lay down on the bed with Gershom in the middle and Junior on the other side. Though the loft was chilly, it was a pleasant place to sleep, for the boys' dreams were perfumed with the wonderful smells of drying herbs and apples hanging from the rafters.

As he waited for sleep to come, John's mind wandered back to that afternoon in the garden with his mother. John rarely asked for time alone because it seemed silly to need her so much at his age; he was eleven after all. But whenever he did ask, she found the time.

John thought about their conversation; he thought about Deerfield and what the village had done to make God so angry. John wondered, as his pastor often encouraged the flock to do, if he loved God to the degree that he ought. Though John could never admit such a thing to anyone, not even his mother or grandfather, he found it difficult to love the God that had smashed his family into dust.

John wondered what on earth had made Mary Brooks think that Jesus loved her? Why did she have such peace, and why did she not mind the death that would send her straight to the very God that had punished them so horribly? John could not understand these things as he imagined Grandfather's sweet little Sarah on the march over snow and ice. He thought of her frozen feet in strange moccasins on the rugged terrain ~ mountains and rivers, brutal…

The image of mountains caused something to flash through his mind, "*nor powers… nor height nor depth, … shall be able to separate us from the love of God…*" Certainly Indian Nations were powers ~ powers which God had used to punish His people. Was it really true that God loved his people so much that even mountains and Indians could not separate them from His love?

It seemed impossible that the good people of Deerfield could have angered God so much. Hungry for God and hungry for the answer to why Deerfield had been destroyed, John had learned the Scriptures far more than was required of him. The people of Deerfield constantly compared themselves to the Israelites whom God had sent into captivity. Yet John knew that the people of Deerfield had not come anywhere near the kind of sin the Israelites had committed. How could they have? Deerfield had not sacrificed their children to foreign gods or given their daughters into temple prostitution as had the Israelites. John simply could not accept that God had been so angry with Deerfield. There had to be some other explanation.

❧

Saturday, March 11th, 1710
Montreal, French Canada

It was an unseasonably calm day in the bustling trade center, and a breeze rustled Red Bear's topknot as he browsed among the tents of traders' goods. At his feet, slushy snow mingled with mud from foot traffic, and though it was chilly, Red Bear wore only leggings and a wide silver band on each upper arm.

Yards of brightly colored European cloth caught his eye, and he stopped for moment. Standing next to him, two Abenaki warriors reminisced about an attack on an Englishman a few years earlier. Red Bear could not help overhearing their conversation as one of the men said, "Do you remember the boy hunter?"

The other nodded seriously, "Yes, he had fine skill, the little white-hair." The two Abenaki were quiet for a moment as they remembered the peculiar sight of an English boy alone in the woods during time of war.

Red Bear interrupted their reminiscing, "This English boy ~ you say he had white hair?" When the Abenaki men nodded Red Bear asked, "What color were his eyes?"

One of the men said, "Ah… strange eyes, very strange, the color of ice." Hearing this astounding news, Red Bear shared with them the story of his father-in-law. The Abenaki braves told Red Bear where they had seen the boy and then one of them added, "The white-haired boy is good. You should take him while your old one still lives." Red Bear nodded thoughtfully.

∽

Tuesday, March 14th, 1710
St. Lawrence River Valley, French Canada

Eager to tell Honors The Dead of the white haired boy, Red Bear stepped out of his canoe, pulled it onto the pebble beach and tied it to a tree. He took what he could carry of the goods he had acquired at Montreal and walked into the camp. Walking toward him down the main path of the village, Red Bear saw Laughing Owl, but as soon as the boy saw Red Bear, the boy looked at the ground. Red Bear scowled, "What is it?"

Laughing Owl looked up slowly at Red Bear and replied, "Swift Legs…" Red Bear ran to the longhouse, flung aside the fur that covered the doorway in cold months, and hurried inside.

Sitting on the ground next to her daughter, Night Sky looked up at Red Bear, the sadness on her face increasing Red Bear's fear. Catches Water sat cross-legged with her son in her lap, the six year-old boy's legs draped across her knee and resting on Night Sky's lap. Honors The Dead sat next to them on the other side of Catches Water while the Catholic priest stood in the background. Family surrounded them all and kept vigil with the boy.

Dropping his trade goods, Red Bear knelt down in front of his wife and son. As Red Bear touched Swift Legs' ashen face, Night Sky softly told him that the medicine man had done all he could and that the priest had given the boy last rites. No one knew what was wrong with Swift Legs. It had appeared to be influenza just a few days ago, but it had not spread the way influenza was wont to do. Having exhausted every avenue of hope to help the child, family and friends now watched helplessly as a precious member of their longhouse faded a little more each hour.

Red Bear watched his son's eyes. Barely conscious, Swift Legs rolled his eyes slowly around, seeming to try to find his father. The effort was too much for him, and he closed his eyes. Red Bear took his son's hand while the loved ones silently watched and waited for Swift Legs' spirit to grow strong again or else depart.

᭥

Sunday, May 14th, 1710
St. Lawrence River Valley, French Canada

Honors The Dead walked out of the camp alone on this warm spring day and moved slowly among the trees. Though he had seen more than seventy-five summers come and go, Honors The Dead had rejected his family's attempts to accompany him and had insisted on going out of the camp alone. Red Bear had waited several weeks after Swift Legs' death to share the news of the white-haired child in the Connecticut Colony of New England. Red Bear had told Honors The Dead privately and had said that he would abide by the old warrior's judgment. Now Honors The Dead sought his God.

Should Red Bear risk his life for the white-haired child, and how could Honors The Dead answer that question for him? If Red Bear were killed in the attempt to take the child, Catches Water would be twice grieved. But it was not only Catches Water who had lost Swift Legs; the whole lodge had lost him. The child's spirit had departed the longhouse before his time, and someone must fill the void.

Honors The Dead walked down into a shallow gully with small round rocks at the bottom and a hill on the other side. He began to climb the hill, stopping every few paces, for his legs tired easily. When he crested the hill, Honors The Dead walked through the trees and onto a great slab of rock which dropped off at a cliff a few yards

162

away. A few feet from the edge of the cliff, he sat down on a boulder to catch his breath.

In awe, Honors The Dead looked out at the beauty before and below him ~ green trees, grey rock, white clouds in crisp blue sky as far as the eye could see. It never failed. When fearful of the future, he would leave the camp and go where evidence of the Creator's power presented itself undeniably. In the village, it was difficult sometimes to concentrate, but up here on this crest, Honors The Dead could think of nothing but his Creator.

⇜

Early in the evening, Honors The Dead walked into Night Sky's longhouse and sat down on a bench in their apartment. He quietly told Night Sky, who was tending the succotash for the evening repast, to bring Red Bear and their daughter. When his family was gathered around him in their apartment, Honors The Dead said in the smooth, soft intonation of his People, "Red Bear has told me of a white-haired English boy in Connecticut Colony. The Abenaki have seen the boy and say that he is brave and a good hunter, which is more than can be said for most English children."

Honors The Dead looked at Catches Water before continuing, "Red Bear has asked me to decide if he should take this child and bring him to our longhouse. I cannot judge this matter, for I fear that in his desire to restore my heart, Red Bear could make my daughter a widow. I honor Red Bear's desire to avenge the wrongs the white-haired family has done to mine. And I honor that he would restore the spiritual balance of this longhouse which has been altered by the death of Swift Legs."

Nodding at Red Bear, Honors The Dead went on, "How can I decide this matter? For I will always want the child, and I will always want to avenge my family. But Red Bear is not my husband, and I cannot ask this of him." Turning to his daughter, Honors The Dead said, "Catches Water, this boy would be your son to gain, and Red Bear is your husband to lose. I leave the matter to you."

With a heart aching for her dead child, Catches Water looked at Red Bear who gazed sternly at the wall of their longhouse ~ strong, quiet, powerful. She loved that Red Bear had offered to risk his life to heal her father's heart and replenish the void left when Swift Legs' spirit departed their longhouse. Yet she sensed that Red Bear's offer was not solely a gift to her father and to those who dwelt in Night Sky's longhouse.

As she pondered the decision, Catches Water studied Red Bear's face. She watched his eyes for any sign of hesitation, but her proud warrior's stare never flinched. How she loved him... Catches Water did not want to lose him in addition to having lost their son, and yet she sensed that to refuse Red Bear's offer might wound him deeply.

Yes, there was indeed more to Red Bear's offer than what he had said, for Catches Water knew that beneath the stoic mask grief raked his heart. In the stern face before

164

her, she saw that Red Bear wanted this boy to heal his own heart … and so did she.

∽

Tuesday, July 25th, 1710
Waterbury, Connecticut Colony

Exhausted and grateful for the break, eleven year-old John followed his father and Junior to the great oak tree in the meadow where they would have lunch. As their father sat down with his back against the tree, the boys sat on the ground facing him. Enjoying the shade, they ate their meal of bread and boiled beef in silence as they surveyed the work they had accomplished and had yet to do in the maintenance of their fence. The day was humid, and thick white clouds passed briefly overhead providing a moment's respite from the sun.

John reached down for the weak ale his mother had sent along that morning. Suddenly he gasped as three painted Indians appeared on each side of the great oak. Two of them grabbed Jonathan Scott by the arms while the third held the point of his knife against Jonathan Scott's throat. Lifting the large Englishman to his feet, the two warriors each as tall and brawny as he, pressed their weight against Jonathan Scott and held him to the tree.

Hoping that there were no other Indians hidden nearby, John and his brother seized the opportunity, jumping up and running across the field toward their house.

With a silver band on each arm and a proud top-knot sticking out from his otherwise hairless scalp, the warrior with the knife grunted in broken English to Jonathan Scott, "Call boys!" Shocked that the savage actually thought he might call his sons, Jonathan Scott shook his head firmly.

Pressing the edge of his blade into Jonathan Scott's neck until a thin line of blood appeared, the warrior repeated, "Call boys!" Prepared to die, Jonathan Scott did not move. He simply waited for the knife to finish its work.

Seconds later, Jonathan Scott heard the warrior cry again, "Call boys!" Surprised that he was still alive, Jonathan Scott thought about Hannah and the children at home. He realized that the boys had probably run back to the house and that as soon as they killed him, the savages would attack his family.

With sickening logic, Jonathan Scott found that he must either risk the lives of two sons or risk the death of his entire family. He knew that Indians did not torture children and that strong children were well treated in captivity. Jonathan Scott's boys were strong, and with his help they could easily survive until they could be ransomed.

Hannah and the young ones had only their aged grandfather to defend them, and he not even having the chance to prepare for their defense. Even if his family were able to keep the savages out of the house and thereby save themselves from the hatchet, surely the savages would fire the house with his family inside.

Jonathan Scott shuddered at the thought, but he realized that he had to call the boys. The Indians would want to adopt them since they were young enough to adapt to their way of life and old enough to march on their own two feet. While Hannah and the younger children had little or no chance of survival if the Indians attacked, the boys could make it, and Jonathan Scott was sure that whether by ransom or escape, he could get them away from any Indian village and bring them home to Hannah.

Yet it was likely that the Indians would kill Jonathan Scott regardless of what he did. In these last few seconds before he died, he had the chance to save most if not all of his family. Resolved, Jonathan Scott bellowed, "Junior! John! You are to come!"

Still some distance from the house, John heard his father's call. Shocked, he stopped running and turned to his brother who had also stopped, "No, it can't be… Did you hear that?"

Breathing hard, Junior asked incredulously, "Can he mean it?"

They heard it again. The command of their father was both unbelievable and unmistakable. Looking back, they could see that the Indians held their father against the tree. With great trepidation, the boys obediently loped back across the meadow. As the boys neared the terrifying cluster of four men, they slowed, wondering when the warriors would lunge at them.

When the boys were within a few feet of them, the Indian with the top knot grabbed John and bound his wrists in front of his body; another did likewise with Junior. As the warrior bound the boys, Jonathan Scott spoke to his sons, and John could hear the pride in his voice, "Boys, you have saved the lives of your whole family, and you can tell them so when you return. Prepare yourselves now, for I think they are about to kill me. They should spare you though, my boys. Keep quiet; do as the savages tell you, and wait for ransom."

Though the knife was off his throat and the chance might come to escape from the two Indians who held him, Jonathan Scott made no resistance, for what could his own life bring but the death of his children? If he ran, the Indians might in their rage kill Junior and John. They might attack his home. It was possible that they might do nothing and simply take the boys captive and leave, but Jonathan Scott was not willing to take the risk. He knew how highly the Indians prized a stoic man who died bravely. If he could die quietly under their torture, his death might even help his boys by making them more prized as the sons of an honorable man.

The two Indians holding Jonathan Scott flipped him around so that he faced the tree. While one warrior twisted Jonathan Scott's left arm behind his back and straddled the Englishman's body pressing him against the tree, the other stretched Jonathan Scott's right arm across the great tree trunk, pressing his hand flat against the bark. This warrior then drew his hatchet and neatly sliced off Jonathan Scott's right thumb, letting it drop into the grass.

Having bound the great dark-haired Englishman's hands, the Indians led their captives away at a run. They

168

disappeared into the woods and crossed the first mountain on their rugged path to Canada.

Chapter Seven

Wednesday, July 26th, 1710
Waterbury, Connecticut Colony

The steady beat of the drum calling Waterbury to an emergency meeting had ceased, and Hannah walked into her hot and humid home with four of her children and her father. The children's shoes shuffled along the plank floors as they filed into the house. It was late afternoon, and Hannah began preparing a meal from the ample food sent home with her by the women of Waterbury. She was grateful that she would not have to cook, that she would have time that night to hold her children close.

The meeting had been called on account of Jonathan Scott and their boys' disappearance. It was obvious to all that they had been captured. Adding to the facts that this was a time of war, and that farmers simply did not disappear with their sons for any reason other than captivity, was the evidence of Jonathan Scott's thumb which had been found under the great oak tree. The town chose a group of men to petition the General Court at

New Haven for a Special Committee of War for Waterbury, which would send scouts and garrison soldiers to Waterbury. The town also returned to Hannah her husband's taxes for the preceding year in order to diminish the inevitable hardship of running a farm without a farmer.

At the meeting, Jonathan Scott's ample family had surrounded her, comforting her, reassuring her, quoting Scripture on the faithful endurance of hardship, and how even the righteous can be afflicted as a test rather than as a punishment. Hannah had not wanted to leave; she had not wanted to return home where she would sleep alone if she could sleep at all.

Now at home, moving slowly and distractedly through the motions of preparing the table, she wondered how her man and boys fared. Though her sister Sarah's case gave evidence to the contrary, Hannah allowed herself to believe that her boys would come home, that the Indians had taken them to adopt into their filthy, heathen hovels. Hannah shuddered. How could her boys be gone, and how could they possibly be on their way to months or even years in such squalor?

Standing before the table, she suddenly broke into tears of worry and anger. Her grizzled old father rushed to Hannah, wrapped his arms around her and held her close, his only remaining child. Seeing his strong mother's crumbling composure, Daniel ran to her and clutched her leg. Hannah lifted him in her arms and tried to smile reassuringly. Sergeant Hawks looked at his grandchildren's worried faces. Kneeling down he opened his arms, and they ran into his embrace. A concerned

Eliezer peered over his grandfather's shoulder asking, "Mama, is Papa coming back?" Hannah sniffed and said, "I don't know, son. Only God knows. We have to trust Him."

Eliezer asked, "What about Junior and John?" Before Hannah could answer, the old sergeant gruffly said, "Of course they are coming back, and so is your father!"

Stunned and disturbed, Hannah scowled at her father. After the solid hope of Sarah's ransom and the crushing blow of her death, how dare he lift the children's expectations only to have them dashed in months to come? It was best to leave things in God's hands and be prepared for the worst.

Desperately wanting to believe their grandfather, the children looked from their grandfather to their mother and wondered who was right. The old sergeant looked up at his daughter and shook his head at her lack of faith. Tenderly he said, "I mean it Hannah. I do believe they are a'comin' back. And besides, is it not better to live with hope for as long as we can, than to grieve for something that has not yet happened?"

Reflecting on the anguish she knew her father had felt at the unexpected news of Sarah's death, Hannah remained far from convinced, and the thought occurred to her that her aging father's mind may have begun to slip. Too haggard to check herself in time, Hannah's countenance took on a look of undisguised pity for the old man.

Gently moving the children aside Sergeant Hawks stood up, and looking his daughter steadfastly in the eye, he boomed, "Hannah, whose God do you think you're talkin' about? Whose God pulled back the mighty Jordan with a crash and a roar? Whose God broke the very chains from Peter's hands? Hannah! How dare you surrender hope? 'Tis an insult to God's power not to expect them to return! For to assume that He *will* not bring them back is to assume that he *can* not, and that my dear child is a grave, grave sin."

The old man threw his arms up and said, "You're not thinkin' about your God; you're thinkin' about them heathens who have no power that your God didn't give 'em. They can do *nothing* without His leave!"

His voice softened as he continued, "Now Hannah, think on your man ~ strong, disciplined, in many ways like a savage. Jonathan Scott has the self-control to submit quietly and wait for the right moment to bring your sons back here. God can do anything Hannah, and believe me, He hasn't nearly the work bringin' a mighty man like yours home that he had bringin' an ordinary man like me home from battle."

She laughed through her tears. "Ah, Father," she said, "Lord, I thank You for my father."

The old soldier took his daughter's face in his hands and locked his gaze with hers, "Mark my words, Goodwife Scott. Your God will bring that man back to you, and He'll bring your sons back too."

∾

Friday, September 8th, 1710
St. Lawrence River Valley, French Canada

On the pebble beach, the Indians who had rushed out to greet Red Bear and inspect his captives began to pull back forming a long path meandering through the village behind them. While the head of the path comprised warriors menacingly wielding war clubs and heavy sticks, deeper into the village the gauntlet was lined with women and children brandishing sticks and green branches. This gauntlet snaked back into the heart of the village of longhouses and then turned left down a wide path ending in an open area before a large Native structure near the furthest extent of the village.

Hands bound behind their backs, the three naked captives stood on the beach among several warriors who held the captives fast. Whoops and screams pierced their ears, and John watched in horror as his father was led toward the gauntlet. A large bruise was just beginning to form on Jonathan Scott's ribs where his master had struck the bearded white man to silence him.

He was as tall as most of the warriors, his body lean and muscular like theirs, but there the similarities ended. While Jonathan Scott's forearms, neck, and face were dark from the sun, the rest of his naked body was pathetically pale against the copper skinned Indians.

Jonathan Scott's master untied his wrists and shoved him to the start of the gauntlet. John watched his father, mere inches from a likely death, stand his ground and focus.

Suddenly Jonathan Scott said aloud as though announcing to his sons and to himself, "Greater is He that is in me than he that is in the world!"

John could see his father's face from the side, and he watched as Jonathan Scott clenched his jaw and drew a breath. Tightening his stomach, Jonathan Scott bent forward instinctively lowering his body for speed. His back strong and broad was chiseled like the Indians' but white and stark in the sunlight. His whole body flexed in preparation for the run of his life, Jonathan Scott's lower back muscles formed a deep groove around his spine, and his bare feet dug into the pebbles for traction.

The captive shot off into the line, his thick legs pumping and carrying him deep into the line before the savages had a chance to swing their clubs at him.

As Jonathan Scott tore through the gauntlet, he turned a sharp corner in the snaking line. A club caught him on the back, and he stumbled with the force, but he caught himself by shifting his leg deftly under his weight. Feeling a thick rod whip his lower back, he pressed his feet hard against the ground, and keeping his head down launched his body forward again. He had sprinted but a few paces when a warrior smashed him on the shoulder, causing him to lurch forward and sending sharp pain through his shoulder all the way to his waist.

Jonathan Scott knew that many died in the gauntlet. If a captive gave up or appeared weak, the Indians would beat him to death on the spot. Knowing that bravery and hopeless force in the face of death were his only weapons, he jerked his body upright and shot his elbow backward, catching a brave in the face and knocking the man off his feet.

In response to Jonathan Scott's defiance, the whooping increased, taking on a tone of praise. He set off again, racing through the gauntlet, missing the myriad weapons swinging at him from both sides until a stone tomahawk came plunging toward him on the right. Seeing that he could not escape the blow that would crush his head or shoulder, Jonathan Scott grabbed the tomahawk with his left hand. His right thumb gone, he wrapped the fingers of his right hand tightly around the base of the club and thrust his weight forward, pinning the surprised warrior against the cheering mob. Jonathan Scott wrenched the club from the warrior's grip and sped onward amid the obscene laudation.

Rounding a curve, he saw women and children lining the path just a few yards before him. Shocked and sickened, he dropped the war club on the ground. He pressed on while they lashed at him with green branches and sticks, cutting his back and limbs.

Several hands grabbed his arms on both sides, and a young woman on Jonathan Scott's right sank her teeth into his shoulder. On the opposite side, another woman and two boys bit his left arm drawing blood as they clamped into his flesh. Jonathan Scott stared a moment in contempt at the heads attached to his arms before violently shaking them off and resuming the stinging, lashing course.

The path straight now to the end, he could see that the gauntlet ended just a few yards ahead in front of a great longhouse. Focusing his aim on the building, he shot off toward his mark. Dashing through the line of savage whoops and pelting children, Jonathan Scott made it into the open where the crowd erupted in cheers.

Breathing hard to recover from the battle for his life, Jonathan Scott squared his hands on his naked hips, a hideous scar where his right thumb had once been. Mottled with bruised skin, bite marks, and bloody slashes, the great stark Englishman stood amid their adulation.

Hatred coursed through his naked body and Jonathan Scott's blue eyes blazed with fury at what his sons would have to endure. Disgusted beyond all caution Jonathan Scott opened his bearded mouth and yelled into their approving clamor, "This is your sport, you sons o' bitches? Bloody wolves you are!"

At the water's edge, John stood with his master Red Bear. Having heard his father's voice, John began to believe that the man was safe. In spite of the trepidation running through John's veins, the sound of his father's voice relieved him immensely.

Only a few minutes earlier, the captives had arrived by canoe on the pebble beach where the whole village rushed to greet the returning warriors and to inspect the captives. A gaggle of Indians had rushed to see John's hair ~ some groping, some stroking softly ~ as clawing hands had suddenly begun tearing the captives' clothes from their bodies.

Gasping, John had cried, 'No!" Yet they had persisted, and within seconds he was entirely naked. Having achieved their aim, the crowd had pulled away from him, and John had seen that most of the boys his age wore not a stitch of clothing. The men wore only loincloths, and to John's great shock the women wore nothing over their breasts, their skirts extending only from the waist to just below the knee.

His hands were still bound, and now as the crowd grew quiet and turned their attention back to the captive boys, John was mortified at his inability to cover himself.

Though John could not see his father in the throng of Indians, he suddenly heard his father's voice again, "Boys!" Jonathan Scott cried. "Be strong, and do not let them see that they hurt you! You can do all things through Christ which strengtheneth you! You are more than conquerors through Him who loved us!" Buoyed by the words, John looked at his brother who appeared to take heart as well. They knew that their father risked further beating by communicating with his sons, for the captives had been forbidden to speak to one another on the journey.

The whooping began anew, and John watched as the Indians pushed his naked brother toward the gauntlet. Though a tall lad and strong, Junior looked frail in the shadow of the long line of warriors.

As his brother stared down the grim line of sticks and clubs, John thought of their grandfather and all the battles he had survived. He thought of what their father had just survived, and now John believed that God would help him and his brother if they called on Him. Growing confident and willing to risk a correcting wallop, John shouted to Junior, "Greater is He that is in you than he that is in the world, my brother!"

No one struck John as Junior looked back at him and seemed to take strength from the confidence in John's face before turning his eyes back to the whooping madness. Junior stood for a moment bracing himself and then dashed into the line.

Expecting a blow that would knock his brother to the ground at any moment, John prayed silently for his strength and for the enemies' weapons to miss their mark. Within seconds however, John saw that this was not the same gauntlet their father had run though it was the same Indians who lined it.

John watched Junior receive an occasional thump on the arms and back, but each hit was slight, almost fraternal. The Indians whooped and danced as Junior ran unimpeded. John lost sight of him as he rounded the corner into the main section of the village. John waited to hear the crushing thuds that had beset his father, but nothing of the sort reached his ears. Then he heard a cheer go up and it was John's turn.

As the Indians led him to the gauntlet, a thrill of hope that he would receive the same light treatment rushed through John. He shut his eyes for a moment and prayed that this was not a cruel trick. His face drawn, John squared himself a moment and bolted down the line, receiving immediately a light thump on the shoulder. As he ran easily, receiving no resistance and hits less painful than those his own brothers at home could deliver, his heart soared with hope. He rounded the corner and zigged through the meandering curves of warriors tapping him gently with their clubs. When he reached the women and children, they fairly tickled him with the branches, only delivering slight scratches, and John reached the end in no time.

His legs trembling with relief, John found himself smiling giddily. The Indians cheered around him, and John laughed out loud in his moment of deliverance. He was alive, and there was not a fresh bruise on his body, at least not from the gauntlet, for there were plenty of bruises from the long march.

In the midst of his laughter, John heard his father's voice scolding him sharply, "John! Remember yourself!" Surprised and embarrassed, he wheeled around to find his father newly bound, and John was shocked at the state of his father. Covered with dirt and bruises and riddled with stripes of dried blood, the sight shamed John.

The thrill of being alive and unbroken, the sickening and sad sight of his father, the shame of laughing with the enemy, and the reality of how very far he was from home ~ all of these things collided in John as he fought to keep tears of joy, sorrow, and shame from destroying the dignity the Indians had allowed him. Nor by the emotions of a child would John rob his father of the dignity he had *taken back* from the Indians. No, John would not shame his father by weeping in front of savages.

The boys remained unbound when the Indians led their naked captives into the large longhouse that formed the end of the gauntlet. As they stepped through the longhouse doorway, a wall designed to prevent drafts blocked their way, and they turned right in order to circuit the wall. Once inside, John saw an old man sitting on a bench at the far end of the building. Down the middle of the longhouse ran the black circles of fire pits. An opening to allow smoke to escape ran the length of the roof and provided the only light in the dim interior.

Made to sit separately from one another, the captives were led to a spot on the dirt floor in front of the old man. Red Bear sat with John while Jonathan Scott and Junior were each with the Indians who had taken them from Waterbury. John watched his father and brother intently. The fear seemed to be over. From the many accounts of captivity he had heard, John thought that the Indians were not likely to kill any of them now. Their father had taken the gauntlet valiantly, and the Indians had given the boys only token hits before receiving them joyfully. Yet from these same accounts of captivity, John expected that his father, his brother and he would be separated and taken to different villages along the St. Lawrence or deep into the wilderness away from the river.

The room soon filled with people sitting on the floor and standing where they could, and the longhouse grew hot quickly. John found the place dark and cluttered with something hanging from every rafter and pole. When the people had stopped milling around and had grown quiet, the old man spoke to the group in their language, saying things that John could not understand. The captives were made to stand naked with their masters, and each master was given an opportunity to speak. Each speech was followed by approving grunts from the large congregation.

John did not understand what was going on, but it seemed that the captives were being assigned officially to their individual masters. There appeared to be some question as to who would get his brother, but in the end, the captives each sat down with the same masters who had brought them in.

After the space of an hour or more, the people filed out, dispersing around the village as the women set to the work of preparing a feast of welcome for the three braves who had returned with as many captives. When they left the longhouse, Red Bear and John went out before John's father and brother. Red Bear walked next to John, holding his arm above the elbow and leading him deep into the village. Awkwardly covering his nakedness with his free hand, John tried to look behind them to see where his father and brother were taken, but the throng had closed around them, and he could see nothing but a sea of curious faces marveling at the white-haired, ice-eyed captive.

As the pair walked through the village that appeared to John to be a series of huts in clusters with no organized plan, several of the village warriors slapped Red Bear on the back and congratulated him.

Red Bear led John into another longhouse. John's eyes had not adjusted to the dim light until he found himself standing before a grey-haired old man and woman seated on a fur-covered bench. Standing next to them was an

Indian woman with dark, lustrous eyes. John thought he saw a great softness in her eyes, and it comforted him.

Red Bear spoke to the old man first, who nodded and examined John intently with somewhat cloudy old eyes. The dignified old man did not smile or frown, and John could not sense what he was thinking. Then Red Bear addressed the old woman who also remained stoic and then grunted at the end of Red Bear's talking.

Then Red Bear took the younger woman's hand and placed John's hand in hers as he spoke. The young woman looked solemnly at Red Bear while he spoke. Then she turned her kind eyes on John and smiled. She led John across the middle section of the longhouse and into an apartment facing that of the old man and woman.

As John looked around the longhouse, he saw that but for Red Bear and the old couple, they seemed to be alone. The younger woman retrieved an earthenware bowl of warm water from the fire, a clean cloth, and a pouch of animal fat. She set the bowl on the floor and dipped the cloth into the water. She stood up and began rinsing the dirt and sweat of three hundred miles off the boy's chest and arms. Taking special care of the many scratches from brambles, she gently cleaned his body but avoided the area he covered with his hands.

When she had finished, the woman handed the rag to John and nodded toward his private area. Humiliated, John nodded respectfully before turning his back to her. He washed himself quickly, and when he turned around again, the woman took the rag from him and gave him a loincloth.

Having seen many naked boys his own age, John was grateful to the woman for her care of his modesty. When she opened the pouch of animal fat, John obeyed her instructions to work the fat into his skin. John guessed that the fat was bear grease, which was commonly known to be the Indian remedy for persistent summer mosquitoes. John found that despite the acrid odor, it gave his skin a handsome sheen.

When the woman was satisfied, she stood next to a fur-lined bench in the apartment and patted it with her hand before walking away. Just as John sat down, a boy about his age peered around the apartment wall and startled John. Laughing at John's reaction, Red Bear crossed the longhouse and sat down on the bench next to John while the Native boy came out from behind the wall and stood in front of John.

The boy smiled at John and talked incessantly, but John did not understand a word. Within a few minutes, the woman returned with two bowls of some kind of corn soup. One she served to Red Bear and the other to John, which he devoured.

Red Bear also ate quickly but with more dignity than John. As the woman brought more soup, John heard a great commotion outside. The old couple followed Red Bear and the Indian boy out of the longhouse, but the woman stayed with John.

With smiles and gestures imitating a fat belly, she demonstrated that Red Bear and the villagers were all going to eat a great deal and their stomachs would be very full. Though John preferred the privacy of this dark longhouse at the moment, he wished that he could go to the feast where he might catch a glimpse of his father or brother, but the woman showed no sign of taking him.

She sat quietly on the adjacent bench and looked at John from time to time. He found it peculiar that the woman sat with no mending in her hand, but John found her stillness soothing in this foreign place.

John's mouth watered as the savory smells of the feast began to permeate the longhouse, for though the woman had given him two bowls of soup, he was not sated. After what seemed like an hour or more, the Indian boy appeared again holding great chunks of meat in each hand. John smiled at the boy saying, "Many thanks."

The boy laughed at John's strange speech, but John sensed no mockery or cruelty in the boy. John was glad that the boy sat with them while they ate. When they had finished the woman shooed the boy, who returned to the feast, while she gestured to John that he should lie down.

He did so and sank gratefully into the soft furs of the bench where he had been sitting.

Wondering how his brother and father fared, John prayed silently that the Indians would relent now that they were home, that they would no longer pin his father to the ground with broad sticks across his chest and legs as they had done each night of the journey.

John had felt guilty on the march, for their father was treated with such gruffness while the Indians were almost kind to the boys and at times even playful.

John and his brother had not been allowed to speak to their father on the journey. John had missed the sound of his father's voice on the long hungry march, and the surprise of hearing it this morning before the gauntlet had done much to encourage John.

For weeks they had marched at a demanding pace through bushes and brambles and over seemingly endless mountains. When they left Waterbury, their Indian masters had tossed the captives' shoes into the Mountain Laurel bushes and had handed each captive a pair of moccasins. Red Bear had given John a pair that seemed absurd in the context of their journey, for they had been carefully beaded and decorated as though made for someone very special.

Having made their way to the Connecticut River, the little party had followed it at some distance in order to avoid English settlements. The Indians had maintained silence most of the time, speaking softly and only when absolutely necessary. They had made no fires and had eaten only the finely ground corn powder which their captors called nocake. Given only a small amount poured into their palms each day, they licked it up and washed it down with river water. Hunger had gnawed constantly in their bellies and exhausted muscles.

When they had reached the White River, the party changed their course toward the northwest. From the widely circulated memoirs of Deerfield's Reverend Williams, the Scotts knew that their own Sarah Hawks had been killed along that river. John Scott wondered if his captors had been among those at Deerfield and if any of them even remembered Sarah.

A few days along the White River, the Indians had begun to relax. Though they did not slacken the pace, they spoke to each other more often and lit fires on some evenings. On the only morning when they did not march, one of the braves had gone hunting. He had brought back a whitetail doe whose meat and a whole day's rest had done much to revive the little group.

Cresting mountain after mountain, expecting each one to take them closer to rest, the captives had made their way tediously across the Green Mountains and on to Lake Champlain and had today at last arrived at this village on the St. Lawrence River.

Lying down now in the longhouse John blinked wearily as he noted how intently the woman watched him. For any of the other Indians to have stared so long at him would have made him uncomfortable, but he did not mind with her. His muscles eased into the furs, and his blinks grew longer and closer together. Soon he could not keep his eyes open.

Long after the sun had gone down, Red Bear joined his bride on the bench next to that of the sleeping tow-head. Catches Water awoke and touching Red Bear's face as he lay next to her, she whispered, "The child is good, Red Bear. He is strong and intelligent. In the coming months, this boy will restore my father, and he will fill the void in our longhouse. We cannot know if he will choose to stay among us, but you have done a great thing, Red Bear, in bringing him here."

Chapter Eight

Sunday, August 12th, 1711
St. Lawrence River Valley, French Canada

John Scott and Laughing Owl walked back to the village from an afternoon swim with the villagers. At the crystal clear pool not far from their settlement, all had shed their clothing and enjoyed the cool water of the wide and deep pond bounded by large rocks. Swimming had become a near daily reprieve from the heat, and John's skin had grown dark in the sun nearly matching that of his copper friend Laughing Owl.

Laughing Owl was the boy who had greeted John on his first day in the village. A grandson of Night Sky, he lived in the longhouse where John lived, and the two had become fast friends. A year younger, Laughing Owl was of the same height as John.

Laughing Owl's hair was cut short on one side with the other side hanging past his shoulder. While the usual practice with young male captives was to cut their hair to be like the other boys, Catches Water had wanted to see John's unusual hair grow long first. As a result John's hair now reached his shoulders. First greased then meticulously combed back from his temples, the top section of his tow colored hair was bound by a thin leather strap leaving the rest to hang thick and brilliant in the summer sun.

More than a year had passed since the Scott captivity began, and John found himself relaxing into the Indian way of life. One of the greatest reliefs John had experienced was that Sunday was no longer wretched. John recalled the interminable Sabbaths at home, with preaching all day; eating lunch in the Sabbath House was almost as bad as sitting through the meetings, so serious and tense was the mood. Even among his friends at home, he had not been allowed to speak of anything other than God on Sunday, could not mention a tree or an animal or the crops unless it was to describe God's hand in making such things. He could not play or even run if he were late, and heaven forbid that he smiled at one of the other children! Even his grandfather, who was the most lenient of the adults in his life, would box John's ear.

Mass was an entirely different thing from a Sunday meeting, and John attended mass with his Indian master's family once or twice each week. Though John had feared the evil power of the priests, Red Bear had insisted that the boy join the family at mass. John had suspected that it was a fight he would not win and offered no resistance.

The first time he went to mass, John had seen a crucifix hanging over the heretical Catholic altar. Before that initial mass, John had never seen an image of his Lord, and its power had stunned the boy. Because of the danger of worshiping the idol rather than the God it represented, there had been no images of God in Waterbury. Throughout his childhood, John had heard that the Devil used idolatry as a powerful tool in deceiving the Catholic heretics.

Yet during that first mass, even knowing the danger to his soul, when he saw the vivid imagery of Jesus' suffering for John's own salvation, it had pierced the boy's heart. His throat had tightened, and he had fought tears of gratitude and sorrow.

John had suddenly found himself capable of the one thing God wanted most, the one thing John had never been able to achieve in the grip of his parents' God. Amid the peculiar ritual and incomprehensible Latin ceremony, John had quietly fallen in love with God.

John's brother and father did not attend mass. In the longhouse where Junior lived, most were not Catholic. Thus, Junior had received pressure only from the local priest whom Junior found easy to refuse.

Their father Jonathan Scott's master, however, was a faithful Catholic like Red Bear, and he had firmly insisted on his new slave's attending Mass. More afraid of God than of any man, Jonathan Scott had suffered beatings rather than damn his soul by attending mass. Disgusted at the Englishman's insult to the only true Church, Jonathan Scott's master finally abandoned the project of saving the man's soul.

Quiet, strong, and reticent, Jonathan Scott served as one of three slaves in the village, the other two slaves being Indian. Though the Indians continued to keep the captives apart, trying to transform Junior and John into viable Indian boys, Junior managed to find time alone with his father whenever possible.

Jonathan Scott instructed Junior to pretend to enjoy Indian life, for their masters would be less and less vigilant over them as time wore on. This had proved true. Jonathan Scott no longer slept under poles. He was however bound and tethered to his master's wrist each night. He could not be trusted entirely because he had not weakened like most slaves, particularly English slaves who tended to fade more quickly than Indians. Being tougher, Indians were accustomed to alternating states of starvation and feasting, and to exposure of the skin to hot and cold weather.

Young John had not made the same efforts to be with his father because he was watched more closely than his brother and father. It was clear to all that John was something special. That was not the only reason however, for John found that he hurt less when he simply played Indian and waited for the ransom that would come eventually.

From many captivity stories recounted to him by the fire in the evenings of his childhood in Waterbury, John knew that ransom always came. Whenever he caught sight of his father or brother, they reminded him of home and his mother and siblings, his grandfather, and the ache was simply too much to bear.

His father and brother's strange appearance too disturbed John. They were filthy and shaggy with unkempt long hair. His father's beard was longer than John had ever seen it even when he would grow a beard for warmth in winter back in Waterbury.

All three had received new names. John's command of the Mohawk language was quite good now, and though he could understand his father and brother's names, he never spoke their names for he was not allowed to speak to his father and brother. Nor did Indian life sit well on them. They were what captives were expected to be by those at home in the colonies ~ quietly resistant and underneath all the dirt and foreignness English to the core. As a result, he never thought of them as anyone but Father and Junior.

John did however tend to think of himself by his Indian name, Restores The Old One. He had not abandoned the name John Scott in his heart of course, for John Scott was who he was. Yet while the Scotts awaited ransom, young John enjoyed the name Restores The Old One, for it implied a power he had certainly never attributed to himself. The name honored John and made him feel for the first time in his life that to someone he was extraordinarily useful. That John could restore anyone swelled his heart and filled him with a feeling of importance and value to those around him. He felt important here in a way he had never felt at home in Waterbury, and John had latched on to this new name the moment he had first understood its meaning.

Knowing that the name was an honor, John understood that he was a critical element in Night Sky's longhouse for as long as he stayed among them, but he did not understand all that his name meant and the boy was afraid to ask. John wondered if the "Old One" in his name might be Honors The Dead, but the old man did not take any particular interest in the boy. Honors The Dead did not ignore John; he simply seemed reserved as though awaiting something.

John and Laughing Owl walked through the thick forest along the oft used path. Fern and bushes and great tall trees enveloped the boys in green abundance dappled with sunshine. As they approached the corn field where the slaves and chatting women were harvesting, John spotted his father among the women. Pity and embarrassment punched his heart, and he looked quickly at Laughing Owl to see if he had noticed the great bearded slave. Laughing Owl was distracted by a noisy, yipping game afoot among the warriors in the nearby meadow.

Red Bear broke away from the game and skirted the cornfield, loping over to the boys. "Cooler?" he asked. Laughing Owl nodded and began to tell his uncle about the day's exploits. Red Bear noticed that Restores The Old One seemed distant. Following the boy's gaze, Red Bear saw the boy's English father at work among the women.

As the three walked together around the edge of the cornfield, Red Bear and John watched Jonathan Scott harvesting among the squaws while Laughing Owl continued to talk. Seeing Jonathan Scott's erect back and clear eyes, Red Bear thought to himself that if one did not see the man at work, one would not peg him as a slave.

Red Bear could see the pity mixed with embarrassment on the face of Restores The Old One as they watched the big bearded man wearing a loincloth, moccasins and a pack on his back suspended by a burden strap slung across his forehead. He walked methodically through the rows of corn, picking then tucking ears of corn into the pack. Though missing his right thumb, Jonathan Scott worked as efficiently as anyone else. But for the beard and the hair on his body, Red Bear thought the English slave looked the very picture of an Indian ~ dark, lithe and proud.

Red Bear understood the boy's embarrassment, for his English father was doing women's work. Warriors conserved their energy, occasionally playing while they rested for days on end. Hunting and war were too important to risk wasting valuable energy on daily chores. Jonathan Scott was not a warrior of course; he was a slave. So though a man, he worked wherever he was needed, and that was usually among the women who did all the labor of the camp.

Red Bear watched as Jonathan Scott stopped his field work for a moment and seemed to be looking in the direction of an older woman. The grey-haired woman was strong as she worked along side her family and friends chatting and laughing. Jonathan Scott resumed his task, looking up at the woman from time to time.

After several minutes Jonathan Scott crossed three rows of corn to stand just in front of the older woman.

Standing in her way, he nodded deferentially to her, and without saying a word, he reached out gently with both hands to lift the burden strap from her head. Shocked by this bizarre behavior from a slave, the woman slapped his hands away. He nodded again and gently but firmly slid the strap over his forearms and walked past her, back to his place three rows away.

The old woman turned to watch Jonathan Scott. Deeply offended and wondering what to do with herself now that she had no pack, she shouted at him. The other women laughed at the absurd sight, as he strapped her pack across his forehead as well. The older woman indignantly left the field and strode toward the village to fetch another pack.

John was mortified, and yet he was touched by his father's act of kindness or … defiance or whatever his father had intended it to be.

Red Bear studied the boy, and part of the brave wanted to tell Restores The Old One how profoundly he respected his English father. This act of taking women's burdens without their command or consent was something Jonathan Scott had done on more than one occasion. Such acts of silent defiance set the peculiar Englishman apart from any other captive Red Bear had met. The man's very survival seemed an act of defiance. For as a slave he certainly ate, but he ate last, and when there was little he received little. Yet the man thrived. It was the most peculiar thing. The man was as brawny and robust now in a cornfield with two burden straps across his forehead as he had been a year ago working in his own field.

Red Bear respected the English slave, and he did not like to see Restores The Old One suffer from shame, yet he could not share this respect with the boy, for Red Bear was Restores The Old One's new father. The more Red Bear saw of the English slave the more Red Bear saw his People's need of this son. With all of the destruction to his People from disease, starvation and war, Red Bear knew that this Englishman's blood was good and necessary.

The English father was strong in body, mind and spirit. He was disciplined enough to keep quiet with no warrior nearby to keep a slave's tongue in check for him. Red Bear guessed that Jonathan Scott understood the language well now as he responded to all commands, but the man never spoke. This slave appeared to thrive on much work and little food; he never seemed to grow despondent. His sons were both strong, and Restores The Old One's heavy jaw together with his nearly Indian-like height prophesied that the young man would one day stand as strong as his father.

Restores The Old One adapted well to the ways of Red Bear's People. It was as though the boy were fleeing from something, as though he found a kind of refuge in captivity. The dark-haired son was another matter. He was very English, and while he did what he was told and lived in the longhouse of his master, the dark-haired boy would probably choose ransom when the war ended.

When this Queen Anne's War ended, ransom would be offered for all captives. Restores The Old One must *want* to stay among Red Bear's People ~ to marry and to raise up strong warriors from his own body ~ and so Red Bear allowed the boy's shame for his real father to grow.

෴

Tuesday, October 9th, 1711
St. Lawrence River Valley, French Canada

Following a shallow stream, John walked behind Red Bear who led a small hunting party. Laughing Owl and his father White Drum walked behind John. That morning, two parties had set out from their hunting camp which lay about two day's walk from their village, the meat supply in their village having gotten rather low. The other party comprising six braves would move faster, for they would not be teaching.

Carrying Red Bear's loaded flintlock at the ready, John was grateful to be away from the hunting camp, for his father and Catches Water were among the two slaves and six squaws who had come to clean and carry the game home. It was growing harder to be near his father particularly at a time like this when John so wanted to let go and shine. But to shine as an Indian was to hurt his father. 'Yet perhaps,' thought John, 'If he sees how well I can shoot, he might see the value of it and allow me to hunt when we return to Waterbury.'

John had hunted many times since he had become a captive, and he enjoyed it immensely. Today was a big hunt, and it was the first time that he and Laughing Owl would be allowed to shoot for something as valuable and fleeting as a deer.

John could not help but thrill at the victory over his brother. Ever since they had come to the Indian village last year, John had thrived and Junior had stagnated. Despondent and thin, it was clear that Junior hated life among the savages. His master struggled to coax him along the path to becoming an Indian, but his poor transformation caused Junior's master to treat the boy more like a servant than an adopted child, and Junior was assigned far more work than John, for John was seen as a future warrior.

As the hunting party walked though the brilliant colors, the leaves raining down on them, they watched and listened, squatting down occasionally to check the moist earth for tracks and droppings. Despite the pressure of potentially shaming Red Bear with an early shot or by frightening the prey with a sudden action, John's focus was immutable. In the woods, on the hunt, a flintlock in his hand, providing meat for those who loved him ~ distilled down to his essence, this was John Scott.

John found it surprisingly easy to be with Red Bear who was so like his real father ~ quiet and pensive yet playful at times. It was not so easy of course when John knew his real father was watching his interaction with the man who made it plain that he wanted to usurp his father's role.

John felt a bit guilty, but he could not resist the genuine desire to achieve success in the ways of this People. They cheered him when he did well, and when he failed they encouraged him to try again. Best of all, when John did something wrong or stepped out of line, they corrected him with nothing more than frowns of disapproval. Knowing that he would not be beaten had allowed John to relax among the Indians.

When John had first seen this form of discipline used on a misbehaving toddler, it amazed him to find that a simple scowl from everyone the child loved could keep a child in line as well as a rod or a belt. John had laughed to himself at the thought of his mother scolding Daniel in this manner, for he knew it would not work in his Waterbury home as it did here. John supposed that when aunts and uncles and grandparents all showed disappointment together, it meant more than if only a mother or a father were to attempt the same thing.

John was also surprised at the respect and honor afforded to him and to every child. Here he was not a sinful child to be kept busy in order to prevent his idle hands from finding themselves about the Devil's business. That this People treated him ~ a mere boy ~ with respect had utterly astounded John.

Soon after the captives' arrival among this foreign People, John had realized that no one cared which hand he used for anything. He had accidentally taken food with his left hand and had looked up to see if anyone had noticed. Surprised that no one had paid any attention, John had begun to test this to see if they truly did not care which hand he used. Finding that they did not, in the space of two months John had picked up a lacrosse racket with his left hand and soundly trounced Laughing Owl.

That the Indians didn't care which hand he used bewildered him. In fact, he began to believe that they wouldn't have cared if he had used his ears to perform a task as long as he did it well. As objects and tasks found themselves in John's left hand, he began to flourish, excelling in everything Red Bear and Laughing Owl taught him. Public excellence was something new to John, and he found it sublime.

John knew it was wrong, that it was a betrayal of his family at home, but he could not help shining in this environment. He knew captivity was temporary, that they would return to Waterbury, and somehow the fleeting nature of this time among savages gave him permission even though he knew his father and brother were disgusted by his assimilation.

Suddenly Red Bear held up his hand bringing the party to a halt. Through the dense, brilliant foliage lay a marshy meadow. As John followed Red Bear's gaze for about fifty yards to the far side of the meadow, he saw a bull moose grazing. The hunters stood stock still as Red Bear nodded to John. They had gone out that morning tracking deer, and John never expected to find a moose on his first big hunt. An animal as massive and cantankerous as a bull moose needed to go down quickly. It often required more than one shot to do the job, and John knew that White Drum and Laughing Owl would be backing him up with their muskets.

That Red Bear would allow John to fire from so great a distance astonished the boy. No one had ever held such confidence in John, and his blood coursed with the thrill of the moment. John quickly and smoothly opened the priming pan by lifting the steel battery which stood at a right angle on the cover of the pan and checked that the powder had remained sealed inside while they walked. Then, so as to prevent the click and snap of the motion to betray their presence, the boy slowly released the pressure of his thumb on the battery and allowed it to rotate silently back to its position covering the pan.

In one fluid motion, he squared his feet to receive the impact of the recoil and slid the butt of the musket into his left shoulder. John loved the feel of a musket against his shoulder. It made him feel strong and useful, for among this People nearly every time John took up a musket, it brought him adulation. Using his thumb, he now pulled back the cock that held the flint in its clamp.

His heart pumping, John forced himself to breathe calmly as he closed his right eye, looked down the barrel through the rear sight and adjusted the direction of the weapon in almost imperceptible movements. The moose stood broadside to them, munching on the tall grass. John waited patiently until he saw in the center of his sights, the precise spot just below and behind the great beast's shoulder where the heart lay. John took a short breath and pulled the trigger. As the flint flew forward striking the battery and opening the priming pan, a shower of sparks fell onto the gunpowder in the pan. Through the touch hole in the bottom of the pan, the powder in the barrel was lit propelling the ball out through the smooth barrel.

As John heard the perfect explosion of the musket, the startled moose looked in their direction. The great beast jerked as a hole appeared just behind and below the shoulder. His legs buckled, and he dropped into the grass.

White Drum and Laughing Owl held their muskets solidly against their shoulders ready for action, but none was needed. The party stood in silent shock for a moment, everyone expecting the moose to rise from where he had fallen in the grass and charge the hunting party. Knowing that the shot had been perfect and that the moose would never move again, John was quietly pleased with himself, wishing that his grandfather could have seen the kill. The hunters waited ~ no one daring to move ~ and as the seconds turned into minutes Red Bear turned back toward John with more animation than John had ever seen on his master's face. Near disbelief Red Bear's whole face opened in joy and pride.

The group quietly and cautiously approached the moose, White Drum and Laughing Owl keeping their muskets cocked. As they neared the spot where the moose lay, they heard no sound ~ no heaving, no thrashing, only silence. Red Bear sent Laughing Owl back to camp for the squaws who would carry the moose while the hunting party quietly honored and thanked the moose for feeding them.

About an hour before twilight set in that night, the two hunting parties gathered at the campsite with the women and slaves. The larger hunting party had taken nothing rather than take small game, for the shots would have scared away the larger game they sought. Jonathan Scott and the women had done nearly all of the work on the moose at the site of the kill. Weighing nearly half a ton, the bull moose was too heavy to carry back to the campsite in one piece requiring it to be skinned, cleaned, and cut into smaller segments before it could be transported.

Jonathan Scott's master had gone with the other hunting party, so Catches Water had directed Jonathan Scott and the other slave in their work. It had greatly diminished John's triumph on the hunt to see his father so demeaned at the beck and call of a woman. Jonathan Scott had bent over the beast, carefully sliding a knife along the hide and pulling backward. It had been difficult to learn to use his left hand now that the right thumb had been cut off. John could see that even after more than a year, it was a struggle, particularly at times like this one that required dexterity. Still, John could tell that even in slavery, his father did excellent work, and he guessed that his father took pride in how neat the hide was.

Now, the entire party of eighteen sat around the fire in the center of the wigwams which the women had constructed that morning, the men feasting on roast moose while the women and slaves listened to the warriors and waited for their turn to eat. The smaller hunting party having taken nothing, John's success buoyed them. Watching the braves feast on his kill, John sat next to Red Bear and beamed at the fuss the men made over him. The men had been crowing all afternoon about John's perfect kill. In all his life, John had never executed any task with such consistent precision as that with which he hunted. It felt so good to excel. Now he knew how Junior felt every day of his life before captivity. John knew that though he was young, he was already a superb hunter because he was consistent and that this was his God-given skill despite what his father might think. John kept his eyes away from his father sitting a few feet to the left of John in the circle. Fortunately Red Bear sat between them and as he leaned forward over his meat he blocked John's view of his father.

Into the echoes of praise Red Bear said, "It is not just Restores The Old One's eye, for surely he has excellent aim, but he also has the patience and quiet heart of a hunter twenty years older." Red Bear paused as the other men grunted and nodded their approval to John. Across the circle Catches Water smiled proudly at John, her thick hair tied back in a braid. Red Bear continued, "Precision is one thing. Calm and consistent excellence are quite another. Restores The Old One never rushes a shot. He is smooth and even in his skill." Red Bear looked at John and continued, "You will make a fine warrior one day. I am proud that you have come to dwell in my longhouse." Catches Water nodded firmly.

John worried about his father's hearing such words, and he wanted to reassure the man that his son had not turned Indian. Making his best attempt to go unnoticed by the Indians, John leaned back and glanced furtively over Red Bear's back. His father's blue eyes, so piercing now against his dark face and beard, met John's glance. John paled, and his heart sank at the sadness, betrayal and worry that he saw in his father's eyes.

Unable to bear his father's gaze, John looked at the ground. Feeling as though he was going to vomit, John squeezed his eyes shut while his thoughts raced. Why did he not resist the Indians as Junior did? Junior did as he was told and that was all. He did not *thrive*. Thriving here was the sin, and John wondered within himself, 'How can I be so happy here? How can I enjoy these savages as I do? Why do I like the name they have given me? Why do I like to hear it? Why do I crave their praise? Why do I want to please them? They are savages and Catholic ones at that! Why do I care what they think? What could be worse? What greater sin could I commit than to venture willingly into the darkness after being taught to follow the light?'

John looked at the fire and hoped he successfully hid the turmoil of his heart as he thought, 'I like it here! God help me, I like it here! And Catches Water… how can I … love her as a mother? For I fear that I do. Oh, Lord God, forgive me! Help me not to betray my dear mother who loves me so.'

John hated himself for the betrayal. He ached for his mother and hoped that once he returned with his father and brother, she would never know how often he had forgotten her. It simply hurt too much to remember, to imagine her alone with his brothers and sister, to imagine them missing him. How he missed his siblings. The Indians had smaller families, only a few children instead of half a dozen or a dozen. He missed sleeping next to his brothers. He missed Martha and Grandfather. 'Grandfather…' thought John, 'you would have destroyed the village of your captors and been back home by now.'

John's inner wranglings did not escape the notice of Catches Water who waited patiently until Red Bear happened to glance in her direction. After several minutes of the warriors' intermittent talking, silence, and feasting, she caught Red Bear's eye; she scowled and nodded toward John, their Restores The Old One. Red Bear saw the boy's evident distress, but he could not tell if it was sadness or worry or anger. He watched the boy awhile longer, guessing that whatever the boy was feeling, his English father was the source of it.

Red Bear had kept Restores The Old One isolated from the other English captives for more than a year. The three captives had seen each other around the central fire of the village during feasts and certainly they caught glimpses of one another from time to time, but they had not been allowed to speak to each other at all for well over a year now. Red Bear had expected some sort of reaction on this hunt when Restores The Old One's father would be so close physically.

In the cornfield that summer day, Red Bear had taken note of Restores The Old One's pity and embarrassment for his English father. The boy had been very troubled by the man's servitude which was doubly thrown in his face on the hunt. It was a precarious time, for Red Bear knew that a son's pity could turn to compassion just as easily as his embarrassment could turn to contempt.

Red Bear had counted on Restores The Old One's success in his first big hunt, and he had counted on the English slave's disdain at the boy's excellence in such an Indian act. Restores The Old One had not let Red Bear down, and Red Bear wondered now if the English slave had already shown John his disapproval. Something was afoot in the boy's heart, and Red Bear would wait patiently to see the outcome. Red Bear cocked his head and watched the English father of this boy who had become so precious to his family.

Soft chatter continued and the fire crackled while Jonathan Scott sat on a great log at the edge of the loose ring of people surrounding the fire. In his usual sitting posture, arms resting on deerskin clad thighs and his back spread broad, Jonathan Scott watched the fire. The air was cold, and Red Bear knew that if this Englishman were at home in his English house, he would be wearing layers of clothing. Here among the trees, he wore what the Indian men wore, nothing more than leggings and moccasins. It pleased Red Bear to see that the cold did not appear to bother him as it would most of the weak English, for this indifference reaffirmed Red Bear's confidence in the English slave's offspring. No goose bumps appeared on his flesh nor did he shiver. It was cold, and it took discipline and concentration to keep the body from showing discomfort.

That Jonathan Scott did not appear weakened in any way since his captivity impressed Red Bear. Many captives whom the nation did not adopt slowly starved to death. Defeat appeared quickly on their faces, but this man receiving the last of the food, eating with the dogs, working among the women, and shamed in his status as a slave, looked as strong as any brave.

As twilight set in, Red Bear studied Jonathan Scott, and firelight flickered across the Englishman's body where dark hair lightly covered his chest. His ribs were visible, yet his muscles were strong and pronounced. He was remarkable especially for an Englishman.

This quiet figure gave the appearance of submission through his obedience, but Red Bear could sense that something was not at rest in the man. Red Bear knew that Jonathan Scott held their ways in contempt. He had watched this Englishman carry women's burdens on more than one occasion. The whole village jeered Jonathan Scott for this, and he had even been struck by offended husbands and sons, but he continued to help the women despite their wishes to the contrary. Though Red Bear thought the man's silent obstinacy foolish, he respected it. He admired Jonathan Scott and Red Bear knew that he, himself, would behave the same way were he ever sold into slavery. In some way Red Bear also would find a way to resist the conqueror.

This business of carrying women's burdens seemed to be a way of expressing contempt for his captors, as though professing the superiority of the English people by saying wordlessly to the braves, "You ought to be ashamed of yourselves, allowing women to carry your burdens." Of course, Red Bear did not see it that way at all. Indian women were respected and allowed far more say in the decisions of the People than English women.

Studying Jonathan Scott who stared into the fire, Red Bear did not trust the slave. Red Bear knew that this man would attempt escape at some point even though he had shown no signs of this since captivity. Red Bear almost preferred the idea of Jonathan Scott's leaving. He could see that the man's influence over the dark haired boy had not waned though Restores The Old One appeared to have thrown himself fully into his Indian home and truly seemed to have *become* Indian. The time was drawing near when Night Sky and Catches Water would want to adopt Restores The Old One formally as their own.

The fire crackled, and Catches Water moved to a spot next to Restores The Old One where she partook of the delicious meal he had provided. Red Bear glanced up and gave her a loving nod. Laughing Owl came and stood behind Restores The Old One, the boys quietly talking as they reviewed the day's events. Night drew in, and shadows covered the wigwams. Forest faded into black, and the wind blew softly through the autumn branches, rustling dry leaves… a low breath of God…

Red Bear continued to watch Jonathan Scott, his hair black now in the fading light, his face cast with flickering light and shadow from the fire, shoulders strong and unyielding ~ a great hulking silence of a man.

Chapter Nine

Thursday, October 11th, 1711
St. Lawrence River Valley, French Canada

The hunting party had stayed another day, and John had had the pleasure of witnessing his friend Laughing Owl take his first deer, a whitetail doe, and having feasted a second night the entire party began the journey home. The party walked single file on the path through the forest. Unencumbered by any burden, the braves led the way followed by John and Laughing Owl. Burden straps across their foreheads secured the weight of the hunt on the backs of the squaws and slaves who were flanked by two braves walking in the rear.

Bearing a heavy pack of his son's kill, Jonathan Scott walked near the rear of the silent party and looked over the heads of the squaws, catching occasional glimpses of John ahead on the trail when the way was flat or when a curve turned just perfectly to bring his son into view.

Jonathan Scott missed his son though he walked mere yards from him. Kept from speaking to his own son for more than a year, Jonathan Scott simply did not know the boy anymore, so vastly had he changed. John did not seek his father out the way Junior did, and it broke the father's heart to see John slide so willingly into idolatrous popery and savage ways. Perhaps his natural tendency toward left-handedness accounted for that desperate gallop toward the gates of hell. 'Why on earth would anyone choose Catholic superstition over the pure and simple faith founded only on the Word of God?' Jonathan Scott had wondered so many times.

Having watched both of his boys adapt in such different ways to captivity, it puzzled him to see John thrive while Junior languished in bitterness. The father wondered if John missed his family at all. John had seemed so close to his mother and grandfather, extraordinarily close. In fact, of all the children, John had always seemed the most attached to Hannah and the old sergeant, and yet here in these savage woods there seemed to be no longing at all about John.

The older boy, Junior, however had expressed to Jonathan Scott many times that he missed his mother deeply and worried about his mother and siblings. Junior was angry at not being able to contribute to their survival. The fourteen year-old boy often spoke with tears in his eyes when he was alone with his father, but Indians did not cry, and Junior kept his emotions in check when he was around the savages. Every time he was able to speak to him, Junior asked his father if they could escape soon. His father always replied the same way, "Watch and wait. Be prepared every moment. For I may call you at any time. You must be prepared like one of King David's men."

Jonathan Scott's stomach growled, and he did not care who heard it. Early in captivity, he had been surprised and irritated to find that he was often hungrier the day after a feast than he was the day before, for now even after last night's feast, he felt hunger, the pernicious, omnipresent hunger of captivity, of slavery, of a body that never receives enough fuel to perform its tasks. Jonathan Scott had found two things to keep him strong, for strength was something he would need if he were to escape with two boys and trek alone for weeks through the wilderness.

The first thing Jonathan Scott had learned was to allow himself the sin of gluttony. The foolish way Indians ate sickened him. Whenever there was plenty, they gorged themselves to such a degree that they could hardly move, and they continued to eat throughout the night, stuffing themselves like hogs. After the feast, they would smoke a fair amount of the meat and use it sparingly, but so much meat was wasted in the first day's gluttony. 'Why could they not be moderate and keep hunger at bay by smoking twice the meat?' Jonathan Scott shook his head at the thought of such sin and waste. And soon after the feast, the endless cycle of privation and wasteful gluttony would begin anew as hunger returned to the village.

Jonathan Scott thought, 'Why do the Indians not improve the land and grow more food? They waste the land that God has given them; they choose hunger when there could be bounty. If only the men would get off their duffs and help the women! Lazy, slothful, wasteful gluttons… Their hunger serves them right.'

Tough and senseless as it seemed to him, Jonathan Scott had accepted this system within the first few months at the village on the river. He realized that in order to survive the inevitable days of lack, he must feed his body as much as possible whenever the chance arose.

He told himself that it was feasting instead of gluttony and reminded himself of the countless God-ordained feasts of the Bible. He frequently tried to convince Junior of this, but the boy simply could not bring himself to gorge himself in the manner of the hated savages no matter how thin he grew. John, of course, had no objection and thus looked as healthy as any Indian boy.

This method of eating was not enough however to keep a slave in the unusual health in which Jonathan Scott found himself month after month, for his two fellow slaves ate this way and still looked gaunt and drawn. So Jonathan Scott meditated on God's Word a great deal, and as he watched his younger son turn into an Indian; his oldest boy grow sickeningly thin and suffer disrespect at the hands of his master; and as Jonathan Scott bit his tongue and endured drudgery, privation, and dishonor, he discovered the second and most important thing ~ that truly the Word was the only thing keeping him strong.

Early on in their captivity, before they had even reached the Green Mountains on their march north, Jonathan Scott had felt the Lord lay on his heart the story of the Biblical captive Daniel's self-imposed privation and the stunning health God gave to him. Daniel had refused to eat all foods forbidden by God even when forbidden delicacies were his only source of meat. In refusing the king's delicacies, Daniel risked his life and the life of the eunuch in charge of him. Daniel had eaten only vegetables and water, and yet he had outshone all those who had feasted on the king's delicacies. Daniel had been strong, healthy, and able to think and reason with unsurpassed wisdom.

When hunger struck Jonathan Scott as it did on the trudge from the hunting camp this morning, or when he began to feel weak, he would thank God for the feasts of worthy food which God provided at the hands of the Indians, and he would meditate on Daniel's strength.

As he plodded along behind the squaws, Jonathan Scott's mind drifted to his own little Daniel back home in Waterbury, whither his mind traveled much of each day. Judging from the fall colors and the shortening of days, Jonathan Scott decided that Daniel must have turned four years old a few weeks ago, perhaps as long ago as a month. He thought of curly-headed Daniel and how he exasperated Martha. 'Ah, Martha when I last saw you, you looked so like your mother... so like your mother,' reminisced Jonathan Scott.

He wondered how Hannah and the children fared. He wondered if Hannah's father, the old sergeant, was still alive, and he prayed that her father was still with her. Jonathan Scott knew that she must be relying heavily on him. With no way to farm their land, he wondered how much the town had been able to help them. He missed his woman and thought of her shapely form as it looked when she would cook before the hearth. He remembered her standing at the spinning wheel, lovely and fair, shorter than the Indian women. He remember her sitting on the older boys' bed in the loft as she tucked them in, and he pictured her fair hair and pale blue eyes and contrasted them with the raven hair and dark eyes of the woman who seemed to have succeeded at stealing Hannah's precious John.

Jonathan Scott looked ahead on the path and saw Catches Water's braid lying on her back just above her pack. Her black hair glistened in the soft dappled light of the forest. Though he could not see her face, he thought of Catches Water's eyes ~ calm and large, even kind. The woman was truly lovely in her savage way, but she was not as lovely as Hannah, and she was not John's mother.

Last night, Jonathan Scott had watched John glow in the pride of Red Bear and Catches Water. He had seen the smiles and laughter, the nods of approval. Worse, he had seen John's deep enjoyment of it all. Jonathan Scott thought about his son's life at home in Waterbury and how he had never done well in Junior's shadow, how learning not to use his left hand had handicapped John. It was natural, Jonathan Scott supposed, for John to do well among people who had so little care for his soul that they did not try to curb this evil left-handedness, which obviously opened the door to and weakened John's defenses against the devil. Jonathan Scott could see that the devil had quite a hold on John now, for the boy had adapted too well to the savages and their popery.

Red Bear having rounded a hill, Jonathan Scott could not see him, but Catches Water was still in view. 'Bastards,' thought Jonathan Scott. 'A thief steals silver or a gun. Only a savage steals a child.'

Deftly Jonathan Scott stepped to the left and around the squaw in front of him. The squaw obliged him and stepped back to give him room. None of the warriors seemed any more concerned about him than about the Indian slaves, and they allowed him the same liberties. Over the course of a winding mile Jonathan Scott edged his way along the line until he was walking just behind Catches Water. They walked up a small rise on the beaten path peppered with stones, green grass edging their way. The St. Lawrence River appeared about half a mile to their right. So as not to disturb the balance of the weight on her back, Catches Water turned her head very slightly to view the forest and shining water.

Taking care not to let his burden strap slip backward, Jonathan Scott leaned forward and held his left hand just under Catches Water's pack. Then he slipped his thumbless right hand, palm facing the sky, under the woven burden strap just below Catches Water's ear where the strap did not touch her skin. With a smooth motion, he lifted the pack with his left hand and grasped the strap with the fingers of his right.

Astonished, Catches Water turned around to see what had happened to her pack. She stopped short in front of Jonathan Scott who stood with her pack suspended over his head by his freakish right hand. Behind him a pair of squaws tripped over each other and one of them fell on the path because of Catches Water's unexpected stop. Catches Water stared in irritated disbelief as Jonathan Scott swung the pack behind him and caught the bottom with his left hand, laying it on top of his own pack. He lay the second strap across his forehead just below his own strap.

A bland challenge gelled in his blue eyes as Jonathan Scott looked levelly at the Indian woman who hoped to take the place of Hannah as John's mother. A few paces ahead, John turned around and watched Catches Water suddenly spit on his father. His musket slung over his shoulder, Red Bear strode quickly back to see the source of the commotion and arrived to see the squaw who had fallen now getting off the ground and picking up her pack again. Jonathan Scott turned his heavily laden head and leveled his gaze at Red Bear whose eyes flashed with fury at the personal affront.

Red Bear knew that this was about John, and he met Jonathan Scott's gaze with ferocity. Red Bear swung his musket off his shoulder, and slammed the butt end of his weapon into Jonathan Scott's right side. The Englishman bending forward, Red Bear drew the musket quickly back to mete out another blow, but the hitherto passive Englishman lunged forward, throwing his shoulders into Red Bear's chest and knocking the Indian on his back. Red Bear tucked his body and kept his head rolled forward as he fell backward, and his head did not hit the great grey slab of stone on which he fell.

The packs having fallen off his back, Jonathan Scott grabbed Red Bear's musket and held the butt end over Red Bear's skull. Jonathan Scott slammed the weapon into the rock a finger's breadth away from the Indian's ear splintering the hardwood stock.

As warriors rushed to Red Bear's aid, invisible hatred dripped from the brilliant blue of Jonathan Scott's eyes while he stood heaving over Red Bear. Turning his face toward his son, Jonathan Scott saw naked fear on the boy's face. Jonathan Scott's hatred softened into weariness, and he asked with a sad smile, "For whose life d' ye fear, lad? For mine or for Red Bear's?"

Warriors seized Jonathan Scott's shoulders as they bound his arms behind his back, and Jonathan Scott ached to hold his son, to run with him the hundreds of miles home. He looked at his son, his savage son, and thought of how little resistance the boy had made, how he now thrived and excelled in all things savage. As John's pale blue eyes in his sun-darkened face looked in wonder at his father, Jonathan Scott thought, 'His own dear mother wouldna' recognize him.' He wondered when John had last heard his name spoken, for the boy responded to the ridiculous heathen name Restores The Old One as though it were his own. Wearily Jonathan Scott said, "*I* am your father, and your name is John Scott."

∽

Honors The Dead sat on the ground outside the longhouse on the brilliant autumn afternoon. The sun shone, and the air was crisp and calm. His legs clad in leggings, he had slung over one shoulder and under the opposite arm to warm his torso a wool blanket acquired through trade with the French. In the distance he heard a triumphant whoop followed quickly by more shouts of success. Knowing that his family returned from the hunt,

218

he smiled to himself and wondered if Laughing Owl or Restores The Old One had had any success on their first big hunt. His neck stiff with age, Honors The Dead turned his body at the waist and called into the longhouse, "Night Sky!"

The village came alive and people returned the joyful whoops as they poured out of their longhouses to greet the hunters. Within minutes Red Bear and the braves appeared on the trail leading into town. Honors The Dead watched as Red Bear stopped and waited for Restores The Old One and Laughing Owl.

Night Sky emerged from the longhouse, laid her hand on Honors The Dead's shoulder and sat down next to him. When the proud boys, who attempted with ridiculous faces to put on an air of dignified stoicism, came abreast of Red Bear he put his arm around Restores The Old One. Honors The Dead and Night Sky looked at each other and stifled laughter at the boys' exaggerated expressions of grave dignity as they approached, for the old ones knew that such faces could only mean success. Red Bear and the boys stopped when they reached Honors the Dead, and Red Bear stood proudly between the two boys.

Red Bear laid his left hand on Laughing Owl's bare shoulder and said, "We took a deer and a moose." Honors The Dead wondered how large a role the boys had played in these kills. Red Bear continued, "Laughing Owl took a whitetail doe. She was not far from us, yet he got the shot off without her hearing a sound. It was a good kill." Honors The Dead and Night Sky nodded proudly as Honors The Dead said, "Laughing Owl, tonight we will eat what you have provided."

Red Bear allowed Laughing Owl his moment of glory in the eyes of his revered grandparents before proceeding. Then laying his right hand on the shoulder of Restores The Old One, Red Bear said, "With one shot to the heart at quite a distance, Restores The Old One took a bull moose." The smile vanished from Honors The Dead's face as he looked hard at the blue-eyed boy in buckskin leggings; then the old man scowled and looked deep into the boy's eyes as though searching for something, as though disbelieving what he found.

At length the old man grunted and gave a solid nod to Restores The Old One. The three hunters ran off into the melee of happy villagers just as their entourage of squaws and the two slaves walked into the village. The women smiled under their burdens, grateful for the female hands that lifted the burdens from their backs. Catches Water and the other squaws who had gone on the hunt now had many hands to help prepare the night's feast, and they quickly set to preparing the meat. Some would be preserved, but much would be roasted or stewed for the feast.

Young John Scott stood with Laughing Owl in the midst of a swell of smiling warriors delivering many tousles of hair. John looked at Laughing Owl and the two boys beamed at each other. John was pleased to share the moment with Laughing Owl, who had become closer to him than Junior had ever been. Laughing Owl was very proud of John and not jealous that John's kill had been such a stunning feat. John stood in the proudest moment of his life, and he did not allow thoughts of his father and brother to creep in and ruin the moment.

The crowd of warriors led the boys to the central fire that burned low on the crisp and chilly autumn day. The men dropped to the ground and reclined on logs or sat cross-legged as the older men of the camp joined them. John savored the chance to rest from the walk as he sat cross-legged a few feet from the fire's warmth. Though he wished to creep closer and hold his hands near the flames to warm them, he resisted for he had learned much of stoicism and refused to show that he needed warmth.

The excitement of the hunters' return having died down, the familiar and gentle sing-song of Indian voices pulsed in John's ears. It was a comforting sound ~ soft and patient. There seemed to be no need to shout to emphasize a point, 'How different from dear old blustery Grandfather,' thought John.

John looked up in surprise as the revered Honors The Dead took a seat on the ground next to him. The old man had never sat next to John, and there was plenty of room from which he could choose tonight around the fire. The old man adjusted his blanket with a gentle tug at the shoulder. He sat facing the fire but with his body turned a little toward John as he watched the fire in silence while the warriors continued to talk. Still looking at the fire, Honors the Dead said quietly to John, "One day you will face a decision Restores The Old One, for ransom will come. Your father and brother will choose to go back to the English." Honors the Dead was silent a moment and stared into the flames.

"You are needed in Night Sky's longhouse. Your blood is strong, and one day your own children will strengthen our People. We hope that you will stay among us," said

Honors The Dead. No Indian had yet spoken to him of ransom or of choice, but John knew that one day he would have to choose between his mother, father, grandfather and his dear brothers and sister … and these people who had stolen him.

Honors The Dead looked now at John as he continued in the quiet, sing-song voice, "I have watched you, Restores The Old One. You are no longer an English boy. Perhaps you never were." John looked into the old man's eyes, brown irises softened with the grey of age, and thought about his words. Honors The Dead and the boy looked back at the fire, and the pair sat for some time in easy silence.

The ever-present aroma of wood smoke filled the air as John looked across the fire where the women worked among the cluster of longhouses where Night Sky's stood. John watched with pride as Catches Water stretched his moose hide on a large wooden frame next to Night Sky's longhouse. Next to Catches Water, Laughing Owl's mother was doing the same with Laughing Owl's deerskin. 'I am twelve years old,' thought John with wonder, 'I am twelve, and look what I have provided for my longhouse! They treat me almost like a man.'

He could hear the women's soft chatter as they prepared the night's feast. Much of the meat they put on spits and roasted for the night's feast while reserving a portion for future use. Hanging from a stripped young tree suspended over the outdoor fire was a large iron kettle, and as meat was tossed into the iron pot, a wonderful smell of abundance wafted throughout the village.

John enjoyed the busy scene for it reminded him a little of his Waterbury home, though it was a very different kind of industry. All his life John had heard Indians described as lazy, had heard that they worked only when they absolutely had to, and that they never improved the land. John could see that some of these things were true, but he could not see how these things were bad. So often even the women simply sat enjoying children, enjoying laughter and old stories, essentially enjoying what God gave them. How could that be sinful? Isn't that thanking God? 'So different...' thought John.

John turned his attention back to Catches Water, who had begun scraping the hair from the moose skin with a sharp stone. Laughing Owl's mother left the fur on the deerskin for use as a soft winter covering, so she was already working the hide with deer brains to render it soft and supple for years of use.

The day continued with the braves relaxing after the long march home and the women preparing the night's feast and slicing thin strips of meat to be smoked for the future.

Even with all of the anticipation, there was no rush. There was never any rush. At length the men roused themselves for a game of lacrosse, and John and Laughing Owl joined them.

Late in the afternoon the women brought baskets of berries and hot bread and laid them on large flat stones. John was so hungry that he could hardly wait, and he kept glancing at the food while he played. He knew that the bread was cooling, and as an English child he also knew that bread was best when warm. He knew that at least the stewed meat in the pots would be hot and ready to serve even if nothing else was. John wondered to himself, 'Why did the squaws not time these things better? Do they not know that food tastes better when hot?'

John had adapted to Indian life remarkably well, but this lack of urgency with food still irritated him. Yet here no one seemed impatient or the least bit irritable, for the entire village seemed to accept that the women served the feast when they felt like it and not a moment earlier.

At last the meal was ready, and the men sat down around the central fire. John watched eagerly for the women to serve the men, but the squaws stood quietly as though waiting for something. In a few moments two men carrying a large drum between them walked into the center of the circle around the fire. A warrior brought the men each a short, wide log and set the logs on end for stools. The musicians sat down and began playing the drum and singing. Not knowing and not particularly caring why the musicians were singing, John had to shut his eyes to keep himself from rolling them in exasperation, for he knew that it would be another hour or more before he would eat.

As the music played John allowed himself to look around the camp ~ a leisurely activity he usually avoided because he did not relish seeing his father or brother. Something in their filthy, unhappy appearance wracked John with guilt for enjoying this new life, but tonight he desired to watch them feed on his kill. John had an unrepentant desire to rub Junior's nose in his success, for Junior would eat with the women and children as always while tonight John would be granted the privilege of feasting with the braves if only for one night.

With their father however John wished only to feed the man ~ to connect with his father in some way after the incident on the trail. Not seeing his father around the fire John guessed that his father was somewhere behind him, and he decided not to turn around. No doubt he would see him when they all sat down to eat.

Spotting Junior among a group of children, John saw that his brother had been watching him. Looking into his brother's eyes, John wondered how the Indians had kept them apart so successfully for more than a year when they lived mere yards from each other. Considering the matter, John realized that Laughing Owl was his only close friend, and when John did spend time with a larger group of boys, Junior was not included for Junior's reticence had made him more slave than child.

It hurt John to see his brother treated as a slave carrying wood on his back and even receiving the occasional beating. For while this People did beat their slaves, they did not beat their children, and John was seen as a child because he embraced Indian life. The only chastisement John ever received was the obvious disdain and disappointment of those in his longhouse. John reminded himself that it was Junior's choice not to follow his master's lead, and that Junior could live the same life John was living if only he would surrender while awaiting ransom.

Junior's dark hair, which the Indians had cut short on one side and left long on the other, was filthy. Seeing his brother's ribs clearly through the grime that clung to his torso and neck, John suddenly remembered the guilt he had felt that first Sunday when he had made no resistance to attend mass.

For months, John had forced himself not to think about these things because it was so much easier and even wonderfully enjoyable to join this bizarre People in their bizarre world that made so much sense to him. A pang of guilt rang in John's chest as he realized anew that Junior had chosen loyalty to his family and Puritan faith over health and any measure of happiness the Indians could offer. It was a noble thing that Junior did each time he refused to give himself to the savage way of life.

At last the music ceased, and John turned his attention back to his stomach. Guessing that a good hour had passed by the time the women brought out the bounteous moose and venison, John sat down between Laughing Owl and Red Bear, allowing Junior and their father to slip back into the recesses of his mind. John and Laughing Owl began to gorge themselves in the early twilight while Red Bear stood up and walked toward their longhouse. John could not imagine what could be more important than eating, but thought no more of Red Bear's untimely disappearance for though most of the food was cold, it was fit for a king even in its simplicity. Reveling in the bounty, John ate his fill and then ate some more.

When Red Bear returned to his place next to John, he held a piece of moose antler in his hand. His mouth full of meat John stopped chewing and looked from the antler to Red Bear who said, "Restores The Old One, I will make you a knife, and this will be the haft. You have done well." John's eyes widened, and he smiled thinking, 'What a knife!'

Women, children and eventually the slaves joining the feast, the villagers sat for several hours enjoying full bellies and the conversation of family and friends while John stuffed himself according to Indian custom. Oh how good it felt to eat and eat as much as one wanted and feel no remorse for it. Red Bear had explained early on that John must eat as much as he could when food was plentiful, for it strengthened the body for times of hunger. He had gone on to explain that while the feast is better, hunger is also good, for hunger teaches an Indian strength in the same way that bare skin in cold weather teaches him strength. Hunger was part of life, and it was a tool to strengthen the People.

As he savored roasted meat from the moose he had killed himself, John thought about how very like the world around them the Indians were. Trees swayed in silent strength as silent hunters walked among them. Deer grazed leisurely just as Indians never hurried to serve a meal. There was no bustling or worry, but there were much beauty and much enjoyment of simply being.

John had been reflective ever since he had watched his father humbly skin the moose John had taken. Not having heard his father's voice nor having heard his English name in more than a year, his father's words on the trail had struck John as a slap to the face. It had not occurred to him that anyone other than Jonathan Scott could ever be his father, yet he could see the hurt in his father's eyes. With but a few moments' reflection, John knew that his father had reason to worry.

It must have been obvious to his father that John was more comfortable among these foreign savages than he had ever been in his own family. John thought about what Honors The Dead had said to him, "You are no longer an English boy. Perhaps you never were." John wondered if his father thought the same thing.

There was a peace about this place, and John realized that he had never known such freedom. Pondering the faith of his Puritan family and how they taught that freedom only allowed a child greater opportunity to sin, John cringed as he recalled the shame and humiliation of his training in all things right-handed.

John thought of how much more *useful* he was among these savages who allowed him the employment of his left hand, 'I do not engage in devil worship as my old pastor in Waterbury said I would if Mother and Father allowed me to use my left hand. These Indians might mix the idolatrous Catholic faith with their own ancient ceremonies, but 'tis certainly not devil worship! Most importantly, they love Jesus, do they not? How can this be evil? Their Catholic priests seem to believe what they believe every bit as strongly as my Waterbury pastor believed his faith. Is Jesus not still Jesus however folks worship Him?'

Looking about the circle around the fire John spotted his brother sitting across from him. To John's guilty delight, he saw Junior's master pointing directly at John as he scolded Junior, "Look. That young English boy ~ younger than you ~ is so strong that he took the moose that now feeds you. Are you so weak that you cannot even eat what has already been killed?" Junior refused to look at John so John followed his brother's gaze to find that it rested on their father now looking steadily at Junior.

John's delight vanished as he saw again the more noble route Junior took, and he watched their father raise a chunk of meat to indicate that Junior should eat. Junior obeyed his father but not his master, and he ate until Jonathan Scott stopped prompting him from across the circle. Unaware that Junior's obedience was not to him, Junior's master patted him on the back ~ the boy wincing at his touch. The master recoiled in disgust saying, "You are nothing but fear and weakness."

John shut his eyes, sad and ashamed for his brother though he chose the noble path of resistance. He wanted to take Junior by the shoulders and shake him, tell him, "It's not so bad. They are not as evil as everyone said. You won't go to hell just because you go to mass, and you won't go to hell just because you do what the Indians want. It's not as though they are asking you to practice witchcraft! Why do you choose to be a victim?"

The two men with the drum now returning to the center of the circle began to sing and beat the drum which was not entirely unlike the Waterbury drum used to summon the towns people to a meeting. Yet the Waterbury drum was firm and crisp while this drum, played with equal largeness of sound, was deeper and somehow softer. The ancient pounding of the Indian drum resonated in John's chest restoring confidence in his choice to do things the Indian way for however long God chose to keep him among this People. As the men sang, at times almost wailing, their visceral cries filled John to overflowing, and he had to fight the urge to echo their song.

John looked over to his father whose clenched jaw did little to disguise his obvious disgust, and John knew that to his father this visceral beauty was nothing more than an infernal racket. Some of the people began to dance around the fire, and John wanted to join them on this wonderful night. Laughing Owl stood to his feet and beckoned to John with his arm, but John shook his head. Were his father and brother not here he would have joined him, but to dance with the savages in front of them without being forced was one step too far for John. With longing, he watched Laughing Owl dance on one foot then the other in time with the eternal rhythm of the drum.

After a few hours of celebration, all of the villagers quieted down to hear the old ones tell the stories of their People. Mothers nursed babies and siblings held sleepy toddlers in their laps while Honors The Dead and Night Sky each spoke in their turn among the elders.

Drifting in and out of comprehension, John would listen intently to their wonderful stories and then his spirit would seem to float on the sounds of this comforting language hearing no words ~ only the calm, quiet voices of age.

Chapter Ten

Sunday, January 6th, 1712
Waterbury, Connecticut Colony

In the freezing meetinghouse, Hannah sat with her back straight and Martha at her left side. Hannah's feet rested on a foot stove, which had been filled with hot coals that had now lost most of their heat. They had been sitting in meeting for a little over an hour now, and Hannah expected their minister to make some reference to her at any moment. In the year and a half since Jonathan Scott and their boys had been taken, not a single Sabbath had passed without their minister making reference to Hannah. She appreciated that his constant remembrance of their plight kept her family in the prayers of the entire village, however she wished that her suffering could be a bit more private.

The haze of a single day's beard growth lightly covered the minister's jaw reminding her of Jonathan Scott, who was never entirely out of her thoughts. Throughout the warmer months his jaw would grow dark and rough every

Sunday, for even the minor work of shaving was not allowed on the Sabbath. Jonathan Scott usually grew a beard in winter to keep his face warm and to protect it from chapping winds. It being winter now and her husband surely having been deprived the luxury of a razor these many months, Hannah imagined him with an unkempt and dirty beard reaching the middle of his chest.

Word had come from the French government in Canada several months ago confirming that Jonathan Scott and their boys were safely in captivity in an Indian village near the wretched Kahnawake where so many of Deerfield's captives had gone. Upon hearing the news Hannah had breathed a sigh of relief, for they were all still alive. Colonial officials had advised her that the colony would ransom her men at some point but perhaps not until the end of this interminable war, and it was now a matter of survival in a less harsh climate than that of the march into captivity.

Though the waiting was a terrible strain, just knowing that her men were alive, if only for the moment, had eased Hannah's tensions immeasurably, and she was better able to enjoy her children and father. When worry harassed her, Hannah found that by singing psalms of praise and by focusing on God's greatness rather than on the helpless plight of her sons and husband, she was able to diminish the fear significantly.

Out of the corner of her eye, Hannah was pleased to note that Martha kept her eyes on the pulpit where their minister stood in his great black robe over a black doublet. His collar was white, and from it hung two crisp, rectangular strips of white linen so fine that they were transparent but for the edges. His hazel eyes were clear and bright under great bushy eyebrows which alternately plunged downward meeting just above the bridge of his nose, and soared into his forehead as he thundered through the sermon.

To Martha he was a frightening man who found far too much fun in yelling, and he sent her away from the meetinghouse each week with fiery new visions for her to drown before they had the chance to become nightmares.

The tow-headed mother-daughter pair sat with tidy coifs, freezing ears, and mittenned hands folded neatly in their laps as they kept their eyes on the pulpit. Martha forced herself to watch the minister, for just below him on the pulpit stairs sat the village boys in full view of the entire town that they might better mind their manners.

Throughout her young life Martha had received many pinches on the leg for causing her brothers to giggle on those occasions when their behavior was so appalling that the village boys all had to leave the men's pews and sit on the pulpit stairs.

For standard misbehavior such as fidgeting or whispering, the children received a sound wallop on the head with the tithing-man's long stick. Martha prided herself on never having received any correction from the tithing-man, for she was clever enough to avoid his notice. Today instead of walking slowly around the meeting house looking for inattentive villagers, the tithing-man stood next to the pulpit stairs with one arm behind his back and his stick, which was taller than he, in the other hand. Martha allowed herself a furtive glance in the tithing-man's direction and thought that he looked rather like a pikeman. He certainly was as fierce as one.

As the sermon waxed on, Hannah glowered steadily at her boys to keep them in check. This was four year-old Daniel's third month of sitting away from his mother in meeting, and so far he had done rather well. Sitting on the pulpit stairs among the big boys, Daniel actually appeared pleased to be among them in spite of (or perhaps because of) the fact that they were on the pulpit stairs for some rather unsavory behavior.

That morning Hannah had bundled her children in all the extra clothing she could respectably stuff under the boys' woolen doublets and Martha's woolen waistcoat. The old sergeant had brought the dog who now lay obediently on his feet to keep them warm. Hannah hoped that her father would not doze off; he was nearly as much a worry as were her boys. Hannah had to stifle a laugh at the image of the many times when the deacon had been forced to tickle her revered father's nose with a fox tail. The good old Sergeant Hawks would snort and then jerk awake sending a swift, involuntary kick to the seat of the pew in front of him. This of course disturbed the men in the pew that had just been kicked and naturally prompted incessant giggles among the children and teenagers. It mattered little how many times these giggles had been whacked away by the tithing-man's stick, for they often reappeared in the form of facial contortions and quaking shoulders at some point in the long day of preaching.

Suddenly there it was; she heard her name from the pulpit, "…who can forget her suffering? Is there any woman more afflicted in all of your memory? Look upon her countenance and see there the affliction of the righteous!"

Feeling the eyes of all Waterbury on her, Hannah kept her eyes on the minister. She did not understand why her suffering was the affliction of the righteous when the destruction of Deerfield had been God's judgment on the wicked. Hannah knew that she was not as good a woman as her Aunt Mary had been, and yet Aunt Mary's pain, which Hannah knew was certainly greater than her own for Hannah's husband and sons were still alive, was deemed God's judgment.

Hannah thought about the day when her son John had asked about Mary Brooks and Deerfield, and how he had wondered what Deerfield had done to receive such dreadful punishment. Allowing herself to escape the moment while her pastor preached on and her fellow villagers stared at her with relentless pity, Hannah wondered, 'If the outwardly good people of that town had been able to stir the wrath of God to such a degree, then it is entirely possible that I have done something or *neglected* to do something which has caused this terrible calamity to befall my husband and sons. Certainly I am no better than Aunt Mary, and yet what has happened to my family is deemed the suffering of the righteous. Righteous Hannah Scott... I think not...'

She hated to be held out in this public way by her minister, and though Martha did not complain, Hannah knew that it made the young girl terribly self-conscious to be stared at as she sat with her mother each week. Hannah was grateful however that their minister had taken this view. Because of it, no one in the village *openly* questioned the righteousness of her family. Yet Hannah suspected that some wondered how on earth three devastations like the sack of Deerfield, the torture and killing of her brother-in-law, and the kidnapping of her husband and sons could touch one family without some member of that family having done some secret wrong to provoke the wrath of God.

Inwardly Hannah wondered about this herself. She alone was the link in the chain of destruction God had allowed to befall her family. Perhaps she had not spent enough time in prayer or perhaps she had been too lenient with her children or perhaps... It *must* be something she had done, for Waterbury's sole connection to destruction at the hand of savages was she, Goodwife Hannah Scott.

This worry haunted her, and she had shared it with her father only. He had asked her to search her heart for any unrepented sin and to ask God to help her search further than her sinful capacity allowed her. When she had been unable to find anything that her father thought could possibly have enraged God to such a degree as to mete out judgment upon her family as punishment for her sin, the old sergeant had said, "Hannah, ye mustn't blame yerself. For who can know the mind of God? All things work together for good to them that love God. All things, child. It will be all right."

Hannah had been little comforted by her father's words for she could see no good from the attack on Deerfield though she knew it must exist. She knew that her father had found good in his living with them. Certainly she needed him, and he could not be with her now if his own wife and young daughter were alive to need him. Hannah supposed that that was good but hardly worth the lives of those who had depended on her father in Deerfield.

A sense of general guilt and worry that she had caused the captivity of her husband and sons gnawed at her, but she had never confided in her minister for fear that he might actually find some great latent sin lurking within her breast and change his opinion about her family's righteousness. Hannah knew that she could not bear to see her children held up as examples of God's judgment on sin no matter how it might help to unburden her soul.

Wishing that she could shrink into the pew itself and vanish from sight, Hannah stared straight ahead at her minister who gripped the railing of the pulpit with his right hand and gestured with his left as he explained, "Recall our childhood verses, 'Many are the afflictions of the righteous, but the Lord delivereth them out of them all.' But this deliverance does not come of nothing, no... No, for Paul tells us in First Thessalonians that we are to *pray* without ceasing. We know from Luke that even though Christ Himself was God, He *prayed* to the Father all night before he chose the twelve apostles. And we know from Matthew that Christ instructed the disciples to use fasting in conjunction with prayer when dealing with a great evil."

Looking out over his congregation, the women on his left hand and the men on his right, the minister spread his hands wide and asked, "How much more then must we, being frail and wretched sinners, fast and pray for Goodwife Scott and her men? This family is the only family in Waterbury to taste affliction at the hand of the savage enemy, and yet when was the last time you fasted for her? Look upon her face once more! The family of her birth destroyed by the enemy, her brother-in-law tortured to death in her own hearing, her husband and sons wrenched from her bosom and now languishing among the heretical Catholics ~ who can know what temptations Jonathan Scott and those boys face in their hour of distress? Who can tell if they will be persuaded by the Devil's servants, those false priests to the savages? How can any one of us dare to forget the Scotts in our prayers? Pray! Pray! Pray without ceasing!" thundered the minister.

∽

That night, wrapped in layers of wool blankets and heavy clothing Hannah sat on a stool in the corner of the fireplace next to the oven. Her household asleep, she held the large heavy Bible on her lap and tried to pray Psalm 139 for her captive men but met with little success. Her mind and body exhausted, she had read the same words twenty times over with little meaning. Hannah knew that she would not be able to sleep, so she avoided going to bed on this cold night. The shutters closed tightly, Hannah could hear the wind howling among the bare branches without. The large room of the first floor was dark as the firelight cast its furtive light here and there.

Hannah wondered how her boys and husband were. She wondered if they were cold and if they slept under furs or blankets. She wondered if any of the blankets had been stolen from Deerfield, and she imagined that a blanket woven by one of her childhood neighbors now warmed her beloved captives. Hannah wondered if Junior and John had gone to bed hungry that night; she wondered what they had eaten. She wondered if they missed her bread, for Indians did not make the same kind of bread. She wondered if Jonathan Scott was tethered to his master and if he had enough covering to prevent frostbite. She wondered how her husband fared as a slave. Was he able to submit? Was he often beaten? Was he starving like most slaves? Would he survive to see her again? Hannah had heard much about the filth and clutter of an Indian house, and she wondered about the health of her men. She suspected, and almost allowed herself a smile, that John would not be bothered by the clutter at all. She leaned back against the stone fireplace wall and looked up the chimney at the stars on the cold, clear night.

Everyone slept in the large downstairs room now, which Hannah knew her husband would think was folly so long after he had been taken but the children needed Hannah and their grandfather, and they too needed the children. The old sergeant's bed lay next to the fireplace for he had grown colder as the years crept on, and each winter his bed was moved from the loft to a spot next to the fireplace. His bed was simple like that of the children, for he was an old soldier and needed "no fancy curtains to keep the heat in." Hannah shook her head fondly at her father's toughness and his inability to admit that he was cold even when his frame trembled from toe to finger.

On the trundle bed lay Gershom and Eliezer, their fair skin rosy against the linen pillow cases. Hannah gazed tenderly at them and bitter-sweet pain welled up within her bosom as she recalled Junior and John lying there on that trundle bed as wee ones.

Tucked snugly in her own bed were Daniel sleeping in the middle of the bed and Martha lying on her side facing her brother. Hannah got up, set the Bible in its wooden box and closed the lid before crossing the floor to her bed.

She slipped off her shoes and climbed into bed pulling the bed curtains closed. Curling up against Daniel, Hannah lay her arm across the pillow above his head and slid her fingers under Martha's nightcap. Hannah stroked her daughter's hair and nuzzled against the tender and perfect skin of Daniel's childhood. She closed her eyes and let her hand slip from Martha's hair. As she drifted toward sleep, Hannah felt her daughter's breath against her hand and she smiled.

∽

St. Lawrence River Valley, French Canada

The day was cold and grey as John walked alone in the woods just outside the Indian village. He could see his breath as he made his way up a gentle incline, his snowshoes slapped and ground a bit on the snow under the great, naked trees. Evergreen trees and bushes dotted the quiet place, and John continued aimlessly. He wore soft mittens of coonskin and a cloak of deerskin with the soft fur against his chest and back. Ever since John shot the moose, he had begun to sport the stoic face of a warrior. He was far from becoming a warrior of course, but he had noticed that Laughing Owl's countenance had changed after that hunt, and John had made a point to behave in a more manly fashion as well. Now John's face was well practiced in stony impassivity, and it required effort to maintain the stoic mask only when something startled or greatly pleased him.

John had seen his brother Junior traipse off in the woods completely alone and unguarded many times, for his master would send him out alone to gather wood, but it was a rare thing for John to be alone for he was highly prized. In the year and a half that John had lived among them Red Bear's family had not allowed him to venture forth alone more than once or twice.

John reached the crest of the incline and decided not to go farther. He turned around and looked back on the soft tracks he had made. Through the naked trees and evergreens, John could see patches of the cozy village below, thin trails of smoke rising from the longhouses that seemed to lie wherever their builders had fancied to erect them. There was no real order or symmetry to the place, yet it was a peaceful sight.

Enjoying this private moment, John smiled to himself and savored the total absence of tension, tension that had plagued him all his life. He was not worried about a thing. Here there was no worry, no fear of getting things wrong, no fear of being late, no fear of saying the wrong thing. What an enormous relief not to be fearful of a whipping for being found with idle hands.

John supposed that it ought to worry him that he was hungry right now and that the entire village was hungry, but John knew that the hunting party would return in a few days or a week. Because of the toughness it gave him, John did not mind hunger for he desired to be stronger than hunger just like the braves.

What John did mind was the constant worry over failure that he had felt every day of his life until he reached this remote village. Among this People, he did not fear failure because failure seemed to be an integral part of learning to excel. He knew that the Indians would teach him whatever he needed to know, and more importantly he knew that he could learn whatever they taught him. To John, it seemed that what this People taught him was almost second nature. He had always been fond of woodcraft but had never been allowed to pursue it.

Above all John knew that he could learn because the Indians allowed him the use of the hand he naturally favored. After so many months of what felt like brilliance to John, a quiet confidence had come over him and he simply expected to learn whatever the Indians taught him ~ and learn it well. It had not been that way in the beginning however. At first, John had been stunned by how quickly and with what excellence he could use a knife or shoot an arrow when finally allowed to use his left hand. What a shock it had been to excel, what a joy to be praised, what a peculiar thing to find people smiling when they saw him coming.

John had to admit to himself that he missed the whir of the spinning wheel and the memories of his mother and sister constantly working, but the pain of missing them had diminished as he grew more and more comfortable among the Indians... 'as an Indian...' thought John testing the idea.

John wondered if it was evil not to miss his mother more than he did. He wondered if it was a sin to enjoy this slow and quiet place. All his life Indian ways had been called slothful and slovenly, but that was not how John saw them. He enjoyed their pace and where Englishmen saw sloth, John saw quiet dignity and tranquility. Except when they sang or exulted Indians were quiet people; even their speech seemed to be still.

Life was so much slower here where he could relax and play. He had never played so much in his life; he hunted; he explored; he swam. What more could a boy ask? This freedom seemed too good to be true, and John knew that it was indeed.

Such freedom came at an impossible price: Mother, Grandfather, Father, brothers and sisters, English bread, apple pie, pumpkin pie... everything that meant home to John Scott.

John wondered for a moment if God had made a mistake in birthing him into an English home. Perhaps John was really Indian at heart. Perhaps this was how God rectified the mistake, and then John recalled, 'No, 'tis blasphemy to think that God could make a mistake.'

After asking his Maker's forgiveness for such a thought, John began to thank Him silently, 'However long it lasts until they ransom me Lord, thank You for this place! For no matter what the English say, it is not an evil place, and

You know that the Catholics love You as much as the Puritans. And look, O Lord, see how the Indians have changed me! Look at the skill they have taught me. See how useful I have become! Thank You, thank You for this time. I know it must hurt my family, but please let it last. I am free here, and here You have given me honor when at home I snuck off in disgrace. God, is it a sin to love it here so much that I want my captivity to last even though my mother must miss us all terribly?'

John heard the sloppy crunching snowshoes of one who does not care if he is heard in the woods, and he wondered who it could be. Crunch, crunch, John looked downhill and to his left, toward the source of the sound and saw his brother appear from behind a fat evergreen.

Completely alone with his own flesh and blood for the first time in so many months, John made no attempt to hide his joy. His face lit up, and he walked quickly but quietly toward Junior. John took Junior's arm and led him behind the evergreen, which was wide enough to hide them from view of the village.

Seeing Junior's pack of wood, John moved his hands up to his brother's forehead to slip off the burden strap for a few moments' rest. Junior reached up and shoved his brother's hands away, hissing in English, "Stunned I am that such a great hunter would deign to help a lowly slave."

Shocked and hurt, John retreated behind the safety of his stoic mask, which he now saw could serve to protect one's heart. John worked his mind to form the English words he wished to say. That English no longer came naturally unnerved John though he showed no emotion at all, "I will gather wood for you today, brother."

Junior replied in disgust, "What makes you think I want your help, savage? How does it feel to watch your father toil all day, to watch the women do all of the men's work in the fields and carry your kill home as though they were dogs or horses? It must be nice to be an Indian boy, you lazy bastard!"

Junior's face was ugly with contempt as he looked John over from head to toe and snorted before continuing, "This place fits you like a glove, you know. You were always lazy. I always had to pick up your slack. You never kept up when work was involved."

As he listened John looked steadily in his brother's eyes and though John betrayed no sign of it, Junior's words cut him to ribbons. When John answered, he disregarded his brother's remarks. "Come. Your master may beat you if you do not gather enough wood," and he turned to walk deeper into the woods.

Junior stood his ground and said, "You'll not escape the truth so easily. When Father saw you go off alone, he found me and instructed me to have you to wait behind this tree for him. I hope that there is enough English courage left in you to face him." The blood drained from John's face though his expression did not change, and turning back toward his brother, John's eyes calmly accepted the challenge issuing from Junior's gaze.

The boys stood silently for a few minutes and John looked into the trees, listening intently in the barren forest for any sign of his father approaching. When the soft, quiet crunch hit his ears, John turned his head to the right and saw his father with an empty pack tucked under his arm only a few yards up the hill from them. John was proud that his father had taken the care to walk so quietly. Of course, John knew that Jonathan Scott had gone on several hunts to carry back his master's game and would have been required to walk silently then. Still, it pleased John that his father was able to come so close before he could be heard.

John hesitated but smiled at the man, John's heart filling with renewed pride at the sight of this bewilderingly healthy man, his *father*. John watched his true father, strong and powerful as ever, his breath appearing in grey puffs and freezing on his long beard, walk over the snow and down the hill toward them.

Wrapped in a fur cloak and wearing leggings, Jonathan Scott stood before his boys with no expression on his face. John's smile faded at his father's seriousness and now the three looked at one another in silence. Such a peculiar sight they were, blue eyes piercing out from behind sun-darkened skin. From many winter weeks spent inside with the soot of the longhouse fires, Jonathan Scott's and Junior's hair was as black as any Indian's while from under the soot and grease of John's hair peeked occasional strands of white. John's face was hard and stony, his strong square jaw set to receive whatever contempt his father might send his way.

Suddenly Jonathan Scott stepped forward and threw his arms around his sons clutching them to his chest. He held them firmly as John looked over his father's arm into the snow-clad wilderness and tentatively wrapped his arms around the man who had bounced him on his knee and tossed him in the air as a child. Closing his eyes, John sank his face against the fur covering his father's breast and clutched him tight. The three Scotts held one another for some time before Jonathan Scott spoke, "John."

Startled to hear his English name, John's eyes flashed open. John pulled back and looked up at his father who said, "We leave as early in spring as we can, but we must wait for enough foliage to hide our presence." John's eyes widened with surprise and his head involuntarily jerked backward. He wondered if his father had heard something troubling about negotiations for ransom of the many English captives in Canada.

Jonathan Scott continued, "I have already told Junior, and now I tell you that you must watch and wait. Be prepared every moment. For I may call you at any time. You must be prepared like one of King David's men."

John blinked in disbelief as he looked at his father, "Do you mean to escape?" Jonathan Scott nodded and said, "I will watch for a night when the guard sleeps, and we will leave just before dawn ~ probably after they are groggy from one of their gluttonous feasts."

Shocked at his father's daring, John looked at Junior to see if this were really true, and Junior nodded at him with an air of self-righteousness. Ignoring Junior's demeanor, John looked back at their father who said, "Ever since we arrived here, I have been keeping back a small amount from the portion of the nocake they give me. It keeps very well, and I have enough now to get us most of the way home. There may also be berries and nuts, and if we can manage to steal a weapon, we can use John's skills as a hunter once we are far enough from Indians to risk detection." Jonathan Scott nodded at John, who was taken aback and touched by his father's acknowledgment.

Jonathan Scott continued, "But it may be that we will have nothing but the nocake for the entire journey. There are many such stories among the few who have escaped. The Lord has honored many of those brave souls and has gotten them home. He will provide for us as well."

John's head swam with the knowledge that his father had so long been preparing for their escape. His selfless sacrifice touched John, and John looked up at his father with wonder, "The Lord has honored you already, Father. You have saved from the little that the Indians gave you, and yet God has kept you so strong."

Jonathan Scott smiled at the lad and said, "The Bible, my boy, think on the book of Daniel." A look of understanding came over John, and he shook his head in awe at the miracle of his father's health.

The trio was quiet for a few moments before the stony look returned to John's face. Though he met their gaze, John's eyes were suddenly far away leaving Jonathan Scott and Junior puzzled. Junior said to John, "You will be ready, John?"

John slowly pulled himself back from the distance and turned a wistful gaze on his brother. Amazed at his hesitation Junior said, "I don't care if I have to wait ten years or ten days, I will be ready! Do you never think of our Mother, John? What about Grandfather and Martha and Gershom and Eliezer, and Daniel? How dare you even consider doing this to them?"

The melancholy did not depart from John's eyes, and Junior and Jonathan Scott looked at him in outrage. Fear gripped John, but he could not deceive his father and brother. He had to be plain with them. Mustering his courage, John managed to keep the trembling out of his voice as he said, "Father, will I be expected to stop doing what I do so well, and will I be embarrassed as you and the schoolmaster restrain my left hand?"

John did not wait for a response, for he knew the answer, "The things I can do, Father, are not the things you need of me. I cannot be what you need me to be. I am not refusing to return to Waterbury, but I will wait for ransom before I decide."

"Decide?" hissed Jonathan Scott, "You insolent child! Who do you think you are, boy? You are my *son!* You are still a child, and you decide nothing. When I command you, you will go home to your mother, my wife, whom I will not allow you to hurt. This is not a choice, John. It is who you *are*."

John did not answer. He could not tell his father that he no longer felt his English blood, and truly there was no defense for the pain John would cause his mother if he did indeed choose to stay behind.

Jonathan Scott shut his eyes and tilted his head back in exasperation, but he held his tongue in check. He shook his head while Junior glared at John, and when he had regained his composure Jonathan Scott said, "It has to be your left hand, son. We did not train it entirely out of you, and the Indians do not care enough for your soul to restrict you. Do you not understand, John? It gives you a propensity toward *all* things evil, and that is why you thrive here among these Popish savages! Without any fight at all, you surrendered to their idolatrous mass. You must resist, son! Have you no care for your soul? If you will just force yourself to stop using that hand, I know that your ability to resist their temptations will increase. God will honor your obedience son, and He will strengthen you."

At the mention of his left hand John began to grow bitter, and in spite of the insolence to his father, John could not resist the chance to tell Junior what he thought of him, "By such an act of obedience will God so strengthen me that I can be a weakling like Junior, despised by all the braves?"

Aghast at his brother's warped perception Junior responded, "How dare you! I choose the path of righteousness. It takes courage to resist them and choose the life of a slave rather than to cave to their idolatry and live the pampered life of an Indian boy. You're a coward not to resist, John. A coward and nothing more! Why do you *care* what the so-called braves think? They are not your People; they are the *enemy!* You should see yourself. You disgust me! You look more savage than the savages. At least their hair matches the filth they allow to pile up in it."

John coolly watched his brother's fit and then turned his attention back to Jonathan Scott, "Father, what about all the children who have refused ransom and have chosen to stay with the Indians? There are so many, and they cannot all be left-handed. There must be something good about the Indians, or so many would not stay. I am not saying that I choose to stay; I am only saying that I will wait for ransom before I decide. For Father... Red Bear will allow me to decide even if you will not."

Jonathan Scott delivered a rough slap to his son's cheek, and without so much as wincing at the sting John looked impassively at his father. Shaking his head and squinting at John with contempt, Junior asked in a low voice, "What is wrong with you? You speak to our father as though *he* were the enemy. Have you never noticed the scalps hanging outside your master's longhouse?"

Maintaining his stoicism John looked at his brother and wondered what he was really asking. John had never looked directly at the scalps, but any idiot would know that they were there. At first, the mere knowledge that they hung from a pole just outside the door had been too distressing, and John had done everything in his power to keep himself from looking at them, but within a few months among the Indians, John had accepted that they were the trophies of war and had allowed them to blend into the village.

Though his expression did not show it John's silence told Junior that he had never looked closely, so Junior whispered sharply to him, "Among all the black scalps hanging on that pole, I believe you will find colors that have never adorned any savage head ~ red, blond, brown, even one of the chestnut hue. Did not Grandfather say that his wife Alice had the most beautiful chestnut hair? And perhaps one of the fine-haired children's scalps is that of his daughter Sarah."

Appalled at the thought and annoyed at Junior's ridiculous assumption, John was tempted to roll his eyes, but he maintained his stony face as he said, "You cannot possibly mean what you suggest. How can you even guess whose scalp is whose?"

In spite of John's patronizing tone, Junior responded with confidence, "My brother, the men here were with the war party that raided Deerfield. I understand enough of their tongue by now to catch what they say to one another. Your precious Red Bear was there…"

Junior paused a moment looking deep into John's eyes, "Why do you think Red Bear gave you those moccasins when they first took us? Those moccasins were not the beat up, second hand kind that Father and I received. Yours were beaded and new ~ ridiculous for any march through the wilderness. From the very beginning, Red Bear claimed you as his own. What does he call you, John? Restores The Old One? Who is the old one, John? Certainly not Grandfather! Red Bear took us because he wanted you. Whatever his demonic fixation may be, Red Bear *chose* you. I do not know why he wanted you, but 'tis clear that he does, and you are quickly becoming *son* to the very savage who may have killed your own family."

Stunned, John said nothing as Junior stormed off to gather the wood for which his master had sent him.

Seeing the boy's bewilderment, Jonathan Scott gently laid his hand on John's shoulder and said, "Whatever you do, please do not betray us in our escape." John stared blankly into the white forest and nodded his assent.

His father having returned to the village, John walked numbly back to the longhouse and stopped outside for a moment to glance up at the scalps. There among all the grisly trophies hung the fine dark hair of a child and a long chestnut scalp that could only belong to a white woman. Unwilling to behold the horror any longer, John lifted the fur that hung over the entrance and walked inside the dark and smoky longhouse, taking off his mittens as he rounded the baffle wall. He kept his head down so as not to engage anyone and walked directly to his bench. No one questioned him as he lay down on his side in his snowy moccasins and faced the wall.

The very act of lying down for no reason in the middle of the day was an act of betrayal to the constant busy-ness in which his mother and siblings were even now surely engaged. For such a brazen act of laziness he would surely have been whipped at home, and yet here no one thought twice about it. The vast differences between the longhouse and his Puritan home exhausted John.

He could hear soft conversations taking place throughout the longhouse, and weary of thinking John's mind wandered as images flashed through his memory ~ his mother standing before the hearth ~ little Daniel tugging on a string and undoing his tape-weaving ~ a white woman's scalp ~ Grandfather smoking his pipe on the settle ~ the imagined vision of Deerfield burning and bloody ~ Martha smiling sweetly at him from behind the flax wheel ~ Uncle Joseph and Cousin John haying with the family ~ the grisly imagining of Uncle Joseph's skinned body ~ Father reading the Bible ~ Father's right thumb dropping to the ground ~ Mother worrying the day he had snuck off to go hunting ~ the minister thundering at the congregation ~ the Indian women and children Grandfather and Great-grandfather had killed ~ Mother sharing a bowl of soup with one of his younger siblings when they were toddlers ~ the bed he shared with Eliezer and Junior ~ Grandfather hunting with him ~ Gershom sitting on the saddle in front of him as they rode to school.

Breaking into a silent swell of tears and mortified that anyone might discover him crying, John reached down for one of the furs at his feet and pulled it over his head. He suddenly recalled his mother racing up the stairs when he would have a nightmare, how she used to sit and hold him until he fell asleep no matter how old he was.

He wept not only because he missed his family but because he knew now that he was an Indian and could never go back. Such a choice would cause his loved ones more pain than any other thing he could possibly do. There could be no greater insult to his mother than to prefer the very People who slew her family. 'Could it really have been Red Bear?' he wondered. 'But what of Grandfather's killing in King Philip's War? Was it not similar? There had been sleeping children at Peskeompskut just as there had been at Deerfield, and there had been scores more women, children and old men killed at Peskeompskut than at Deerfield.'

How he wished that he could tell his mother that it wasn't she, that he loved her still. It was not his mother at all; it was John himself. He belonged here, and it was nothing she had done or left undone. He knew it would not matter though even if he could tell her. How could a mother understand such a thing? How could anyone understand it? Yet John knew that he was not alone in this choice, for he knew of children from Deerfield and elsewhere who had chosen to stay with their captors. It was inconceivable to choose savages over one's own parents, and yet it happened.

Someone touched his shoulder causing terror to sweep over John. For an Indian boy to weep like a child was weak and shameful. He grabbed the edge of the fur that covered his face and clung to it. To John's horror, a hand slipped under him and lifted his torso off the bench. A woman sat down under him and lay his shoulders and head in her lap. Though his face was still covered, John realized that it must be Catches Water. Leaving his eyes and all but his cheek covered she pulled the fur away from his hairline and tenderly touched his face, her fingers lightly caressing his skin... just as his mother's had.

An ache wrenched John's heart. He clenched his gut and swung his knees up against his stomach as he stifled a groan. This was a pain unlike anything he had ever felt for it was the physical manifestation of loss, the severance of his bond to all whom he loved ~ even to his Grandfather who alone had believed in him. This was the insufferable anguish of choosing to break his mother's heart.

John knew that the choice was made. He could never return for he was no more English now than he was a cat. Yet John knew it was a choice. He *could* go back, and he recalled how his mother had sat on a stool next to him in the evenings. Sometimes she would lay her mending in her lap, put her arm around him, hold his head close and kiss his hair. As John thought of her needing him and missing her boy, the pain of it racked his body in silent sobs. She had done nothing to merit losing her beloved boy. How could he do this to her?

Catches Water stroked John's cheek while tears streamed down his face onto her cloak. Surely she knew that he was crying but she did not falter. Her rhythmic, gentle touch never changed.

The longhouse having grown dark, Catches Water held John even after he had cried himself to sleep just as she had held Swift Legs when he was alive. She knew John's pain. She knew that her father had felt the same thing when the Narragansetts had taken him.

Catches Water wondered about John's English mother, wondered how like her this boy was, wondered how she fared with her husband and sons gone. Feeling some sadness for the woman who had borne this remarkable boy, Catches Water whispered into the darkness, 'This is war. It is a hard thing, but you have come to us, white woman. We did not go to your England. You have brought your kind of war, and we have returned with our kind.'

As she looked down on Restores The Old One she smiled with bittersweet gratitude for her years with Swift Legs and for this new son whom the Great Spirit had brought her.

Chapter Eleven

Tuesday, August 28th, 1712
St. Lawrence River Valley, French Canada

John stepped out through the doorframe of the longhouse into a foggy morning. The sun had just risen, and the world was dewy and warm. Upon waking this morning John had found himself feeling something peculiar, something that he could not quite name. It was not fear, perhaps nervousness or sadness; he could not tell.

Up before anyone else in the village, John took the opportunity for reflection as he looked up at the pole on which hung the ghastly cluster of scalps taken by the warriors of Night Sky's longhouse. With so little time completely to himself, for someone was nearly always up and about in the village, John had only occasionally glanced at the scalps since the conversation in the snow with his father and brother. John had wanted to stop and examine, to contemplate and somehow honor the former owners of those scalps.

John imagined the people and what they looked like. He wondered where they had lived and how old they had been. He wondered about their surviving families, wondered how long ago they had been taken and how many were from Deerfield. He imagined six year-old Sarah Hawks, the child of Grandfather's old age, and wondered how she had spent her last day among family and friends. He imagined her by the fire, perhaps carding wool or grinding spices.

Among the layers of black hair interspersed with red and blond and brown tresses, some short some long some curly, John found the long chestnut strand that Junior had mentioned and the fine dark hair of a child. He wondered if these two could possibly belong to Grandfather's wife and daughter, and he thought about how improbable that was, how ridiculous it was that Junior would make such an assertion.

Suddenly a voice behind him said, "Take a walk with me." John wheeled around to see Honors The Dead sitting on a stump off to the side from the longhouse. While John wondered how he could have missed him, the revered old Indian stood up and started toward the woods opposite the river.

Still strong though he was in his late seventies, Honors The Dead led John through the thick, misty woods and down into a shallow run-off bed full of rounded rocks. John stood next to Honors The Dead at the bottom of a hill which rose from the bank of the run-off bed. Not wanting to insult the old warrior's strength, John cautiously extended his elbow in front of Honors The Dead, who immediately grabbed the boy's upper arm. John slowly led him up the hill and into the fog, stopping to let the old man catch his breath every four or five paces. As they crested the hill, Honors The Dead let go of John's arm and walked out onto the great rock that formed a cliff just a few yards ahead. He sat down on a boulder and held his arm out toward a large stone next to him indicating that John should follow suit.

As John sat down on the stone in the fog surrounding them, he could see only the green of the bushes and trees nearest him and the grey slab of rock under his feet. John had been to this spot himself and he looked to his right, where he knew the cliff was just a little distance from his foot but he saw only fog.

Honors The Dead said, "You want to ask me something. Go ahead."

John had lived with this candid old man for nearly two years now, yet Honors The Dead's incisive words still caught him off guard. Not wanting to offend the man, John looked at Honors The Dead and pondered how to ask the question. So many things were simply not talked about in this place just as there were things at home that no one discussed. John decided to adopt the old man's bluntness and asked, "The white women and children ~ where were their scalps taken?"

As though he expected the question Honors The Dead answered without pause, "From many places Restores The Old One, but that is not the right question."

John hesitated for a moment, for he was not certain that he wished to know the answer to the right question, "Did any come from Deerfield?"

Nodding, Honors The Dead responded, "Eight winters ago the French raided Daughter of War, the town called Deerfield by the English. Red Bear was among the war party. In a house with a dark haired woman and her daughters, Red Bear saw a child with eyes the color of ice just like yours. Red Bear killed the dark haired woman, and a warrior from Kahnawake took the older daughter to sell for ransom back to the English. Red Bear took the ice-eyed child to be his daughter and to be my granddaughter."

Junior was right then; the scalps of Grandfather's beloved wife and daughter adorned the very longhouse in which John lived.

Honors The Dead continued, "But as they journeyed north, Red Bear saw that he could not carry both his pack of loot and the child. She could not walk in the deep snow, for she was too small, and there was no one to share his burden. Even if he dropped his pack of goods and left them on the trail for some other warrior to find, Red Bear could not know that she would survive the march. He knew that his pack of goods from the raid would survive and bring good trade for the family, so the pack must be what he would carry. But the child would only weaken and fall behind. Eventually, she would have been all alone. Rather than leave her to starve alone or be torn apart by wolves, Red Bear killed the child swiftly and prevented her suffering."

John stared at Honors The Dead and waited for further explanation, but the man spoke no more. Hiding his confusion under the dignity of a practiced stoicism John thought to himself, 'That's the whole story? She was to be Red Bear's daughter, and he killed her because his pack was certain to survive the journey and she wasn't?' John was stunned as he realized, 'Red Bear would have done the same to me… and he thinks himself my *father?*' Rage and bitterness crept into John's veins as the pair sat silently for several minutes watching the fog lift.

John could see the cliff now just a few steps from his right foot when Honors The Dead spoke again, "Who were the women?"

"My grandfather's wife, daughter and step-daughter," John answered.

The old man said, "It is hard for you, Restores The Old One. I do not expect you to understand this yet. But one day you will be a warrior yourself, and then you must understand."

John had heard this talk of his becoming a warrior before, and he had always ignored it because it seemed preposterous. How could he fight on the side of Grandfather's enemies? How could he fight against his own Cousin John, who now fought against the French and Indians and whose father had been skinned alive by Indians? It was ridiculous, and he had always before simply dismissed it. Now however, he could not. Sickened at the idea of his taking scalps and torturing settlers, John did not care that he would offend Honors The Dead. 'He *needs* offending,' thought John as he opened his mouth to shut the man down.

Before John could speak Honors The Dead said, "Think on this. What do we do when we take captives, and what does the white man do?"

John knew what the Indians did from so much of his own family's suffering, but he had not thought much about Indians in the hands of the Dutch and Spanish and English. Now he reflected on Grandfather's stories from King Philip's War. Before Barbados stopped accepting Indians, the English had taken hundreds of Indians prisoner to be sold into slavery. Further south from New England there was a great deal of rape as well, but now the English simply wiped everyone out in battle ~ man, woman and child. While scores died in an Indian led assault, hundreds were killed when the English attacked.

As he considered the way Indians took captives, John could not imagine a white soldier taking an Indian child home from battle and expecting his wife to raise the child as her own. Perhaps there was mercy in the way the Indians took captives even to make them slaves like his father was now, but John did not think he would ever understand the reasoning behind killing Sarah Hawks.

The fog had cleared a little more, and now John could see the fringe of the great green expanse beneath the cliff. John thought about the oddness of this moment. They had no task in their hands, and they had been sitting on the hill top for an hour or more and yet had spoken little. John could not imagine such a moment in Waterbury.

Honors The Dead appeared perfectly content to sit there all day with John, and John knew that he might not have such an opportunity to speak alone with him again for quite some time. He also realized that if he chose to stay, and his staying was no longer a certainty in his mind, he would be adopted soon and then it would be time to put away the memories of home.

John knew that this was a rare opportunity to speak with the old Christian Indian and this was probably his only chance to ask the man about Deerfield. Wondering if Honors The Dead believed that God had used his People as an instrument of judgment on Deerfield John ventured, "My family…" the boy broke off for a moment before continuing, "They said that God was punishing Deerfield for her sins."

Honors The Dead did not respond immediately. He looked in John's eyes in a way that made the boy very uncomfortable, but John held his gaze steadily. At last Honors The Dead spoke, "So I hear. They said the same thing about the Indians in King Philip's War. The English will not even give us credit for having a valid reason to make war against them. To them, we are nothing more than the scourge of God ~ mindless bloodthirsty baby killers ~ instruments of God's judgment with no reason of our own to hate them. They call us savages to our face, but *they* are the savages. Savages… baby killers… they seem to forget that they too kill infants and many, many more than we have ever killed.

"Restores The Old One, you know our complaints against the English are many ~ their endless hunger for land; their false justice against us in their courtrooms; even their own Praying Indians should not trust them though many of the fools still do even after the English betrayed so many of them in King Philip's War; they do not respect our ways and traditions..."

He stopped for a moment to allow the fury to seep away before he went on, "You see the English cannot understand why the French Governor is powerless to return this English captive or that English captive when the time for negotiations has come. The English do not understand why the French Governor does not simply deploy his troops to remove all English captives from Indian villages. Do you see? The French honor us and respect our ways. They understand that they can no more take an English captive child from an Indian home than they could march into a Frenchman's house in Montreal and take the man's own French child. Though the English came to *our* land to live among *us*, the English do not try to understand us. They try to make us understand *them*. The French understand us; they do not call us 'subjects' for they understand that we cannot be their subjects. This is why we are their allies.

"Restores The Old One, you said that the people who raised you believed that God was punishing Deerfield. In all our warring on the English, whether we went on the warpath with our French brothers or with Metacom the Wampanoag chief, we chose to go to push the English back and stop their hunger for land. It was not God, Restores The Old One. *We* were punishing them."

Honors The Dead's words surprised John, and they brought him comfort, for he had never understood his mother's belief that God had been so angry with Deerfield. The old man's words made sense to John. Honors The Dead turned his gaze out over the cliff again and said, "This is my favorite place. I come here to be alone. Sometimes it is too distracting in the village to hear God."

He looked back at the boy and spoke what he thought John needed to hear if the boy had ever believed for even a moment that God hated Deerfield so much, "Jesus the Christ is good, Restores The Old One. We must know that we sin; that a just God must punish sin; and that He loves to forgive us because Jesus has already received the punishment for us all."

John knew these things, and he nodded as Honors The Dead continued, "Surely we anger God at times, but to think that God is universally wrathful at all times and that He is just waiting for an opportunity to strike us down is a foolish notion. I suppose the French priests have a tendency to think that way too, but they believe that their rituals keep them safe which is nonsense as well. Ritual and tradition are important, and honoring God through such things pleases Him, but the Christ is not powerless to help us if we do not follow every rule of the Catholic Church. Nor is God angry with us just because we exist, Restores The Old One. He made us, did He not?"

Beginning to understand something wholly new and refreshing, John nodded as the old man stretched out his arm over the edge of the cliff and went on, "A God like the Englishman's God could not create the beauty you see around you. This beauty comes from peace and a great love, not from a rage-possessed God. Look at His power, His beauty, and sink into His peace. It is safe, Restores The Old One, to love this God."

John looked out over the edge of the cliff and saw more of the vast green tree tops far below. He thought about Honors The Dead's words and began to feel the powerful joy of loving a God who did not hate him. How much less work, simply to look out on God's creation and adore Him for it without worrying about not adoring Him enough or adoring Him rightly. What freedom finally to love God as he had always been taught that he must and had never been able.

A peace seated itself within John, floating down like a leaf deep beneath the beating of his heart. The knowledge that it had not been God's wrath that had wiped out so many of his family calmed him, relieved him. As the fog lifted, the great plunging depth of the cliff revealed itself fully, and a Scripture came to mind. John translated it softly into the Indian tongue he had spoken now for two years, '...*neither height nor depth, nor any created thing, shall be able to separate us from the love of God...*"

Honors The Dead looked at John in wonder as another passage came to the boy's lips, "...*to be strengthened with might through His Spirit in the inner man, that Christ may dwell in your hearts through faith; that you, being rooted and grounded in love, may be able to comprehend with all the saints what is the width and length and depth and height – to know the love of Christ which passes knowledge...*"

They savored the beauty of the morning, and Honors The Dead asked, "Who told you those words?" Surprised that Honors The Dead did now know, John recalled that

Catholic priests did not allow their congregants to study the Scriptures. With a smile John said, "God."

Honors The Dead not understanding, John explained, "That is the reason my family came to your land ~ for the right to interpret those holy Words as the Lord leads us." He paused, expecting Honors The Dead to understand, but he did not, so John went on, "Those are the words of God, Honors The Dead, from the Holy Bible."

The old man looked back out over the lush forest and said, "Those are indeed the words of God."

The old man said, "Now I have a question for you." John looked at him curious and a little worried that the old man might ask for a commitment of some kind. John was not ready to declare that he would stay among the Indians forever.

Honors The Dead asked, "Who was at Peskeompskut?'

Stunned that Honors The Dead would know that anyone in his family had fought there, John kept his dignity and responded smoothly, "My grandfather Sergeant John Hawks, for whom I am named, and my great uncle Eliezer Hawks were there."

Honors The Dead nodded thoughtfully and asked, "Did they both have your hair and ice colored eyes?" When John nodded, the old man asked, "Was one clean shaven and the other bearded?"

Unnerved John answered, "That was many years before I was born, but I can tell you that my grandfather has worn a beard for as long as I have known him. I do not know about Uncle Eliezer, for I have never met him."

Honors The Dead said, "Who was at the Pequot Fort?"

Nausea swept over John as he answered, "My great-grandfather was there."

Honors The Dead wanted to clarify, "Hawks? He was the father of your grandfather Sergeant John Hawks?"

Not wanting to continue the conversation but curious to discover Honors The Dead's story, John nodded and said, "My great-grandfather's name was John as well."

Honors The Dead thought for a moment, furrowing his brow then he asked, "Did your grandfather, the sergeant, have no sons?"

As ire began to simmer in his belly at the thought of his dead uncle and family John replied, "He had one son."

"The white man is not very creative in naming his children. All the French children are Jean or Marie and all the English children John or Mary. I wonder if this son's name might have been John Hawks," said Honors The Dead.

Insulted, John said nothing so Honors The Dead asked, "And where is this John Hawks, son of the sergeant?"

John looked away from the old man and down into the green trees below. His face betraying none of the anger he felt, John responded, "He, his wife and their children suffocated in the cellar below their burning house when your Red Bear attacked Deerfield."

The two were quiet again for a few minutes before Honors The Dead broke the silence, "Your great-grandfather was there the day I received the name I bear today."

John looked at Honors The Dead's weather-worn face and waited for him to continue. "On that day every one of my family was taken from this world ~ shot with muskets or arrows, burned alive, hacked down with swords or hatchets ~ all killed. I was a boy of three or four summers, and I saw my father after he had been killed and beheaded. Standing over him was your great-grandfather, and thinking that he had killed my father I chased him with my father's hatchet. The Narragansett man who had indeed killed my father, and who also adopted me and became my new father, saw my attempt to avenge my father's death at such a tender age. He picked me up and spoke my new name as we walked through the burning homes of my family and childhood playmates."

As John wondered how Honors The Dead had gotten so far north from the Pequot Fort in southern Connecticut Colony, the old Indian continued in the soft voice of his habit, "In time, I became a warrior among the Narragansett Nation, and I joined the cause of the Wampanoag Chief Metacom whom you probably know as King Philip. It was a noble cause, and we had great success for many months. Had the other nations joined us... had the Mohawk joined us instead of picking us off, we could have driven the English from our shores. They might have come back, but if we could only unite under that one cause... But our nations are as separate and headstrong as France and England, and at last we splintered apart."

To John, Honors The Dead suddenly appeared weighed down by a great sadness, and the old man paused for a moment looking into the fast fading fog, "I had a wife and two daughters. Our daughters were about the age of you and your brother. That winter our Narragansett fort had been burned by the English, and many of us fled to Peskeompskut. I am sure you know the story of that battle, but now we both know that your grandfather ran my younger daughter through with a sword, and your uncle beheaded my wife. Another Englishman shot my older daughter in the back."

Anger welled up within John; his jaw clenched and his face grew tense. He did not know at whom he was angry, for he was angry with his grandfather whom he loved so dearly, but he was angry also with Red Bear who had killed Sarah. John wanted to stand up and scream, but his body was rooted to the stone on which he sat and he could not move.

Honors The Dead cocked his head to the side and scowled, glaring at the rock slab as he continued, "I could not reach them... The warriors... we had all gone to gather for an orderly counter-offense... This is what protectors do. It is what the Englishmen of Deerfield did too, the men rushing together to protect the whole, leaving their wives and children undefended. To save many, protectors must often risk the lives of the few...

the most precious few..." He trailed off, still looking at the rock and not seeing it.

John had to fight to keep his decorum, for such contradictory feelings of fury and grief, helplessness, shame and justification all warred against one another within his bosom. Tears finding their way to his eyes, John clenched his jaw until his teeth ached. Balling his hands into fists and digging his fingernails into his palms, he constricted his throat and fought the tears. No matter what, John would not allow the dishonor of tears to come upon him.

John spoke softly almost whispering, "Are you the Old One?"

Honors the Dead looked up at him and said, "I am."

John waited, hoping that the old man would say more, and he did, "On the few occasions when I have told my story, I have called your family the Ice Eyes. This is how Red Bear knew that the girl from Deerfield belonged to your family, and she was meant to restore my heart from the losses of so many of my People at the hand of your family. When Red Bear heard of an ice-eyed boy in Connecticut, he went in search of you. Your father and brother and you ran the gauntlet to avenge my Pequot and Narragansett families, and you will replace the spirit of many if you stay among us. Do you see the restoration?"

The anger had diminished, but it was still present. In awe at the irony and strangely grateful for the opportunity to heal this old man, John nodded gravely in answer to his question. A peace settled over him and with it came a solid purpose, an understanding that he was a unique tool in the hands of God. John knew now that he was where he belonged and that God had made no mistake in birthing him into the English family of Hawks. Twisted and cruel though it seemed, this was perfect justice. He was sorry for his family. He wished that Sarah could be restored to his Grandfather, and in all of this wreckage his sweet mother had done nothing except to be born a daughter of war.

Suddenly shouts from the village reached their ears; John's body snapped toward the direction of the village, and the old man and boy looked at one another wondering what was the matter. They were silent, holding their breath and straining their ears for signs of attack. Honors The Dead stiffened his back and looked to John to see if he had missed anything for his hearing was no longer so keen, and with a look of astonishment and terror, John turned to the old man. The blood had drained from John's face, and Honors The Dead tensely waited to find out what had so unsettled the boy. John's voice could hardly be heard as he whispered, "They have escaped."

Relieved that there was no attack, Honors The Dead's body relaxed but he watched the boy intently. As shouts and whoops continued to rise from the village and from the forest where the Indians searched for the two escaped captives, John slowly turned his body back toward the edge of the cliff. Nearly all the fog had dissipated now, but John saw a pocket of mist nestled among the lush ferns and trees on a hillside below them. Panic fluttered in John's bosom as he realized that he was alone in this alien place, this place that had seemed so savage and wholly incorrect when he had first stepped out of that canoe two years ago.

John prayed that God would protect his father and brother, hide their tracks from the Indians and feed them for the month or more that it would take to return home. A pang of longing shot through John. The suddenness of it caught him off guard, and for the second time that morning, he nearly lost the fight to keep tears in check. He kept his eyes on the hillside below and tried to pull himself back from the pain, but his heart swooped so far away, driving on the wind, racing, soaring, pounding, pushing home toward his mother who had done nothing to deserve this rejection from him.

Honors The Dead got to his feet and walked over to John and laying his hand on his shoulder said, "I do not know if they gave you the chance to go with them, Restores The Old One, but you do not have to stay forever, for ransom will come. I hope you will choose to remain in Night Sky's longhouse with us; you have brought peace to us all. You do not know how much you give us."

John looked up at the old man standing over him, and saw peace in eyes that he knew had swallowed more pain than he could ever imagine. This man and his world needed John far more than the English world would ever need him, and yet Honors The Dead had confidence enough in the boy to allow him to choose. Suddenly sensing that with his brother and father's departure he was free to be as Indian as he wished, to dance when the music moved him and to smile as often as he as was happy, John relaxed into the freedom to become entirely who he wanted to be.

Honors The Dead and John heard someone rushing up the hill behind them and Red Bear appeared out of the brush. Red Bear spoke to John, "Your English father and brother have run away and left you."

Unwilling that they might be remembered as cowards John said, "Punish me as you will for not telling you this earlier, but I cannot allow you to imply that my *father* and *brother* were cowards. They have been watching for the opportunity to escape since spring. They told me, and I refused to go."

John watched Red Bear's face for any sign of what he was thinking but the Indian maintained his composure. By not informing anyone of their plans, John had essentially stolen the ransom money that Jonathan Scott's and Junior's masters would have received, and he had furthermore removed from their homes laborers who did much work. A tense silence hung over the three as John wondered how severely he would be punished for not informing his father's and brother's masters.

Bracing himself for a blow to the chest from Red Bear's powerful fist, John faced the warrior who had brought so much pain to his family, then said, "Red Bear, do you not see? I choose to stay."

Epilogue

Tuesday, November 14th, 1743
Waterbury, Connecticut Colony

The day was cold, and the leaves were all gone from the trees as Goodwyfe Hannah Scott sat alone in her home busily spinning at her flax wheel. Her fingers calloused from many hundreds of yards of flax and wool twisting between them, her face had aged and the skin about her neck hung loose.

She had just seen her sixty-eighth birthday, and she still kept house for her husband Goodman Jonathan Scott who in his late seventies spent his days at the gristmill he had built with Junior. Jonathan Scott came home in the afternoon to nap on most days and then stayed home making himself useful about the place.

Daniel had not yet married and still lived with them working their fields and assisting his parents like so many dutiful youngest sons of the time.

The Scotts had built a large home on the west side of main street in town, for the dangers of Indian attacks had grown more constant. Less than a decade after his return with Junior and only a few months after the death of Hannah's father, Jonathan Scott had been taken captive again, this time being sold immediately to the French.

Without the comforting words and touch of her father, Hannah had never felt so alone in her life as she had during her husband's second captivity. The Lord had blessed her with Junior's presence however, and the absence of his father made her treasure Junior the more. All of her children had still been living at home when Jonathan Scott was taken the second time and they had been old enough to help pick up the slack in supporting the family during their father's absence.

The French had allowed Jonathan Scott no work while he was kept a prisoner at large in Montreal. Leaving him wearing only a loincloth, the Indians who had captured him had sold Jonathan Scott to the French, and in order to eat and clothe himself he had been forced to go into debt while the French waited to ransom him back to the English. When he was finally ransomed safely back to Waterbury the colony had reimbursed him for his costs enabling him to repay his Canadian debts.

Jonathan and Hannah's children and grandchildren all lived in the area, allowing for frequent visits from them. Shortly after Jonathan and Junior had built the gristmill to grind corn for the local farmers, a young man named Joseph Hurlburt fell in love with Martha Scott.

When Joseph Hurlburt came courting to the Scott house in the evenings after his work was done, he would often bring his sister Mary Hurlburt.

While Joseph Hurlburt wooed Martha, Junior Scott found himself rather smitten with the lovely Mary Hurlburt, and two months after Joseph Hurlburt married Martha Scott, Junior Scott wed the groom's sister.

Mary had died a year after the birth of their only child, a son, whom they had named John Scott for Junior's lost brother.

On rare occasions, usually in summer when they would not need to try to squeeze into the house, the whole clan would gather at Jonathan and Hannah's house.

Gershom and his wife had four children and expected another or perhaps twins. Joseph Hurlburt and Martha had three children while Eliezer and his wife had none. Having married again Junior had a brood of wee Scotts, for his second wife Rebecca Frost had borne him six children thus far.

When her grandchildren were present, Hannah would lay aside her handwork to hold the young ones on her lap. Their oldest grandchild John Scott now a strapping seventeen year-old, frequently spent his evenings at Jonathan and Hannah's house.

Sometimes he would stay the night sleeping in his namesake's old bed and helping his Uncle Daniel in the fields the next day. These visits from her grandson John allowed Hannah the bittersweet pleasure of saying a name she had missed saying for so many years.

She thought of her lost son often and worried about his soul. She prayed every night and throughout each day that God would keep the teachings of his youth foremost in John's heart and that God would keep his soul from sliding into the gaping maw of hell offered by the papists.

During the lulls in hostility between French Canada and New England, her husband had persistently attempted ransom through the French government at Montreal. The French had done all they could for the Scott family, but John refused each attempt.

Hannah thought of her Aunt Mary Catlin who still had four granddaughters among the savages and the French. She half-envied her aunt the luxury of death, for she did not feel the rejection now.

The old goodwife stood up from her work, put on her wrap and walked to the door which she opened onto a cold grey day. The fields behind the houses of Waterbury were stubbly, and the woods beyond them brown and grey and green with naked maple, oak and birch limbs among the evergreens.

Standing in the doorway she looked across her neighbors' fields into the incomprehensible expanse of wilderness that separated her from her son. Hannah had stood this way hundreds of times since her husband and Junior had straggled out of the woods, bruised, cut and starving. Year after year she watched and hoped for John's return.

Hannah's anguish at her son's rejection of her clean, loving home for a way of life that could not possibly be more different from what she gave him, had never abated. At times she felt betrayed, for John had seemed to need her so much as a boy, had seemed to need to touch her when he was afraid, had seemed to need to speak with her when his soul was troubled. She had given him all the time that she could as she had been running a household of nine, and yet he apparently did not feel the connection to her that she had felt to him.

Her father Sergeant Hawks had never gotten over the boy's rejection of him, for in rejecting ransom John had rejected them all wholly and individually. The old man who had lost so many now lost the grandson whose mere presence had had the power to break the oppression of memory. The old sergeant had never gotten over it and had died soon after John's rejection ~ broken and distant, unwilling to give himself to anyone.

Standing at the door Hannah shook her head, a lone tear sliding down her cheek. Though she rarely cried in these later years, it never got better. It never got easier. There was no peace. John's absence was worse than death because of the undying hope that he would miss her and come home. Her blighted hope knew no end.

Hannah wondered if her son was a fine Indian, and she wondered what that meant. She wondered what his chosen mother was like. Hannah wondered if it was only the enticement of the devil or if perhaps there were something truly good in the woman that had caused John to prefer her home over the home of his birth.

Though deeply hurt by her son's betrayal the Lord had long since removed bitterness from Hannah's heart, and when friendly Indians came to town for trade Hannah would gaze at the strong young braves and imagine her son's back straight, strong and bronzed from the sun. Hoping somehow to send her love to her lost son, Hannah would seek out the notice of these friendly Indians and smile at them usually receiving a stoic grunt in return.

Looking out over the bleak late autumn landscape, Hannah imagined the young Indian women, and she wondered what beauty had captured her son's heart. What did she look like, the woman who now bore and nursed his children?

Hannah imagined her Indian grandchildren and wished that she could hold them, wished that she could sit with one of John's toddlers on her knee, feeding the child from her own bowl.

She looked at the doorpost that Jonathan Scott had ripped out of their home in the wilderness when they moved to town. Hannah had insisted that he put the old door frame in the new house so that she would never lose the post on which her children's growth was marked.

Now she laid her calloused, wrinkled finger on the lowest set of initials "Jn" and smiled as she recalled John and Martha napping together in the trundle bed when they were little. She passed her eyes over all the marks and initials, stopping briefly at one and then another, remembering her children as they had been so long ago.

When she reached the last of John's hash marks she closed her eyes and pressed her thumb hard into the initials. Looking out again on the bleak November day, Hannah rubbed her thumb back and forth over the letters that called her back to a time when her son had loved her.

The old woman bent slightly, her gut wrenched with longing as she continued to gaze into the punishing wilderness. Tears streamed down her face and she whispered, "My boy..."

Author's Note

Following are details regarding those parts of the book where the story evolved from theory and guess work rather than specific facts.

The numbers of those slain or taken captive at the Pequot Fort, Deerfield, and at Peskeompskut vary from source to source.

Waterbury was still known as Mattatuck during Queen Anne's War.

Martin Smith, the man staying with John and Thankful Hawks on the night of the Deerfield Raid was also slain.

As to the fate of Metacom's wife and son, that is a matter of speculation. We do know that his young son was shipped off to become a slave though his mother's fate is unknown. That they were thrown overboard from a slave ship is one distinct possibility addressed in Jill Lepore's remarkable work, *The Name of War*.

The exact means of Joseph Scott's death also is unknown, but we do know that he was tortured to death, that there was very little of his body left to bury, that skinning was not an uncommon means of torture among the First Nations, that his fellow colonists heard his screams throughout the event, and that the colonists feared a larger attack.

That John Scott stayed among his captors is known, but it is uncertain as to whether he was taken in his father's first captivity or his father's second captivity. Regarding the captivities of the Scotts, little is known including whether there was ever an escape versus ransom. We simply do not know although ransom appears the most likely end to Jonathan Scott Sr.'s second captivity based on records of debts he incurred. For more on the Scotts, I refer you to Edward R. Smith's *The Family of Edmund Scott: An Original Proprietor of Farmington and Waterbury, CT* and both Bronson's and Anderson's histories of Waterbury, Connecticut.

It is possible that the Scotts may not have been required to attend meeting during the winter months while they lived outside town.

Waterbury had a school as early as the era of this book, and girls did indeed receive education if only in the area of reading. Connecticut was premier among the colonies in providing education for all classes of society.

For those seeking more information about the events in this book, I refer you to the following Acknowledgements section of the book which lists several resources on daily life, the Pequot War, King Philip's War and the 1704 attack on Deerfield.

Acknowledgements

Had my great-grandmother Florence Orcutt kept her memories locked in her head, had she never set them on paper, if her son Fred Scott Orcutt Sr. had not copied and circulated them, this work would never have been written.

My infinite gratitude to:

my husband for his stalwart belief in the critical nature of preserving our children's heritage, for his many sacrifices in order that this work should be completed, for his knowledge of weaponry and his insight into the warrior mind

my mother and editor-in-chief for the countless hours she gave to this project both inspiring and encouraging me at every turn, for her true partnership in this effort

all of the many teachers who shaped my thinking ~ in particular these four superb teachers, mentors and friends: Carol Rice, Patrick Evans, Lowell Gorseth & Cindy Hummel

my siblings for their support, interest and input

Reverend Lili Bush for her time, care, and
critical eye

Judy Orcutt Holy for her shared interest and
enthusiasm

Lee Meade, my fellow genealogist and editor of
www.meadnewsletter.com, for his editing
skill and support

For their expertise and help in research, I am indebted to:
Edward R. Smith, author of *The Family of
Edmund Scott: An Original Proprietor of
Farmington and Waterbury, CT* available
from author at edwardrsmith@msn.com

Allan Clark

Florence T. Crowell, author of *Images of
America: Watertown*

Phil Konstantin, author of *This Day in North
American Indian History*

Linda F. Skarnulis, Regent of the Trumbull/Porter
Chapter of the Daughters of the American
Revolution in Watertown, CT

So many works have aided my efforts to understand the
world of our forebears that I cannot list them all. I would
like to name those works most indispensable to this
endeavor: Imogene Hawks Lane's *John Hawks: A
Founder of Hadley, Massachusetts;* Rev. John Williams'
The Redeemed Captive Returning to Zion; Laurel
Thatcher Ulrich's work, *Good Wives;* the captivity
narratives of Mrs. Johnson and Mrs. Rowlandson;
George Sheldon's *A History of Deerfield, Massachusetts;*
Alvin Joseph Jr.'s *500 Nations;* George Bodge's
meticulous compiling of *Soldiers in King Philip's War;*
Reader's Digest's *Through Indian Eyes;* Joseph

Anderson's *The Town and City of Waterbury, Connecticut;* John Demos' *The Unredeemed Captive;* Sylvester Judd's *History of Hadley, Massachusetts;* Douglas Leach's *Flintlock and Tomahawk;* Patrick Malone's *The Skulking Way of War;* Jill Lepore's *The Name of War;* Schultz and Tougias' *King Philip's War;* Mashantucket Pequot Museum and Research Center; Memorial Hall Museum; Daniel Gookin's *An Historical Account of the Doings and Sufferings of the Christian Indians in New England, in the Years 1675, 1676, 1677;* Alfred Cave's *The Pequot War;* and Rev. William Hubbard's *The History of the Indian Wars in New England from the First Settlement to the Termination of the War with King Philip in 1677.*

A Resource For Those
For Whom I Wrote This Book

Borrowing the Iroquois tradition of tracing lineage through maternal lines, the following pages lead back to the characters of this novel through the

Grandmothers

of
Lisa, Jake, Lindsay, Brycie, Clay, Ben,
Alexis, Alek, Samantha, Rachael, Drew, Thor, Elizabeth,
and Alaric

Pictured here your great-great-grandmother
Florence Orcutt holds her daughter, your
great-grandmother Helen.

296

Generation 11:   *Your Nanna*

Generation 10:   *Helen Elizabeth Orcutt Wilson*
"Granny" to her grandchildren
1906 – 1993
Wife of Harold Dwight "Pete" Wilson
Mother of your Nanna

Generation 9:   *Florence Pluma Waters Orcutt*
"Ghaki" to her grandchildren
1871 – 1962
Wife of Robert William Orcutt
Mother of Helen

Generation 8:   *Martha Janette Scott Waters*
Known as "Nettie"
1841 – 1916
Wife of Darwin Whiting Waters
Mother of Florence

Generation 7:   *Dolly Wright Scott*
1808 – 1870
Wife of Frederic Scott
Mother of Martha Janette

Generation 6:   *Sarah Hard Scott*
1780 – 1859
Wife of Aaron Scott
Mother of Frederic

Generation 5:   *Lydia Reynolds Scott*
                      1748 – Unknown
                      Wife of Eber Scott
                      Mother of Aaron

Generation 4:   *Rebecca Frost Scott*
                      1701 – Unknown
                      Second wife of Jonathan Scott Jr.,
                      *   called "Junior" in the novel*
                      Mother of Eber

Generation 3:   *Hannah Hawks Scott*
                      1675 - 1744
                      Wife of Jonathan Scott Sr.
                      Mother of Jonathan Jr.,
                      *   called "Junior" in the novel*

Generation 2:   *Martha Baldwin Hawks*
                      1647 - 1676
                      Wife of Sergeant John Hawks II
                      Mother of Hannah

Generation 1:   *Elizabeth Browne Hawks*
                      ca. 1621- 1689
                      Wife of John Hawks I
                      *   called "Hawks" in the Prologue*
                      Mother of Sergeant John Hawks II

Compiled from the notes of Florence Pluma Waters Orcutt; Edward R. Smith's *The Family of Edmund Scott*; Imogene Hawks Lane's *John Hawks: A Founder of Hadley, Massachusetts* from Gateway Press, 1989; and *History of Hadley, Mass* by Sylvester Judd, Picton Press, 1999.